SON OF AMITY

Este libro es para mis hijos,
Guillermo y Pedro,
Los dos campeones.

CONTENTS

PART I
Yesterday

PART II
Today

Darkness indeed came near. It buried its eye
against the eye of the child's own soul, saying:
Had ever breathed, had ever dreamed, had ever been.
—James Agee, *A Death in the Family*

PART I

Yesterday

Pika

May 6, 2006

He entered the town of Amity, Oregon, in complete accordance with the law. Fifty miles per hour, no faster, no slower. The '74 Datsun truck couldn't break sixty, anyway—he was grateful this lifted ride made it all the way up from Cali in one shot. Ten hours from the Bay, half-hour pit stops every hundred miles at the tweaker-infested rest stations. He'd have brought a gat if he'd known this. Pocketed a bag of rocks to toss into the grass like pellets of fertilizer just to watch the twacks set chase. Shit, he should've jacked one of those peeled-back crater-faced mutherfuckers on principle: let me do something valuable with those dimes and pennies you got baggied in your Goodwill socks, friend. Allow me to interrupt your discussion on shape-shifting zombies and accept your involuntary donation to the universal cause of goodness and peace and soundness of body and mind and grill.

Now the 99 wound around a glistening LDS church, its phallic spires sprouting for the vaginal folds of heaven, then a weather-beaten farm falling in on itself apocalyptically, everything even well-done man-made buildings the subject of time's bulldozer (Somehow, he thought, all y'all gonna end up in the ground: Mormons, farmers, atheists, capitalists. Me.), when he saw the trap pop up to his immediate right, calmly downshifting from fourth to third to second in almost a single motion, the cliff-drop to twenty a steady ride on the engine's maximum rpm capacity—*mmmmmmmmmmm!*, almost as if he were test-driving for some local yokel civic official this thirty mph reduction in speed over a mere hundred yards of road.

Scams, he thought, are everywhere. No one owns scam. Every people on the planet—every race, culture, every little two-bit mapdot—has scum in it.

Wanna get rid of scam? he thought. Get rid of scum.

Right on cue, he passed the police, sitting there under the massive split log whose bark-face read in chiseled etching, Welcome to Amity, "A Nice Little Town," Home of the 8-Man State Football Champions 1991 2003 2005, plus the half dozen charity outfits endorsing the welcome, the claim and the team, the set-up only notable—he saw in his cracked rear-view mirror—in that the cop car was empty. This was a first, an officially unmanned speedtrap, something he'd believed to be an element of small-town myth, colorless Andy Griffith BS.

Just the ghost in the machine today, he thought, operating on the street and jungle law of a legit threat to your safety. This squad car right here won't getchu, yo, but someone else down the way sure as hell will.

Where he came from, the idea would get looted before the day officially died. King and Story, East Side San Jo, the Bay, Norcal all the way. Right when the moon stepped in and the city lights palpitated on, everything even the rubber of the tires would be straight-up gone. Like the copper-dense railing on the 580, unscrewed from the structure like a Lego piece. A one-car junkyard rooted out right there on the side of the road, redeem-for-chump change feast, stripped down more thoroughly than a pole dancer, the quaint notion of a tourist destination an urban planner's joke. Nasty community policing—he put the bet to himself—didn't happen in Amity, Oregon.

Still, he had to admit, this stuff right here—the clean, smogless, Northwestern moisture in the air, these ten-acre fields of alfalfa shining like Astroturf, cluster of oak trees as leaf-dense as the thick lifetime growth of a Punjabi's beard, and everywhere the evergreens arrowing out of the earth—this was real-deal green no doubt. A blessing from someone. From something. He'd never seen this kind of straight-up authenticity of the color of money, this hardcore blue-yellow combo. It was like that scene from the *The Wizard of Oz*, his sister Sissy's favorite movie, Dorothy and her crew of benevolent male protectors sprinting through the poppies to the gates of the Emerald City.

Pretty easy to see that this place was bursting with water. That much

was clear. Which explained the green. You took your eye off it for a minute and the green expanded. He didn't know much about the planet's
heating, but he knew enough to get that it was *happening* (Am I blind? he
thought. Stupid?) and what this meant in the most basic terms was that
a lotta people would be flooding this corner of the country eventually.
The sedentary, the plugged-in, the settled—tenth-generationers content
to call home the family house astride the family graveyard—all of them
would have to get off their backsides and move, play the nomad and load
up the truck for a Joad family ride to another side of America. Arizonans
and New Mexicans and Texans roadtripping to the state where it's either
wet, or about to get wet.

He hadn't really been anywhere else unincarcerated except Hawai'i
for the year and a half that his grandfather'd sent him to the islands to get
some basic respect. Unfortunately, his makeshift chaperone was Aleki
Masalosalo, ten years his senior, street-corner hustler extraordinaire. Not
even out of his twenties, Pika's cousin could care less about Fa'a Samoa,
which he called FOB Samoa, Fresh-Off-the-Boat Samoa: "dat backward kine immigrant stuff, Pika," like bowing when passing an elder on
a bench or a couch or fine-mat fala on the floor, de facto housekeeper
daily cooking the ten-course meals and cleaning up the aftermath, madly
husking coconut like a Polynesian ancestor trying to make fire on the
beach. It was egoless service to someone else, "every day all day like dat
until you make die die kaput, Pika," all that beautiful indigenous tribal
shit that can't mathematically make it in America, everyone elbowing
each other for a little bit of space in the storybook.

"Leai kaukala Samoa," his grandfather used to tell him, "leai Samoa
oe."

Took him a decade to learn what the words meant. Can't speak Samo-
an, you're not Samoan. Went off to the joint in '98 and a lifer Crip named
Tut from Riverside, Socal, told him in the dry-heat oven of Avenal Two
Yard, "Shit, Pika, I'll teach you how to speak your native tongue, uso.
Don'tchu worry bout that. Those other ufas over there charge you ten
soups, cuz, but I do it on the strength, uce."

"Fa'afetai lava, Tut."

"Call me Utu."

"'Kay, Utu."

"That's on the invite, Pika. I like how you do your time. Reading your books. Working that heavy bag. All these other bitches out here—let em all call me King Tut—bow down."

"Feel you." He waited, unsure if he should bring up what he knew. "Tut's a anagram, right?"

"A what?"

"Anagram. They just mix the letters up."

"Mmmm. That's right. Like alphabet soup, home."

"Yep."

"Goes back to the schoolyards of R-side, Pika."

"Yeah?"

"No one out there could say my name right, cuz, and then one day some kid said, Tut."

"Probably dyslexic."

"I didn't know who Tut was, Pika. Thought he was making fun of me. Calling me a chicken and shit. Tut tut tut tut."

"Funny, man."

"You know us American Samoa hamos, we get issues with the chicken. Put that shit on our flag, man. Mutherfucking moa up there, uce."

"You mean the eagle?"

"Whatchu think them kefe Kogas say about that? 'Those Samoan rednecks put a big chicken on their new flag. Stupid farmers. Let's go conquer their island.'"

Pika laughed and laughed.

"What the hell is that governor or that committee of matais—what are those *fools* saying about our people? That we gon' run like chickens when the Tongans come over on their boats? Or what, Pika?"

"I don't know, home." He was chuckling at Tut's face, the fake amazement in the wide brown eyes. Tut was the only lifer on the yard who'd sling it once in a while to kill time. If there was any self-pity, Pika never saw it. "Maybe those fools were saying they wanna eat some chicken, or something?"

"Chicken, Pika!"

"'Ey, man—"

"Forget that, sole!"

"—I didn't design that flag, Utu."

"We get enough moa here in Avenal, Pika. Stinking chicken farm for the whole CDC."

"Right."

"Just do the right thing and put a mutherfucking pig on there, Pika! Two hundred-pound pua'a puka, sole! Stripped down, ready for the umu! Fire pit of our people. That's right, y'all. Put that big fat slab of pork on our flag."

He was cracking up, bowled over right there in the joint on a yard where everything you had was at risk 24–7, a straight laugh attack over the image of Porky Pig's grill on the flag of an American territory.

"Hey, sole."

He managed between coughs to get out a, "Yeah?" Then he looked out at the space of dust, making sure it was clear before loogying into the yard. The spit evaporated even as it boomeranged through the dry heat.

"Hey, Pika."

"Hah?"

"That's not the worst part, uce."

"What, man? I can't breathe, Utu. What?"

"Those breads made a holiday, Pika. Actually *celebrate* that chicken on Flag Day. Whatchu think o' that? That's your people, Pika. That's who you wanna be. Every hamo, every family comes out to the beach, sole. Every village. Bringing the family couch to the beach, feel me? Even the old ladies come out, uce. You can hear them talking shit: 'Look at that stupid chicken, Malia. Oh, valea moa.'"

"Shit."

"And you know what's worse?"

"Mmm?"

"I'll whip a mutherfucker's ass who disrespect that chicken, Pika."

He'd smiled, looked over. The playfulness should have been dead in Utu. The rules in any CDC Level III penitentiary was that, one, you called every lifer "Mister" plus his last name and that, two, keep right on walking after you said it. Avenal Two-Yard had a hundred lifers on a thousand-man yard, and so 10 percent of the time you had to apply these rules. And yet here he was with King Tut, shooting it as if they were both free men, pounding 'ava on the malae, all their folks at peace in safety around them.

"I know you will."

"That's *my* chicken, Pika."

"Ioe, Utu. What the hell else we got, right?"

He'd nodded, sadly. "Right, Pika. Right. The illiterate ufas on this yard, Pika—they never gon' make it on the outs. Too busy play-acting for everyone. For each other. And how you gonna stop speaking your own language when you don't have to?"

"My grandpa once told me something like that."

"The faife'au?"

"Ioe."

"Well, shit, Pika, the old reverend was right. Don't worry, cuz"—he started laughing—"we gots lots of time to learn you the lingo."

"Right, right."

"Get your hamo ass a PhD, CDC."

"Yep."

"Like yours truly."

"Yep yep."

"California Department of Corrections, Doc-tah of Philosophy."

"Samoan Schopenhauer."

"Doc-tah of Penology."

"A Polynesian Freudian."

"What's all these names you dropping, Pika? They punks on this yard?"

"Nah, Utu. They nobodies, man. Got everything squared up in their minds. Life straight figured out. Know-it-alls."

"I don't like those kinds of ufas, Pika."

"Me, neither."

"Cops are like that."

He'd laughed. "Yep."

"Bring their ass in here and make em bend over for the leo leos. Just to see your family on Kerisimasi, we get to look into your asshole, fool. Make em spread singing *Jingle Bells*. We got to get them on their PhD, CDC program, Pika."

"Phucked, California Department of Corrections."

"Clean up your mouf, Pika. Lesson number kasi. Dose goodie breads like our mommies and daddies don't like that kind of talk, uso."

He'd had good time-killing laughs with Utu, some of the best in his life, rolling dice for penny stamps against the gray indecorous slabs of concrete, Block 230 higher than the breaker walls in a man-made harbor. The only plane of space in the state naked of graffiti was ironically where all the "urban artists" were locked up, their skills relegated to wild, demonic, medieval illustrations on yellow pieces of canteen paper and undercover tags needle-gunned onto whatever plain of skin their homies hadn't tagged already. A dollar in soups for the former, a hun spot in soups for the latter.

Amity, he guessed, ain't got public art problems.

He looked around at the town without looking—(something's changed, he thought, the dollar's dropped) head steady but his eyes moving, utilizing his mirrors—at the first row of shoddy houses into town, the wide porches deceivingly framing the tiny square footage of land.

Poor white people lived down here. Undernourished, overfed, jobless white people. HHS-invested white people. Gelatinous-spined, weighed down stooping from Ding Dongs and Swanson's TV dinners white people. For all he knew, he could have been in the West Virginia Appalachians, the Arkansas Ozarks. Strings of spat Cope on the lawn, rusting tractors posted up in gravelly driveways. A trampoline with duct-taped springs and grips sitting on the fenceless divide of shared property lines, dozens of plastic toys scattered across the yards like miniature tornado towns post-blast, spotted beards of clumpy moss uprooting the tiles of rooftops. The white people were out there on the dipping, slanted, paint-chipped front porches, ass-planted on cushion-smashed chairs like toads on a rotting log. The chronically obese and tweaker-thin were both watching him come into their town without connection or invitation or permission, suspicious brown man in a beanie up to no good in his beat-up truck from post-war Japan. Fifteen miles an hour the legal cap, car show investigation of anyone entering the town limits.

He wasn't sure how he felt about what he saw. He knew being poor, but this was a different kind of poor, maybe even a worse kind. Seemed stagnant around here, like he was driving through a time warp, the people sitting in their own shit. In the city, everyone was moving on poverty. Sidestepping it, passing it on, lugging it across a borough for deposit.

But one thing he knew for sure: these white people were his white mother.

She and Sissy lived in a run-down, crook-roofed, pre–World War II logging house. Like these places right here. He'd seen the house in the one picture his mother had sent him on his fifth birthday, pale white knees pulled into her chest on the porch. Every one of these palagis probably know the little lady, he bet, the way everyone in small towns supposedly knows everyone else.

Shit, he thought. They talk to my own mother in one day more than I ever done my whole life.

Only recently had he learned some of the story's complexities from Sissy. Their mother'd been through it, no doubt. Just like they had, just like these people he was looking at had. Even when he was born, even when the celebration should have happened. In the maternity ward, the day-old baby latched to her breast, Pika's paternal grandfather had come in and scolded her for being "too loud," too "by herself," too palagi. She only knew what the word meant because she'd been called it before by one of Pika's territorial girl cousins.

But the old man might as well have told her she was being too much *herself*. Yes, she talked loud compared to these new relatives of hers, but she also loved to find solitude on a random urban corner of a midday intersection, just plop down on a bus bench and watch in silence the busy people go rushing by. It was lovely in its own way, the opposite of Amity. Sometimes she'd even close her eyes, find solace in the buzz of it all.

Did they know that? Did they care?

And that's right, she was *palagi*: What else could she have been? You are what you are, born into the skin you're given. You add to the story you've inherited. What else—upon his father seeing her bodysurfing the waves on Seabrighton Beach, glistening white where she wasn't burnt pink—was she supposed to be? Moreover, a person had to *be* what they *were*: anything other than that was a formula for disaster. She didn't know this with certainty, but she deeply suspected it.

Still, Sissy had said, their mother tried. That's the kind of woman she was, unafraid—at least when she was young—to go against her own terms. Was courageous in its own way, was American. Cultural entrepeneur, the centerpiece of fusion, hostile parties coming together over her body. The solemnity of the grandfather had scared her. The few words he ever said echoed with old-world wisdom. The tonal intransigence was somehow perfectly natural, like a three-day surge of Oregon rain: you have no say when it stops. Be happy you're alive.

If a train, she'd newly thought, could switch tracks, why couldn't she?

Conform to Fa'a Samoa meant—in real ways—learn what the hell it is. She didn't know a damned thing about Samoans, except she liked how the young men's shoulders—especially Pika's father's—were wider than any other men she'd ever seen. Also that they did the cooking at home, and not the women.

She officially started by abandoning her favorite time of day: the tendency since mid-teens to wander alone into the cool winds of early morn given up for good, the moon the only witness to this apostasy of ritual. She was needed now, her safety was important. She had to play a part, be a member of the family, she was a mother.

This lasted less than six months. Her feeling of being pinched by the strictures of the culture—breathless voiceless selfless throughout the day, colonial roles reversed: now the white girl served the savages— was so upsetting to her sense of self that she'd started hitting the night clubs when everyone was asleep, a perverse, customized twist on the traditional version of "moonlighting." On the strength of her long Irish legs and basic American late-teen curiosity, she'd gotten a stint as an up-and-coming "folk singer"—as if anyone did this type of nonsense amid the glittering disco ball of the mid-1970s, in the about-to-become-the-Silicon Valley South Bay no less—and then one night without any warning ran back to the tiny Oregon town she'd come from, hitching a ten-hour ride to Amity for the fair trade of a blow job and a few taught chords on her acoustic.

"Little lady middle-fingered my grandpa like that. She got some nuts all right."

"Yes. Our mother was very stubborn, Pika."

"He was about six feet two—you know that, Sis?—and thick. Typical hamo. Strong, steady. The old man used to beat all the young hamos in arm wrestling, all the way into his sixties. Mutherfucking forearms looking like Popeye, and shit."

"You take after him, Pika."

"I don't know. Probably a little bit."

"But you know, Pika—"

"Yeah."

"—what sixteen-year-old *isn't* too loud?"

"I didn't know she was sixteen."

"Yes."

"Good point, Sis."

"I mean, what does anyone know about life at sixteen?"

"Nah," he'd said. "Not a goddamned thing. I don't give a fuck what anybody says about this latest generation."

"Don't cuss, Pika."

"Not cussing don't make my analysis any different."

"It does to me."

Those days in his youth when he'd wonder why their mother had done such a thing, how she *could* have just up and left him, he'd take out her picture, kiss it without thought, slide it back into his wallet. She looked like hell at twenty-one, no getting around this, so strung-out and peeled-back you saw the pronounced jaw bones before you could really take in the face, and foresaw an OD'd body in the ditch of a creek, beads of frothy water trickling into her gaping mouth.

He came out of the heart of the town now, thinking on how culturally locked down this place seemed. Not a single brotha or chino but especially not a single hamo in sight. He could well be the first hamo on this part of the hallowed road who wasn't just passing through. But the eses—the paisas, his órale homies from Sinaloa and Michoacán— had to be around here somewhere, he knew, since there were all kinds of crops to be picked. Paisas to the rescue of the native-born lethargy. Paisas picking up where someone left off. If this place was like Cali at all, they were probably out in the fields already, bent-backed at the hottest point of midday, grapes on the vine, corn on the husk, beans sewn like tapestry through the diamond holes of the fence: that's profit in your bucket, Corrales, and it will add up like pennies in a piggy bank.

And crystal meth—Pika could *feel* it—the ma'a was here. A few shirt-less tweaks with their pants falling off were strewn across the side of the road, speed walking with hummingbird feet, yelling out to one another as if they were football fields away, and not side by side. Their heads popped and jerked like weasels out the hole. The devil's candy, he thought, the evil pill. Bone and teeth eater. The maʻa in barns out back, the maʻa in sheds on the side of the house, the rock in the middle of mutherfucking living rooms, kids revolving around a hot stove like little planets unafraid of fire. Meth out of WD-40, meth out of Pam spraying oil, meth out of generic weight-loss pills.

Sad how it swallowed isolated places. He'd had homies who'd moved it into Salt Lake City, Denver, Kansas City, and all kinds of tiny towns across a Midwestern plain none of them had ever seen. They were shameless. He had cousins who even hit the homeland, smuggling meth in boxes of macademia nuts to Pago Pago International Airport. Right when he'd shown up in Hawaiʻi, the maʻa was eating it like a cavity. The northwest side of Waianae and Nānākuli overrun with Polynesian zombies. Even Aleki the hustler had disappeared before he'd returned to Cali—most likely *been* disappeared. A deal gone bad, an unpaid debt. Who would've thought that crips and bloods would occupy opposite sides of that paradise? Shabu, shabs, batu, ice—whatever you wanted to call it—trumping pakalolo—aka good old weed—as temporary remedy from rock fever. Maui wowie the little leagues. For mainlanders cruising the strip on Waikiki or skin diving in Hanauma Bay. Paka had no pull with the locals anymore. Maʻa was everywhere on the island, the brown-skinned chronics slamming ice in the very sugar cane fields where their fathers and mothers used to break their brown-skinned backs for Mister Dole.

The same way, he thought, that these tweak palagis' ancestors probably logged the mountains.

He was coming out of the funk of yesteryear, awakened from his dreaminess by new surroundings. He ascended the winding road at a steady speed, passing the next plot of land every hundred acres or so, the erect immovable trees protecting the investment like toy soldiers standing guard. The few land-owning wealthy on the hill's crown. A vineyard claimed the highest point of the rain-smoothed hill, its endlessly rolling symmetry meeting at the mansion of a tasting room.

The valley's old colonial on the manor, Pika sneered.

These are likely white people, too. Maybe a few land-buying out-of-staters, maybe a few LA Jews. Retired to a place where you could get high on the oxygenated air and a good dark beer. That was the great delin-

eation among these people, he guessed: Oregon for Oregonians, something real subtle like that.

Rich, been-here-since-Lewis-and-Clark Oregonians versus all you vi-
ticultural transplants from Napa Valley.

He looked at the address written on his hand—54 Cottage Grove
Lane—and pulled up to a trifecta of mailboxes—42, 48, 54. A dirt road
tunneled into a canopy of trees. He drove it as calmly as he'd driven the
99 earlier, the dust kicking up around and behind the truck. After a few
hundred yards, he came into a clearing, a mansion centering the space.
He parked and killed the engine, pulling the e-brake under his left knee.
He got out without thinking of this Michael mutherfucker, but of his
old friend from Avenal Two-Yard.

"C'mon, Pika," Tut would tell him. "What's the matter which you,
fool? Whatchu doing, man? A three-spot of time wa'n't enough for you?
Thousand days behind bars don't cut it? You need what I got, that L with
the 25? Need a fence around your head and heart, too? Every day the
same day: no mutherfucking hope. Shit, sole, you acting like a dumbass
bread, homie. DOA immigrant getting got just to *get* got. Don't know
how to look around and find a different hole to burrow into. You go it all
on your own, sole, and you gonna die on your own, believe that."

Despite the made-up speech in his head from a man he'd probably
never see again, Pika came up the bright, wide, horse-accommodating
walk of the mansion, anyway, upright and chest out, eyes alert for whatever shit was about to go down. Truth was he could feel Tut's point, that
was real talk his old homeboy's ghost had just given him: don't look for a
fight from the start, man, but a reasonable out to this thing you're about
to do. The world was already messed up enough without you adding
your two-cent complaint to it, right? Somehow put the thing on the side,
if you can.

But how was that even possible?

This one was too big to ignore. Even a pacifist would have to address
this reality. If you don't deal with it now, the goddamned thing is still
gonna follow you around like a stray dog, especially once you're living
here in the happy little town of Amity, Oregon, holed up in your twacker
mother's shack.

Kick that mutherfucking dog right in the mouth, he thought.

He couldn't hit up any outside parties to negotiate his needs, anyway, buffer this beef of his with this Michael mutherfucker. He knew no one back there in town. Shit, he didn't know anyone in the whole goddamned state of Oregon.

Maybe, he thought, I wouldn't even know *how* to know them.

He couldn't go ring the doorbell on this mutherfucker, either, get at his rich-ass uppity family, who might do something for Pika's cause on the strength. If they were squares, that is, which meant nothing more than if they put the law above their own blood. Which happened every day in this country, amazingly. Roll to save your own ass. He could wash his hands of this shit if this Michael mutherfucker's family put their own collective boot in that punkass's backside, kick him to the curb accordingly, blacklist him indefinitely, etcetera.

But then: even if Pika could get at their ears, why would they believe *him*? The well was contaminated anytime he tried to "participate" in society, play it straight. Acclimation to the way the world worked. This source, ad eternum, was felonious. Who in this two-donkey town was gonna listen to the brownest newbie in a five-mile radius, Maori tags on his face like some Tysonian tribute, rap sheet longer than a Costco receipt? Nah.

Nope.

He stood by a stark black Hummer in the driveway—even its hubcaps were black, even the decals—looking into the passenger-side window. A question of the reflection: Can't you outsource like other mutherfuckers in this situation?

Normal folk get on the horn and 911 the leo leos. Already the idea was getting hijacked by his battered brain's easy institutionalized cynicism. Inflated donut-eating gods to the rescue! All hopped-up on their second-string junior varsity authority. Some of these po-lice even called themselves "soldiers." This was funny. This was *tragic*. On a daily basis, Pika thought, some poor nigga pays the price for that identity crisis. Do their job all gung-ho and hard core so the vets—their third-cousins in sanctifying the world—could return back stateside to a clean parade on clean streets.

Calling the cops on this cat would be like wiping out his whole life in the ten seconds it took to drop a dime. Would be the last time he'd ever say a word to anyone, saboteur of his own belief system.

Fuck, he thought. Did I drive up here for nothing? Maybe he could feed this dude some truth?

Get him on his knees beside the Hummer and order a lifelong apology to Sissy. Maybe he was that kind of a punk, bullying women until he's bullied back. He'd make the mutherfucker show up Monday through Sunday at Sissy's doorstep with a bouquet of beautiful flowers, the ones that you could find on the side of the road in this "nice little town," and then pick the rocks out of the grass, too, homie, and when you're done with that, go polish the stones. With your own spit. With mine. Penance until you die, whatever your end, and however your end happens, homie.

The jailhouse tattoos tagged to his forehead were coming into full effect in the Hummer's window. He pulled his beanie down over the map of green ink. Maybe in New Zealand, Pika joked, I'd get a few words in. That's where they'd hear me out without judgment. That's where I'd get a second sentence out my mouth. A third. A fourth. Actually form a statement, tie down an argument. Could make a real case, he thought, like they been making real cases against me since the day.

Well, here's what he'd say, this was the sum of it: only thing I know and care about concerning this Michael mutherfucker is that he raped my sister, Sissy, okay? I don't care about anything else: Would *you*? That's right: Judge *that*. What else do you good people have to know from there, man? That's all the bit of info you *need* to know. I've driven five hundred miles in that stolen piece of shit you're looking at, friends, just to address this, and now I expect you to handle him as is. Nip it in the bud, or whatever you farmers say up here in Ore-ee-gone.

"We're not hiring," he heard. "We pick our own fields, understand?"

He turned to face the words. Somehow he knew this was the mutherfucker of the hour—a brotherless, siblingless, homeless punk this Michael was—with a .45 conspicuously tucked nose-down into his beltline, redneck prick, (as if you know what to do with that, Pika thought) his T-shirt featuring a yellow bulldog on a faded red backdrop (maybe he knows *exactly* what to do with it), some souvenir from Marine bootcamp, or else a purchase at the nearby Navy Exchange (and maybe not).

My circuitry is seared, Pika thought, but is it sealed? Is this the last deal for me, all that I am when it comes down to it? I can talk to this mutherfucker straight, right? Get him to sack up and reverse course?

"Michael?"

"Who wants to know?"

A saying he'd memorized locked up popped into his head—too much analysis, it went, begets paralysis—but he shook it off and said, "You know Sissy O'Sands?"

"Michael!" A high-pitched, nervous voice from inside, scared, having sent out this guard dog of a son, or grandson, to toe their property line. "Is everything okay, Michael?"

"Oh, yeah." He looked Pika right in the eye. "Not a thing wrong here. Don't get yourself in a bunch over nothing. Go back to bed."

"Oh, mister? Mister!" A definite first, being called mister. But maybe, Utu's ghost whispered in Pika's ear, not the last. Mr. Tamavavae: keep on walking past this lifer on the yard. "I want you to know I called the police—"

"Asked you a question, homie."

"*Homie?*"

"—and you can explain to them why you're here, okay, mister?"

"Prefer mutherfucker?" he asked.

"That lady inside thinks you're a lettuce-picking spic," he heard, "but I like to give thieves scoping out our property the benefit of—"

"Michael!"

He hit the punkass so clean that he fell forward from the momentum, thinking only of the gun in the waistband, and was already centering himself to address it before they struck ground, the hollow thud of this Michael mutherfucker's head hitting brick and mortar even cleaner bringing out no sympathy in Pika whatsoever. The eyes fluttered and it seemed in that split second that the punkass was already coming back to consciousness and so he reached down and pulled the gun out and hit him once with the butt in the mouth. He threw it off into the bushes, and now heard what had been screeching there all along: paranoid woman sounding out the alarm of invasion.

He stood up to run—"You son of a bitch," came the five words from the ground, the mutherfucker propped on an elbow, plugging the font of blood at the back of his head—and then stopped at the absurdity of escape. This place was a straight-up trap, if ever there was one. Kefe badge-stuck billy club pua'as gonna getchu in Amity.

"Hey, man," he said, breathing hard already. Losing it. "Fuck you think you doing, homie? You ain't getting up, you punkass rapist."

"Fuck you."

"What?"

He walked over and shoved the mutherfucker back down, making immediate peace with whatever price he'd have to pay for the mayhem he was about to unleash. Right on time the birthing screams of the authorities coming to life, nearer than a buzzing bug rimming the microscopic hairs of his ear. This awareness made him neither slow nor stop his ravaging, accelerating instead—*right, left, right*—to get in all the shots he could before the cops mobbed the scene. Wasn't like a city grid where you had all kinds of options to run and hide. Leo leos don't get lost on hot pursuit around here. Might as well getchyo money while you can and take it out on this fool's head.

His punches were pacing his stuck-on-one word thoughts—*Scum! Scum! Scum!*—until the country's blurred colors surrounded him, drowned his eyes, the suddenly rubbery body flaccid in the psychedelic glitter of disco lights, spineless it seemed, without resistance, with nothing holding it together tight, and now he freakishly heard his own brain out loud—"You scum! Get on your face! Touch this war hero, Mexican scum?"—and with it the tingling cymbal of handcuffs, like heavenly pinions only he could hear, and therefore pity the sound, and therefore seek again.

His old friend.

Michael

March 21, 2006

NOTHING CALMED HIM MORE than pushing the treadmill to its limit, PT'ing the hell out of this machine. Three-pound weights strapped to his wrists, mph blasted to a 10.2, twenty minutes into it, 1 percent incline to make up for his easy-does-it shoes. The Nam guys had qualified for jump school in combat boots, he'd been told by the old schooler Tophats after he'd graduated second in his class, one of the select few who got to drink with them at the bar before going over. That was five years ago, and nothing had changed. Although maybe things had worsened. He increased the speed to a 10.4, feeling the same guilt in his favorite pair of ASICS, be it there at Fort Benning, Georgia, or here at Camp Gannon, Husaybah, Iraq.

Couldn't ever get around or past or make peace with the idea that this wasn't exactly what he'd imagined he'd be doing for his country when he'd signed up, daily working out in untainted air on a three-thousand-dollar machine, the kind you'd find in a big college town for the football team. This a far better facility than anything he'd ever been in in Amity, Oregon. To-the-hour current magazines and newspapers, ice-cold Dasani water shipped in by Haliburton. Artificially cooled and generated air the exact opposite of the natural desert reality outside. No sand in here. No bearded shepherds, no Mohammedan prophets. No sandals turned up in the corridors, the locals telling him he's the dirt and shit under their feet. Everything about this place bothered him, that's for sure, but he felt especially torn about this gym right here, having heard all the war stories from the Nam guys about shit-hole DMZs on the 38th parallel. Greased up VC in black ninja robes slithering through barbed wire like snakes through a bed of sticks. You didn't hear them back then because you couldn't hear them. No infrared cameras on your helmet, no motion sensors in the no-man's zone.

But at least if he was running in here and not talking, he figured, he could look down at Sissy and keep his priorities in order. Her photo propped like a trophy between the sixteen ounces of Dasani water he'd yet to sip from and the beeping digital mountain of his progress today. He could miss her the way he imagined GIs from World War II had missed their girls: five years in Europe, a thousand days in the Pacific. They were all just as young, but they were older, too. More serious, he thought. More wounded?

If he ran and didn't talk, he could feel the real physical pain based directly on however much suffering he could take from himself, which meant in a weird way how much suffering he'd *impose* upon himself. At least if he didn't socialize or pay attention to the news, he could focus on Cano with both his legs blown off from an IED on patrol last month, and this reminder would help him remember where he was at, what he was doing here. This wasn't at all clear anymore but—as near as he could figure—he still had the goal of personal survival, which linked to the goal of going home and—this time, anyway, for Sissy—staying home.

Too little of what constituted his war was what he'd imagined so many years ago. Was he wrong? Even the "patrols" weren't anywhere close to what he thought he'd be doing. He didn't feel like a warrior policing these tribal towns; he felt like a mark, a target on display for the masses.

He'd listened to enough old-timers anytime they were honest and critical about the "new bullshit military," and they'd talk about how the VC would penetrate the south, run operations in, and out of, Saigon.

But that wasn't even close to Iraq, he'd think back in his head, defending the "toughness" of the war he knew best. Even the majority of the South Vietnamese had little love for the north. The sympathy for the enemy is higher here than it's ever been. Why? Because *everyone's* the enemy! Here, you go on patrol and everyone you cross paths with—young men, children, old ladies, even—could kill you just the same as the next young man, child, old lady.

So in a way, he thinks, it takes more courage to go on patrol because the factor of the unknown is greater. I still don't truly understand, he thinks now, the stories behind what I see out here, what everyone else dismisses as inevitability. It's still foreign to me. We'll never acclimate.

No one's "winning the culture" here, he thought. The notion of converts to Christianity a total impossibility. That was what irritated him most about reading the paper and seeing the leftist protesters back home. Sure, Bush might be a Methodist turned sober by a vision, but that doesn't mean he's pushing his faith on the populace around *here*. Aren't any tent revivals in *Iraq*. No one standing up from their wheelchairs to walk again, hugging the preacher for his prayers. If anything, he thought, the number of Christians around here is *diminishing* from our presence. Been here longer than anyone, been here almost ten times as long as we've been a *country*, but are now getting chased out by the hordes for sharing the same religion as the invaders.

But then, he thought, plenty of tents. And plenty of *zealots* in the tents. Talking in tongues, pumping their fists. Saying things about me, he knew, that I'm better off not hearing, let alone understanding.

He strode out, pushing the pace. Beeped it up to 10.5, not really feeling it yet in his racing heart, a new guilt, a guilt every exhalation, and so it was up to 10.6 just like that, a tiny touch of the thumb.

And those rightists pissed him off, too. All those flag-wavers from little towns like the one he grew up in. The same one Sissy was in now, waiting for him like that play they'd all watched at base last month, the heroine in Japan mourning ten years for her GI to come back like he said he would. Good-bye, good-bye, Madame Butterfly.

People should do what they say they'll do, he thought. Countries, too. Countries, especially.

The rightists had it all wrong with the Grecian notion of democracy they were throwing around on the television news back home. Acting like these people were hiking up to the Acropolis to pitch their votes for some Peloponnesian War. If anything, this place proved the *limits* of democracy, how the vote goes the dominant group's way, how no Shia around here would vote a Sunni into the newly formed office of the prime minister. Now that's a modern miracle: right down party lines to the death, perfect conformity to the group. How that had been the exact problem, he thought, with the setup here in the first place. When a minority governs a majority, whether they're backed by Uncle Sam or not, forget about it.

And so, sure, he thought, all the Shia went to the booth this last time round. Hell *yeah*, they did. What a success! Seventy-five percent of Iraqis turned up to vote. Because all the fucking Sunnis stayed home, that's why, all 25 percent of them.

If I hear one more politician talk about Athens and Jefferson and Franklin, I'm going to catch the next troop transport home and put a slug through the talk box in their craniums.

He was smoking this machine now, driving it into the ground. "Driving their dicks into the dirt," the latest commonly heard line on this side of the war. Owens said it all the time. As did Alvarez. But sometimes the line hazed. He came here not just to take lives, but to save them. Save the ones on this side of the line. And yet. But then: there was too much "yet" to think about. Everything was "yet" when he thought about it, just like everyone on the other side could kill you. His brain was separating itself. He not only couldn't turn it off from wondering about the lives of the dead bodies—be they American or Iraqi—or from the comparisons of this war to the ones before it—Vietnam, Korea, World War II—or from who he was then—a virgin recruit dizzy on 9/11 images falling in on themselves—to who he was now—a five-tour vet "yet" unkilled—but it seemed as if his brain actually got off on tormenting him, almost as if he had no control over its impulses, an unstoppable entity unimpressed by the larger body subsuming it.

That's what this war is, he thought. They'll never stop. However many Amity, Oregon, recruits you sign up and bring here. I can't stay this course much longer. My reason for being here weakens by the day. My reason weakens by the day. They're unimpressed by our larger body, our bigger guns.

He turned the machine out full speed now, thirteen mph for ten seconds, and then twenty seconds, and then half a minute. Ripped like a soldier should be ripped, vibrant, legs strong. Six feet, 168 pounds: lean. This could go on forever, he thought, until I break the strap itself, or my own knees rip apart at the cap, self-imposed IED casualty on a treadmill. Inglorious, ironical ending for a warrior. Another minute, and then he looked down at her again and saw a foreign thumb just inches from his girl's face, pressed into the digital chart button like a little dick: beep beep beep beep beep. Black, bigger than his own clenched thumbs, slowing the pace, holding it down with authority.

"You all right, Mikey?"

Beep beep beep beep.

He pushed the thumb aside. "I got it."

He was slow-jogging and then speed-walking and finally the crawl-walk. Two mph. Mumbling to himself, head down, frowning, teeth grit behind sealed lips. "Yeah. Yeah, yeah, yeah, fuck yeah."

"Why don't you take a blow, man?"

"No, no. I'm all right, Lt."

"Sure you okay?"

The long pause to fight the brain in his head trying to sabotage his stability in answering a man who not only recommended him for the Silver Star for Valor he'd won but who wrote his mother that stupid letter she'd framed and hung over the fireplace. A body in the battlefield: you run out and drag it back. That's it. That's what he's said over the phone because it wasn't that nothing more need be said. It's that the question ought never to have been asked.

"I don't know."

"I know."

"Just."

"Hey. It's me, Mikey. Don't need to put up a face. We seen each other soil our pants in the field. Don't worry about that Semper Fi shit right now, okay?"

"All right."

"It's cool, Mikey. I got your back, man. I'm all about hoo-rah out there, but we can breathe right now, all right?"

"Okay."

"Thinking about Scanlan?"

"No."

You never said you were because that showed no focus on the mission, whatever it was, whatever it had ever been. Even if it was driving your treadmill time down by a fraction unmeasured in minutes and seconds. That split second could save a man's life. Which meant, conversely, that the same split second could cost a man's life, too. Scanlan might've died, but Scanlan lived. Or both, rather. Death and life not mutually exclusive then, but held inclusively together by the alit skin of one body. So if a part of Scanlan had died, what was left was forced to hold tight to life without any contribution from the dead half.

In a place where there'd been commerce before they'd come, Scanlan's half-life had happened. You could see the possibilities of yesteryear in the architecture, under the delicate craftsmanship of rows of ornate Arab arches, in the refusal of a near-dead vendor to leave his cart. He wouldn't care if you took his newly killed lamb back to camp, hung him the same way the meat was dangling in the heat, chopped his body to bits like little human steaks and then went on—that starved native son's stubborness made Michael freeze in his boots for the war-time eternity of a split second, double-take the setup and wonder, Why did he? How can I?

Meanwhile, Scanlan crawled like some miserable primordial creature less than twenty-five feet from where they'd set up. As the dusty street was coming alive with whatever had eaten Scanlan's lower half. The pek pek pek of popping gunfire not yet infecting Michael's sense, no, but giving rhythm to his fear almost, a pacemaker sucking the lifeblood of his heart. Scanlan was getting nowhere, trapped beneath the weight of his pack, the air's lazy dryness rising all around him, blurring the ground. He was so near Michael could see the trigger hand melted to the stock of his .60.

"You feeling it, huh, Mikey?"

"Just a little worried, Lt.," he whispered. "That's all."

And this man here, he remembered, called in the CASH that preserved Scanlan after I'd dragged back his living remains, whenever I'd had the courage to go had actually been. He honestly couldn't remember—not an epiphanal moment then, but maybe freed, merely that, from the blackout of his own half-stepping hesitance. Whenever he'd stopped using the fearless, aged, foreign vendor as excuse, he'd risen from squatting on his half-ass heels, and soon Scanlan partly on fire partly crippled was planting in his head that same question: Am I okay? Am I okay? Am I o—

As the transportable hospital, noosed by a steel thread to the chopper, was buzzing its overhead arrival. If no one knew but him, everyone got alerted in a neck-snap—Puooowwwwwww!—as it dropped aground with seismic force. We bring the longshoremen to Iraq, he'd thought, and throw crates around like building blocks. We bring the oilmen. Bring surgeons. Doctor and her nurses operating right there in the middle of a flammable desert, no time lost, two legs and two arms gone, but alive, Scanlan was, he is, still with us, still o—

"Mikey."

"Yeah."

Before boot camp, when he was young, a civilian uncle had invited him to his studio in Portland. A send-off of sorts, a last farewell. He'd watched *Forrest Gump* with his cousins and then shaken each hand at the door. He'd left with no clue what the point had been. One scene from the film had stayed with him, though: the sergeant yelling for the aimless idiot Gump to leave him there in the field, armless, legless. Another gimp, a different war. Casualty a word Michael didn't care for. Couldn't say why, and yet.

"You know, Lt. Uh. I don't know, you know?"

"Yeah."

"I'm not trying to act special—you know that."

"Course I do, Mikey. Go ahead."

"I'd never do that, but I. You know. Well: I'm really fucked up in my head."

"Yeah."

Am I okay? Am I okay? Am I okay? is the question that can't be answered. The legs and arms are gone. Okay is not the issue. Ask if you're alive. Ask if I've done my job. Have I earned my stripes, a claim on brotherhood?

"Got some real bad things going on up in there. I mean, don't worry, Lt., I'm not gonna go AWOL on you or anything—I'm not off the farm or anything like that, you know I got your back, too, I just—"

"I know you do, Mikey."

"—feel really afraid inside, not of death or pain, you know, not anything like that, but I want to keep something to believe in—"

"Yeah."

"—and I'm not doing a good job on that front."

Lt. Terrell backed his men on paper and fought alongside them in the field. Naval Academy or not, no enlisted man could disrespect Lt. Terrell if they knew him, or if they saw him fight after the accusation in this same gym sixteen months ago from a steroided machinist running down officers. "Too much muscle, too much down time," was all the Lt. had said, helping the man up, ordering him back to his barracks. And now he was thinking, Lt. was. He was strategizing for an answer, calling in the flying hospital.

"This is five for you, Mikey?"

"Deploys?"

"Yep."

"Yes, sir. Twenty days to wrap number five."

"Don't do six."

"Six."

"What's going on with your girl, Mikey? Still hanging in there, right?"

His eyes widened in reverence and the Lt. nodded. "Oh, yeah, Lt. Yes, sir."

"Well, that's something."

"Yes, sir."

"That's a lot, actually. A hell of a lot."

"Yes, sir. That's right. It is."

"So how's she doing?"

"Ahh, she's great, Lt. Let me show you." He reached out to the center of the rack and pulled the laminated photo of Sissy out of the water bottle holder, and held it out to Lieutenant Terrell.

"Yes. Very good, Mikey. Semper Fi girl looks like to me."

"Through and through."

"Very good."

"She keeps me alive."

"Right."

"I mean inside, Lt."

"I know what you mean. Unless she's about to sign up and walk point, we keep each other alive in this godforsaken dustbowl."

"Yeah."

"Mikey."

"Yes, sir."

"Let me get a little down home on your ass, okay?"

"That don't sound too good, Lt."

"We Georgians got a saying, you heard it?"

He looked over at the lieutenant, nodded. "All ears, sir."

"You all *don't* come back now, you hear?"

He nodded again. "I hear."

"Well, enough of this shit, huh, Mikey? I'm gonna run one more with you for old time's sake."

He climbed aboard the treadmill next to Michael's and Michael was already increasing the speed. Nothing ever felt right except driving himself to his knees. "Yes, sir. That's right."

"Let's blow this treadmill up, what do you say, Marine?"

"Yes, sir."

"Go on and max this goddamned machine one last time. See what you've got, son. Get it, soldier. Get it. Earn those legs o'yours."

"Aaaahhhhh-ooooooo-rrrraaahhhhhhh!"

Sissy

April 29, 2005

SHE WAS IN THE SAME CLOTHES as the night before—red and white tube top, white tube mini skirt, red plastic ice-pick heels, and nothing else— and the stains had dried into her skin, powdered by the dirt she'd slept in after running away from the house party at Danny's. She had tried to dust off before coming into the church, barely having the nerve to pass beneath the unreadable inscription above the door: *Terribilis est locus este.*

She'd known about this place since the Christmases of her childhood when she'd see the fudge and trussels sold in the Amity Grocery Store. The monks, she'd read on the back of the boxes, made the chocolate to eke out a living. Every note on every box was handwritten, calligraphy from another century. Any profit they made went to charity at St. Vincent de Paul's, a safe haven of grain, canned corn, rice, and mac and cheese any time the food stamps the state gave her mother weren't enough. This made her sad, knowing that devotees of God were the same as she was, one rung up from begging. At least a hundred times on foot at the Bellevue-Broadmead crossing, she turned right en route to the vacant shores of the South Yamhill, where she'd first met Michael. Until last night, she'd never turned left at the sign that fingered the way to the monastery.

This wasn't the first time, though, that she'd tried to leave her life. Sometimes she'd spend an entire weekend on a friend's couch in a house barely seven doors down from her own, pretending to be three states over in the Badlands, say, which she'd once learned about in a documentary on the History Channel. She'd get so consumed by the dream that she'd turn the friend into a Lakota Indian, and the two donkeys outside into domesticated buffalo. If a town named Amity is like this, she'd thought, imagine a place called the Badlands. Or Nitro, West Virginia, found in the dusty atlas in the Amity Public Library—another faraway place whose nomenclature fascinated her: you light a cigarette and the whole town's legacy of coal-drilling for a few years shy of a century goes up in retardant-immune flames. Hell on Earth was the Nitro of her nightmares. Hell in America. She could relate to those people; she knew what it meant to be trapped. Even if they wanted to, no one could sell their houses in Nitro, the arsenic-laced water spotting the skin from casual contact, the lobster-red rashes a kind of coal-dust psoriasis. Paper plates and plastic sporks to avoid washing dishes. Bird baths with bottled water to stay clean. She'd fall asleep with the *National Geographic* article spread across her fatless, post-pubescent chest, thus gone into the dark places of her mind the way bats disappear into caves. From darkness to darkness. From the uncontrollable darkness of the world to the familiar darkness of her head.

Other times she'd sleep on the banks of the South Yamhill, her camping bag usually where she'd left it the month before, tucked under a wild tangle of dogwood. Sometimes she had to carefully shake it out, worried about animal droppings and burnt spoon remnants and discarded needles. She liked to collect the shotgun shells and pile them in the middle of an ash-gray firepit. You could see where the bullets had made fist-sized holes in the dirt wall across the water. The wide-open sky of stars and moonlight sheen made her think of things she never thought of in town. Once in late summer she got to see the same dancing lights Michael had described in a letter years ago, crab fishing in Alaska—The Boring Yellow Borealis, he'd adorably but mistakenly called it—and she'd thought, I'm in the middle of these gases of space. I'm stuck here in Amity, Oregon, while the spirit of every other living thing is zipping around me. I'm on the edge of my life but no one knows it. No one cares. In early morning the laser of the sun would stir her into half-consciousness, and she'd rub her eyes, think of Michael "soldiering on" in the war-torn land of a half-dozen lasers of sun, and then roll over to push herself up, thus forced to awaken from the rest she always desperately needed, but never seemed to get.

She was only nineteen, but was already tired of her life. Being in the church didn't change that—in fact, the lingering mist of altar incense

calmed and then seduced her into sleep, which she was going in and out
of now, her skin tingling from some strange sense of awareness that this
could be her last chance to get things right, however that might happen.
If at all. So maybe being here made her think it was wrong to be tired.
That that's what they meant by carrying your cross. Maybe. Every time
she nodded off, the other parishioners in the tiny chapel stood, and she'd
stand with them, listening to the mysterious verse, swaying in the oaken
pew.

The priest was walking slowly around the table, shaking a wand of
water at it, and somehow she went to her knees—still tender to the
touch, sore from the rug burns—at exactly the right time. Everyone but
the priest was kneeling, even the real-life mutes in their ash-gray robes.
She looked across the aisle. A plump abuelita kindly pointed twice at the
ground in front of her. She thought it an indirect suggestion to close her
eyes and pray, but the streak of redness at her feet caught her eye, and
she got off the floor, pulled out the kneeler with the bridge of her big toe
and sank into the cushiony pads, her body resetting like the earth after
a quake.

Her elbows were propped on the pew in front of her, and she hummed
to the whispering at the altar, losing herself again somewhat, as if she
were at a concert and not a mass. She opened her eyes and deeply inhaled the scents, like she'd seen the yipster patrons in the window of The
Blue Goat Restaurant nose the steam of their chamomile tea. One lady
in the front pew—horn-rimmed spectacles, companionless, manless,
childless—was turning in piety: even a little chapel in Amity, Oregon,
had its etiquette police, didn't it? The rules didn't bother Sissy so much.
The spirit of them didn't bother her either. If only there were rules somehow devoid of human meddling.

Was there such a thing as a law handed down on high?

Kindness, she immediately thought. Kindness is universal enough
to be—if there be such a thing—holy. Kindness to anyone was the law,
kindness for whatever reason, however little kindness returned.

She looked around at both ends of the chapel, she looked up toward
the ceiling. These were the images of joyous birth and joyousless death,
the two extreme ends of human awareness that had plagued her for so
long. She was lost between the poles, could never find her true north

bearings, she was centered only by the need of Michael's touch, which had been absent now—as it was—for a fifth consecutive tour.

Gone again, as of this morning. Off to the desert-dry part of the war-troubled world. Drowning-in-itself-Amity's arid opposite.

"So whatchu gonna do with your life? Just keep bumming off me?" This was yesterday. This was last year. Was there a difference? This was every day of her life with her mother. They'd been in the Ashes Café getting a free EBT meal off the beneficent state of Oregon. An episode of Maury Povich was blasting away above the bar, the television staticky. As if even that box of bolts and glass and tubing, she'd thought, is having a tough time sharing this show.

Her mother looked like a past guest of Maury Povich, like infamous alumni. Sissy never said aloud—and tried not to think—what everyone else in Amity knew: here was the most tore back, beat-up, fifty-looking thirty-five-year-old in town, Ms. Lucille Shevon O'Sands.

"Gonna be a tramp forever, Sissy? Eventually you're gonna have to get off your knees and live like the rest of society."

There was no refutation to put out—the truth was the truth even if the source was your own mother, from whom the basis of a person derived—and so she'd said the first thing that came to mind, a modest lie she knew wouldn't be checked up on: "Been going to church. I like it."

The coal-black irises set back in the hollowed-out sockets were loveless. You're a hater, she'd thought, of your own daughter. Even the ex-con fry-cook in the kitchen, popping their greasy meal to life, couldn't stand her mother.

Another customer came in and she tried to nod at him with kindness, but he ignored both of them, the way she was used to, as if she and her mother weren't there at all. Something she'd always known about poverty: the occupants of the ladder's rigid bottom rung adhere like moss to its slopes and ridges of condescension. Ignored by every other higher rung, but vital and inevitable to the bottom-dwellers.

Michael would have told him, You're eating in the same damned low-down restaurant she's eating in, huh, Mister? Then he would have gotten louder if no apology were rendered. Or else did you miss out front the video poker signs blinding even the blind of this town?

"Which church?"

The same old question from above: "Who is . . . the father?"

She took in the grease-browned walls wherever there wasn't a chain-saw or a flea market photo of John Wayne on it, and then finally considered the show. Despite a feeling of disgust for the host, who was leaning away from his guest the same way this other customer was leaning away from her and her mother—toward the door like, just in case—she was mesmerized. Taken in by the idea that people did this to other people, embarrassed them for money or notoriety or insecurity, and that still yet other people came, too, to see it all in the studio, to hoist themselves up on another rung of that inescapable ladder, as she and millions of other Americans were also doing now, peering over the edge at this nineteen-year-old black girl strangling a twenty-year-old black boy for disputing her claim that he'd fathered her baby.

"The monastery," she said, squinting at the ensuing chaos on the screen, humongous black men pulling on the arms of the young mother, big white smiles on their faces, the audience cheering for the bouncers eighty-sixing both parties to either side of the stage.

"Sissy. What are you doing with those—wait."

Sissy looked over at the other customer. He could hear them perfectly—was close enough that she herself could hear his labored breathing. But he wouldn't tip his hand, either out of respect—their business; or disgust—his judgment; or nosiness—to hear every last word. She couldn't tell. She didn't know him, although she'd seen him around. Everyone in Amity—whether they knew each other or not—had seen everyone else around.

She whispered, "No."

"Please tell me you're not."

"Stop it."

"*Are* you?"

"Please stop."

"My God, Sissy! What are you doing at that place? Are you—"

"Just praying, Mom."

"—fucking those horny monkeys out there? Servicing the virgin freaks? Jesus Christ! How many more—"

Sissy stood, right hand pressed against the bridge of her forehead, as if shading her eyes from the sun. Shielded from whatever that other customer was now doing, even if it was nothing but eating his meal. She started toward the exit, her mother attached magnetically to her heel, maternally insistent when it didn't matter any longer. She felt burnt in her core, and now her mother was just piling the pain on, throwing out any punitive measure to see how the fire could rise, how much of Sissy's skin would burn. The words from above made Sissy wince, as if she'd just sucked on a slice of lime: "You ARE the father!"

At the door she went right on Main Street—"Jazelle. Jazelle. It's a 99.997 percent certainty that you ARE the father"—picking up her pace, trying to ignore the cadenced sound stalking her from behind. Harassment was like this. Torture was like this. Life would never change. For someone who hadn't held down a job as long as Sissy could remember, her mother sure worked hard at destroying what little she had.

"Goddamnit, Sissy. You're gonna ruin my good name in this town. You've already ruined me, Sissy."

She inhaled deeply and accelerated, focusing on a green ridge cresting the horizon, way up by a blood-red grape patch at Amity Vineyards.

"Everyone knows my daughter is a whore. Everyone knows my daughter can't keep her legs closed."

She was jogging now, her heels clicking in time on the pavement.

"Everyone knows I should've *never* given birth to you."

She'd turned and shoved her mother. The flat, splattering-of-an-egg sound of her mother's head crashing into dry wall was so sickening that she stopped and reached out for a shoulder, the imprint of her hand already reddening on her mother's hypersensitive skin. The dormant bruises and busted capillaries coming up would never go away for good. She straightened her mother upright. She kept her head down doing this, knowing she was marinating in the judgment of townies with the blinds pulled back, knowing she'd collapse if she looked into her mother's face, only able to move after giving herself official permission out loud and nodding twice: "Okay. To go. Okay."

She sprinted off. With each step, she imagined her mother coughing up the dust of her storming feet. The shame of this vengeant thought only pushed her onward. She came out of the town and passed the Amity firehouse, descending down a trampled slope of ash swale and then up the other side. She ran behind the mishmash of yards overrun with brambles of blackberry bushes scratching at her knees, and the waist-high weeds tickling her lower back, slowing to a pedestrian jog at a hidden, overgrown vineyard. She'd always loved to inhale the sweet blueberry scent of the grapes—even now, especially now—and so she walked for a few minutes, paralleling the staid Amity divide between business and indigence, promise and collapse, money and nothing.

She went into the woods without reservation, the ground softening from the long furrowed bed of moist needles and muddied leaves, an overgrown path moist and unkissed by sunlight, untouched by any mammal without hooves and claws. The catch-me vines of the blackberry bushes grew even this far removed from the sun, and she knew from having eaten the fruit all over town that these berries were worthless, water-logged, no chance for natural light to get the sugar process going.

She walked for a hundred count and then ran for a hundred count, a game she played for at least ten minutes. There were tiny holes in the cobalt blanket of the trees overhead and this lit her path enough until she emerged onto a plain of grass shining with moonlight: the apex of the Eola Hills. For a brief respite, she stood on this familiar terrain, the southwest end of Michael's farm, which was just as black and vast in the distance, except for the square of light promising tonight's peace. The grass, she could feel with each step—she could *smell*—had just been cut, smooth like wet turf beneath her feet. She didn't run, but went directly to the light, his bedroom. She knew what he was doing. What else was there to do the day before but pack? She didn't bother looking into the window, merely tapping on the glass with the edge of her filthy nails, and then sat against the wall.

"Sissy?" From above again. Always on the bottom rung, even with the boy you love. "That you?"

"Yes."

"Be right out."

She got to fifteen in her head before the bitch of a mother shouted the same old caveats at her only son, and twenty-two when his predictable loyal two-word dismissal came, and then the door slam, and then his footsteps.

"Sissy?"

"You shouldn't tell your mother to shut up, Michael."

"Come on. Stand up."

"Okay."

"You walked here again?"

"Yes."

He dusted her off gently. "You're telling me about should and shouldn't?"

"Had to see you before you left."

"I thought we agreed you wouldn't do that anymore. I worry about you, Sis. I can't protect you like that."

"Are you mad at me, Michael?"

"Of course not." He looked her up and down. "You all right?"

"Is *she* mad at me?"

"I don't give a fuck if she is or isn't, Sissy."

"Well, does she think you're going back because of me?"

"Don't know. Don't care. Oh, please don't."

She wiped at her eyes, but it kept coming. "I'm sorry. Just hold me, 'kay?"

"You been crying a lot."

"No."

"Yes, you have. I can tell. Your eyes are all swollen like a boxer's." He kissed one and then the other. "What the hell happened this time?"

"Nothing. It's okay now. Tell me it's okay, Michael."

"You know it's okay when you're with me."

"Always?"

"You know that. Stop asking questions like that."

"I'm worried, Michael."

"I'm not gonna die, okay? God's not gonna let me die."

"Don't talk like that, Michael."

"Okay. Sorry. You're too cute when you worry about me. Let's just say I *hope* God's not gonna let me die, okay?"

"Michael."

"What?"

"I'm worried about *me*, too. This is your fifth tour, you know, and I . . ."

"Sissy."

"I don't know what to do when you're gone. I'm so lonely I ache at night for you."

"Hey—"

"Not like that, I just mean. Well, I don't know. I spend the whole day praying for you."

He pulled back his face, pet her on the cheek, pulled her back in. "Thank you."

"I feel like my life stops when you leave."

"Yeah."

"I don't have any backing, Michael."

"I know you don't. You're the only loyal chick I've ever known. You're a Semper Fi girl, Sis."

"No, I mean—"

"Just don't listen to them townie assholes, Sis."

She separated from him and looked down. "It's not that easy, Michael."

"Yes, it is. You have—"

"They're everywhere."

"—to be strong."

"Your *mother's* everywhere. She's their leader. And I *am* strong."

"I'm gonna talk to her. I know you're strong, Sis. Come on. It's me, Mikey. Don't worry, okay? I'm gonna address her bullshit tonight."

"Please don't. She already hates me enough. She told Officer Yackup that I was using meth."

"She said that?"

"And it's not just that, Michael. There are other lies, too."

"That's so goddamned mean."

"I think she wants to hurt me."

"Look. She'll listen. Trust me. Got no choice—"

"She thinks I'm my mother."

"—but to listen. She's gonna *have* to listen to me."

"Okay, Michael, but it's more, you know—"

"What? Than my mom?"

"Well, yeah. It's way more. Everything. I can't, you know, I can't . . . well, I was thinking, Michael."

"Yeah?"

"Well, it's kinda crazy, but I don't know, you know, war's crazy, too, Michael, and here you are on your way to another tour, I mean, it never ends, you know, and it's like we can't beat the past enough to just live right here in Amity—"

"Sissy."

"—and be ourselves—Yeah?"

"Tell me what you were gonna—"

Her face brightened and she jumped up into his arms, face to face, nose to nose, and then a woodpecker kiss on it, the very tip. "You wanna move to Portland, Michael?"

"Portland?"

She pushed off and dropped back down to the ground. "Downtown. Or you know, like a little studio in Chinatown—wouldn't that be just a complete blessing, Michael? To wake up and go eat some dim sum for lunch?"

"Dim sum?"

"Those little Chinese burritos you loved in Salem, remember? Like little crepes with spicy chicken? Or take a walk along the Willamette at sunset? We could jog across the Old Iron Bridge! Look for DB Cooper's money bundles."

"DB Coop—"

"Well, it doesn't have to be Portland, Michael! Can be Seattle! I can be a barista, yeah, and you can, well, you can fix cars, or even drive a bus, or something like that. You could get a job real easy with your war record. It's not like the olden days when they used to spit on you guys. And later—later, we could go to school together, you know? Didn't you say your GI Bill will pay for everything, even living expenses? And just think! You could walk me to class, Michael. Oh, God. How romantic! Wait for me outside class, carry my books. All the stuff we never got to do here. Or we can even go south. Why not? We're not stuck in rain country just cause we been here our whole lives. Let's be the first in our families to cross the border for good. You know? I mean, what about San Francisco, Michael? 'Member when we followed the path of that cable-car online? How much you loved it. Up and down those beautiful hills! Or we could—"

"Slow down, Sissy."

"—leave the *country*! And not for that stupid desert they keep sending you to. Didn't you say you wanted to see Italy, Michael? Or Ireland, or something? We can go on your GI fund, can't we? But if you want to move to another—"

"Sissy, calm down."

"—small town in the Midwest or something cause you like the small town life—I understand. I do, too, Michael—we could do that—I don't mind—maybe in Nebraska or Missouri or once I heard this lady say that the most beautiful state in America was Maine—or was it Vermont?—oh, I can't remember, just as long—"

"Sissy!"

"—as it's not *here*. Not *this* small town. What, Michael? What?"

He was gripping both her shoulders, she now realized. "Stop this crap right now."

"Oh God, Michael. I hate it. I hate this town."

"You live here in Amity, okay?"

She was aware of her breathing now, rabid and short like a winded dog. She turned her head to the town down below, and its scattering of lights along the two-hundred yard stretch of the 99. "No. No."

Michael reached out and lightly clapped his hands on either ear, and forced her to look up at him. "This is where you live. And you gotta face it, Sissy. Just like anyone else in Amity does."

"Please, no. I can't take being here alone, Michael. I can't do—"

"You *got* to, Sis. I want you to. *Need* you to. Why *else* would I come back from that shithole in the sand? You gotta live in Amity the same way anyone from Amity lives."

These had been the very words she didn't need to hear, from the only other party, except for her brother, whom she ever really listened to. But Pika wouldn't know what to say either way. Not only had she never met him face-to-face, but he was from a city one quarter the size of the *entire state* of Oregon. How could anyone envision a town like Amity unless he'd seen it for himself? But Michael's version of comfort brought no comfort at all: he was pulling up the weeds in the yard, telling her to dump the refuse in the river.

You gotta live in Amity the same way anyone from Amity lives.

Wasn't this exactly what she'd never wanted? And didn't his love for her root in the good dirt of her deep-down refusal of inheritance, the way she tried, every day, to deny the accusation of being white trash. They liked to call each other rednecks now, as if that changed anything. Did he even *know* her? Or, if flipped, what she was *capable* of? How easily the world could be *wrecked* in a ten-minute bout with recklessness?

How loosely to sanity she—or anyone else they knew in this town—was tied?

The same way anyone lives jumpstarted a prologue to the story she'd always known she could write, a public outing of her need to be touched by an Amity audience more than willing to listen, to watch, to join in. Approval in the loving palm of your hand. Yes, she had that in her, too. If she'd gone up through the dark woods alone, why wouldn't she go back down them alone, too? The hard work was already done, this was the easy part. She'd worked against the pull-down of her inheritance for so long that she privately craved to give in to gravity, to free-fall earthward groundward backward downward.

And she was rising from her knees again in this goddamned quarter-filled medieval church, conceding to an outside momentum. The same way she'd risen last night at the urgent tug of the high school quarter-back, Danny Lee Martin, his parentless house party about to really blow up. Kid Rock rapping on the soundsystem, Pabst Blue Ribbon posters scrunched against the wall. Was only thirteen hours ago, less than a day. She'd been taken right to the center of the room by a host of strong, lustful, post-adolescent hands, nearly levitating, the latest immaculate messianic miracle of Amity, Oregon, in the body of a nineteen-year-old girl. Usuram corporis. Ephemera ad eternum. Only half the eight-man football team was there, but each matched the other in breathlessness, the uncontrollable kind after the big run.

"Hey, Sissy."

"Whatup, Sis."

"Shit, man."

"Smoking. Hot. Fuck yeah."

Not the way she was walking up the center aisle of the church now, weeping into her palms, then pulling down on her skirt as she passed the horn-rimmed lady, the one hissing like a desert snake.

"No respect, Magdelene."

She barely made it to the base of the pulpit, the endlessly naked legs endowed by her mother showcased for anyone not praying like they were supposed to. This not the clarity of last night—of purpose, of self. Of power. When they'd let her down in the living room's beer-soaked center like some Egyptian queen she'd seen on the History Channel. Except that her subjects stood, and she was the one kneeling. They worshipped her. They touched her. Grabbed her.

Not merely immodest now as she took her knees at the priest's behest (a gentle nod, not what she'd expected)—but almost laughably present in this church, if anyone were vicious enough to point it out. Maybe even *inexplicably* here.

Like the mysterious flash-dream she'd just had—Right there! Gone!—as yet another human being entered her mouth, this time supposedly for her soulful good and not his lustful own, the dried white wine-dipped wafer powdery as the bubble gum in Michael's packages of old school baseball cards—the dream, her one-second dream might have gone like this: a jury-sized congregation pitched in joyous peals of pious laughter, all at hearing the truth of her harlotry from the night before.

Well . . . she'd confess!

Even then in the squall of their judgment!

If only they'd listen!

If only—

That she'd hiked in the dark to this place for a reason. The only born-and-raised kid at the party not high on cheap Irish whiskey, or made-in-the-outhouse-barn-crystal meth or ripped-off-from-an-old-lady-oxys—stupid one-horse Amity, Oregon, parties!—and that she'd stripped down to her pale-white skin—sober clairvoyance, gutteral yearning—for nothing more than the love of her life.

Michael

May 1, 2006

He lay there on the bed of his childhood not so much in recall or in mourning or out of malaise or conscious political disengagement, but in the feeling that the notion of movement—mobility, he meant— certainly *action*—putting out in the world, that is, the physical manifestation of your own piddly *wants*—was utterly pointless. Between here and there is closer than one thinks. Sitting beside you in mid-yawn, cross-legged, fiddling its thumbs, is disaster. One geared oneself over the course of a life to perpetuate life itself, to sanctify and protect life, wage surface philosophical apologies for life, and there were so many American men and women morons, he knew, who attached their every action to this assumption of life as the basis for all argument outlook belief breath of air that he wouldn't get anywhere, anyway, trying to explain what his non-statement statement meant, given that they'd listen, given that they'd care.

Definitely couldn't get his mother to sign on to this theoretical void of self, the other planet out there in the other solar system of the living room. That redneck, he thought, who thinks she's an aristocrat. Shit. Money won't save you, lady, he thought further. Money is a part of the illusion.

Plug status into the formula, get the same result.

Nor had he any interest in discussing the pointlessness of action with anyone professionally inclined to butt in, a licensed expert on the landscape of the mind and its unforeseen ills, some laywoman virgin with an unbroken hymen between her legs, irises dancing with her need to be your savior; or how stupid he looked prostrate on the same bed he'd nightly peed fifteen years ago, that any challenge put to him about the war—"Get up, man. You can walk, can't you? You're still whole, right? There are vets who can barely move their heads, asshole"—was—provided it came from a born-into-the-world cripple stuck there in his wheelchair, or else another vet face-scorched and body-mauled by the oil-driven flames of another continent—dead-on accurate.

He didn't even dare roll to his side. Not even that was sanctioned, not even that brought back the cause. Nothing could open up a glimpse of the day's promise. There were no flames to flee from here on this side of the world; the buzz on his L5 (the columns learned from a medic in Iraq pointing out the numbers of the lumbar on a corpse they'd just made singled out of the two dozen dead they'd also made by the open perforation just above the hip bone bleeding out the body like the ooze from a trash bag)—that little buzz was a tickle. His lower spine sticky in this position he'd held for the last seventeen hours or so was no concern in the larger scope of things—was it? when it came down to it: *was* it?—that larger scope through which you couldn't help considering *everything*—even the most minute detail, even minutiae, most especially the secondly grinding of the clock—once you'd been to war.

Which meant once you'd had true illogic visited upon your safe and deathless world of logic.

He even despised—if one had the minimal imagination to understand the line of demarcation he was lying across; if one had ever swallowed at the sight of a beheading, reaching for and clutching one's own Adam's apple which was still there rolling beneath one's palm like a baby trapped inside a blanket; if one had hated the species-at-large just barely more than one hated oneself, fifty-one to forty-nine it went, the nod of hatred toward the ninety-nine cowards who'd never gone versus the all-voluntary force coward who did—yes, he despised the melodrama attached to his self-removal. That it had to refract against his mother. She was like an enemy soldier picking up a dud of a grenade, pulling the pin, and throwing it back at the former idiotic American owner. She loved to make drama where there didn't have to be any. The pin was in there, lady, he said to her all day long in his head from his back on this piss-soiled bed, before you went and pulled it out. Men and a few women had gone and fought and died and ruined the world for no other reason, he knew, than people like her.

Bitch, he thought. Then mumbled: "Bitch." The movement outside his door meant she was on her way already.

She knocked as if she were disturbing a world leader, and he laughed aloud at this knee-jerk, middle-America, ultimately ignorant hope of hers to reverse course, saying, "Don't you have anything to do with yourself? Sit around and monitor me all day. Ever heard of a wasted life?"

She opened the door slowly and he yelled, "Open it up, for fuck's sake, if that's what you're gonna do! Can't even do that directly, huh? Can't even be honest about it? Who the hell are you performing for?"

"Hi, honey."

Like she was deaf to his tone, which didn't need the meaning of the words. Didn't dare process the words, whatever they'd meant. Deaf and dumb to anyone's but her own cries.

Oh, he thought, but she can see all right, can't she?

He could sit here in absolute monastic silence, slow his heart rate to a hibernating polar bear's, think shit, say shit, bother no one who didn't enter this house and follow his mother's finger for a nose-probe of this room, and it would make no difference in her mission to get him up and out into the world. Up and out of this house. The problem of the war and more importantly anyone near enough to have their world view obliterated would then be conveniently killed of her daily tea-time considerations, her sewing circles with Coelho Vineyards' biggest supporters, uncramped by his style—a glorious return to the provincial safety of her own Amity, Oregon, world view.

She's a hick, he thought, who thinks she's a queen in a storybook.

In the long run—which basically meant when he got out of the town for longer than a minute—nothing she'd taught him about people had been right. She'd made him feel like a fool in boot camp. He'd been raised in de facto white-flight paranoia, his LDS mother taboo-divorced from the father he rarely saw in Utah. Sent off from the pathologically homogenous state with enough family money to hide the reason, his hairless little boy chin on her shoulder at breakfast for ten years running. She'd prim horrified at the morning paper's daily negativities, levying so much fault on the brown people in nearby cities, brown people in other countries—everywhere the world was corrupted by some degree of tint of that shit-starting color—that every now and then his little boy mind wandered against its own sense of sense and moral justice into a biblical realm she had always claimed, but never partook in while he'd been alive, and had maybe been banished from before he was even a seed, even a skein of protein. His best friend growing up, an LDS named Nathan, told him that the reason blacks couldn't be deacons in the Mormon church was that black was the color of the devil, and it clearly said so in this book right here, see?

Brown, he'd thought back then, is in between black and white. But more black than white for sure.

Then he got to boot camp at Benning and all the badasses running it were brothas from the liberated deep South, deep-voice ghetto-basso legitimate threats barked from a drill sergeant with the biggest biceps he'd ever seen. And the biggest lips, too, his mother would've added. Sergeant Liston. Thirty-six pull-ups from a dead-hang. The sweat splashing off Sarge's lats like the Umpqua waterfall off the rocks. Damned near thirty-seven, shy by the inch of a stretched-to-its-limit chin. In the humid Deep South heat, no less, peach-pink Georgia sky breathing down on him like the warm breath of the maker they all believe in down there. Believe in up here.

On the best day of my life, he thought, with the wind at my back and only a splash of water in my belly, I did sixteen. Couldn't have ripped out another one if her life was on the line.

Everything goes down, she'd said one day to him before his first day of high school, worried about the three Hispanics newly admitted to Amity High, after they come in their filthy swarms. She still thinks blacks and Mexicans are the same, he thought, even after I've gone there five fucking times. Just like she thinks Shia and Sunni are the same. An average American. Average uninformed idiot calling all the shots around the world.

He was shirtless and pantless and sockless in his tighty-whities, head propped, hands laced behind the rear of his skull, arms numb, staring at the ceiling for seconds at a time, counting the various amorphous communities of dust around the fan (Sunni minority right there, he thought. Shia majority over there. A few unlucky Orthodox Christian communities surrounded by dirt on every flank: theological claustrophobia: dust to dust, ashes to ashes, we all fall down!), and then he turned his eyes on his mother, no other movement, and held the stare because there was no reason at all not to hold it.

"You were gone a long time, honey."

He waited. His eyes the same. Muttered, "Not that long."

"Well, five years total, honey—that's a long—"

"Some people never come back."

"—time for a mother to—"

"Why don't you think of them, huh?"

"—have to—well, I do."

"Cry about them."

"Okay, Michael. I will."

"I ain't going back. So don't worry about me, okay? I'm a coward. I'm your son. Chicken-shit right out your chicken-coop womb."

"Don't you talk like that! You're a hero, Michael! They sent me the medal!"

He laughed so loud his bomb-damaged eardrums rang hollow from the echo, emotion spurred by the kind of downward, uncontrolled, inner hilarity he'd felt the first week back at the Amity Patriots Parade, Wounded Warriors Project toll-booth operator named Laird saying without pause in his presence, "Well, it's not heroic of me to sit here all day in the sun, no, but would someone mind getting me an ice-cold Coke?" and then looking up at Michael, unblinking. Then seeing the other Amity sheep run to the market, one by one, after he'd told Laird to stand up and get out of his chair before he blew his fucking brains all over Church Street.

Then he'd laughed even harder when he saw what they'd brought back: giant bag of lime-flavored tapatío Cheetos, Reese's Pieces, Tilla-mook beef jerky, *and* the ice-cold Coke.

You doormats, he'd thought, the hilarity dying into little chuckles, his lashes rimmed with tears from the laugh attack, the 99 percent civilians around him unable—unlike his mother now—to even look upon him. You do know your heroes, don't you? Pray! Eat! Celebrate! Squeeze every one of your fat asses into line! Lower every fat face to the trough!

"You stop that right this minute, Michael!"

He smirked, but didn't smile, and this appeared to calm the woman who'd birthed him, and raised him, and claimed him ad nauseam. Until this time home, that is. When he said he was done going back. When he said he had no intention of doing anything for as far ahead of today as he could see.

"You can feed me," he'd said, "whatever leftover scraps you'd buy without me here, and would otherwise throw out. You could feed me your waste, in other words, the slop. Just like you've been doing since day one."

"Honey, I want to tell you something." She came over to the bed in four steps as determined as they were cautious, bent down recklessly, and kissed his cheek. He didn't move. "It's so good to have you back. I think we'll have a barbecue or something with your cousins."

Worse than hometown civilians. At least slugs like Laird shut up when told to shut up. At least Laird the slug could still well enough conceptualize a headless human body—his own. See the chicken about to be fed to the pigs, zigzagging around the pen like a tweaker in a cornfield maze, blood dribbling out the bird's finger-thin neck like a broken water faucet? See it? Let me give you some shades, cherry, if you can't stomach the splattered blood.

Of his blood or not, that city his cousins lived in made him as sick in his stomach as he admittedly was in his head. Freedom's urban scum discharge. Rich kids dressing and acting like they're poor. Not a single Portlander in Iraq or Afghanistan for half a year running—now there's a stat to be proud of—not unless leading some lame-duck apolitical NGO like Women Without Borders, flat-topped face-pierced Anglo-American wannabe sheebas in half-ass burkhas that never covered their coveting eyes.

Pussy city of Portland, he thought. Average, too. Who cares if you're so "informed" you've turned into a pussy. Used to be tough—like the Barbary Coast—when you had loggers and maritimers running it.

Unsafe to your average Portlander, he scoffed, was a Plaid Pantry at dark with the "darkies" in Northeast.

"I'm not interested in talking to any of those hipster commies."

"Well, Michael, I—Michael."

"So what'd you—"

"They just have a diff—"

"—want to tell me?"

"—erent point—What?"

"You said I was gone a long time."

"Oh, well, you know, I just mean a lot of things happen when you go away, honey, and I don't think that you really, well, I just don't think you . . ."

Now he moved. At last was jostled. His hand over his eyes, closing them both. Not wanting to see this woman, even in peripheral shadow. He knew her better than she knew herself. Wasn't especially special. She'd never know how she came off, how predictable and transparent her needs were. How her needs weren't *even* needs. How she was about to stuff her "needs" down his throat, just the same, with the desperation of one in need.

"So what happened?" he asked.

"Have you talked to that girl since you been back?"

He looked up at her again, waiting.

"Well, I think you should. Right this minute, Michael. You should go find that girl—"

"She's got a name."

"—and ask her if she's been—"

"Just like you've got a name. Maybe you have the same name, ever think of that?"

She stopped, her lip trembling, a finger quickly pressed against it, not a bit of difference. Now she put her whole hand over her mouth as if she were her own kidnapper, and then seemed to free herself of the hand by pressing her chin up, and then down again.

"Michael."

"Let me ask you something."

"Please, Michael. Please stop with—"

"Why should I go anywhere when I can find out what I need to know right here?"

"That girl is no good, son."

"Oh, that again."

"No, it's not 'that again.'"

"Hmmph. Thought I went over there to make this a better place."

"It's worse, Michael. I can't believe that you have no clue what's been going—"

"Just say what's on your mind."

"She's a whore! A white-trash whore!"

He didn't move at this outburst, he didn't even blink, level-eyed as he'd ever been taking in his mother's predictable weekly bombastics. If it wasn't this BS, it was his second-grade teacher, Mrs. Garcia. His mother always pushing up her tail feathers when even obliquitous attention got thrown at her son from a member of her own gender.

Or else, something else. Maybe something worse, a weird third leg on the monster. That whatever gender, whether or not native to Amity, black was to Hispanic was to—no difference to her, ultimately—white trash.

As far back as high school, he'd tired of tracing his mother's words and attitudes to the source of prejudice. Did it matter? Who cared whether it was mercury or asbestos polluting the water? She returned him, again, to the casual nihilism.

Get out of here, he thought. Go pitch a tent outside this Eola Hills mansion you never earned.

"You *know* I'm right! In your heart, you *know* it, Michael."

He pushed himself up into a sitting position, sniffed, and considered his own hands.

What did he know any longer? That was the point. Sounded melodramatic, sounded hyperbolic, sounded hackneyed, an old black-and-white movie scene or something, but as he stood up, he more or less posted by his claim of unknowingness as resolutely and stoutly as he'd signed up after the buildings came down in Manhattan. He knew now he didn't know shit. No one did. Even if you were just a C-minus student of the theatre, that's what war taught you. You could only know the small things. The big philosophical things were unattainable. And then: you could only know the small things your own hands perpetrated. Or else your unknowingness, as it was, was actually the very last thing you'd *ever* know, as all the lines in your head had been erased on the other side of the world by every side of the argument—each time you'd tried to keep a flag of belief in shape, the patriotic pyros of your own country torched it to ash, or the First Amendment maniacs in the media perversely ripped it down with a propagandistic six-minute segment, or a sand-people nightmare of eyeless soulless spineless jidhadis crumpled it into t.p. right before your astonished face, and the worst part of it all was that—as signee who hadn't stayed back in the safety cradle of Western civilization, as one who'd gone and done things immeasurable and untraceable and irreversible, had pushed into the belly of the beast with the index finger of his gun—you'd contributed to your own unknowingness.

But Sissy. Sweet small-town Sissy. Ahhh. Well, maybe he *was* involved in hyperbole. "Nothingness" covered a lot of terrain, didn't it?

He still relieved himself of the shit in his stomach—didn't he? Still ate a meal of Top Ramen now and then, had enough of a caloric intake to lie there awake on the bed all day and night. He had enough energy to be an insomniac, right? Not sleeping required energy. Was ugly to watch maybe, ugly to see, but the assumption was that he was so *damaged* he couldn't sleep, which was true but incomplete. Damaged or undamaged, staying up around the clock required energy if you wanted to take your next breath of air.

Even this second right here, he thought, turning his hands over, palm to knuckle one hand, palm to knuckle the other, even this minimal movement right here takes a minimal belief in the movement itself.

Or else how did it happen?

How did any of it happen?

He swiped his slacks from the top of the chest of drawers, slid both legs in, brushed his slacks, walked around his mother without touching her, picked his boot-camp T off the floor, and put his head and arms through the holes.

"Can you say something, hon?"

He put his index finger to his lips, and looked up at her. "Shhhhhhhh-hhhhhhhhhhhhhhhh."

"Please, Michael."

"Means shut up, Mother."

"Don't you talk to me like that!"

He walked out the door, not because he didn't want to fight, but because he didn't care at all about what she'd have to say. You had to care to fight. Had to think it mattered.

"You're the only fool around here, Michael Anthony! The whole god-damned town knows! My own son's a cuckold to a piece of trash!"

Pika

August 29, 2010

HE WAITED.

What else did you do in the joint but wait? Oregon, Cali, was all the same when it came to the literalness of doing time. Waiting for the next meal, waiting for an escort, waiting for a love letter, waiting for an out date. Holding your breath for a bogus charge delivered by a bogus DA, or the big riot over an undelivered penny stamp. Looking for drama to kill the time, riding through holiday events and shaking your head at relay races, breathless at the monthly shanking—thankfully in another man's neck—on the end of the tier. For a message encrypted on a sheet of paper with a thousand centimeter-high words, for photos of loved ones spray-painted with crystal meth by wives and girlfriends and hookers, or else by hooker-wives and hooker-girlfriends.

Here, man, go ahead and eat my beaming ten-year-old son in his little league all-star uni for that dozen coffee shots and a half dozen soups you owe me.

Scum, he thought again. Thought always. Put your own kid in another man's mouth like a mutherfucking communion wafer? Never eat again? Shit. You should never *breathe* again after that, mutherfucker. Should never come near me—near no man—at arm's length. Gimme your chow, scum. Gimme those coffee shots and soups you owe your kid.

With the exception of the meal—which always came and accumulated, always drowning in some flavorless colorless nutritionless gravy or bagged with a sandwich consisting of mystery meat zit-dotted with big black peppercorns (you pop the zit and there's a big hole in the pink skin where it used to be)—*other* than the meal, you get lax with expectation, not that you forget about where you're at, no, *impossible* to forget that, but backpocketed deep enough to get through the bulk of the day on the surface, enough to function and program and get the checklist checked off of reading seventy-five pages of Baldwin and writing a letter to a cousin in New Zealand (never met and, thus—you hope—leastly judgmental) and ripping out your pull-up routine surrounded by homies face out to the yard for safety measures and running a game of handball with the lifers. The concentrated hatred and routine deceit like LA smog on a summer day: taken in and processed on assumption, minimally intellectualized—you cut right through it and, later, when you won't know it, anyway, die from it.

"What you thinking about, Pika?"

He turned and stood, robotic, soldierly. "Hey, Sis."

"Hey. You all right?"

"Yeah, yeah. *You* all right?"

"When I came in, I watched you waiting for me. You were gone from this place—I could tell. Well, not completely gone. What was it?"

"You look good, Sis."

"Pika."

"Well, I don't know."

"Yes, you do."

"Well. Guess I was just thinking. Places like this, you know what I mean?"

"Okay."

"You don't do the time, Sis, the time does you."

"Mmm."

"Does *us*. I mean, I'm locked up in this mutherfucker, but you've been in here, too, you know what I mean? Or a part of you, anyway. And poor Benji. Take a look around some time at these fucked-up families that come through here. They can't stand against this thing. They try, with everything they got, but it crushes em, man."

"Well, we're not like them."

He smiled. "I just never wanted Benji raised up in here, you know?"

"He wanted to come today, but he's got a soccer game."

"You and Benji are all I got to believe in."

"Well, we believe in you, too."

"Sissy. Listen. Do not spend Labor Day in this fucking hole. And don't you dare bring the kid. I mean it, Sis. I'll be out of this bitch in a minute, all right? Two weeks ain't shit to me. Do this time standing on my mutherfucking head. No one gonna hear me whimper one goddamned second of it."

"I know we won't, Pika."

"You just keep cashing those checks I send you—okay?—and please do what I ask, Sissy."

"We're coming on Labor Day."

"Even though I know you won't do what I ask."

"Well, not Labor Day. But Labor Day weekend."

"Goddamnit. You're not feeling me, Sissy. You stubborn as your mother. Shit, I can't—"

"Don't cuss, Pika."

"Sorry."

"We got to get you to practice talking clean so Benji won't hear it, okay?"

He smiled, nodded. Looked around, looked at her, nodded again. Took in a deep breath, smiled.

Is that what goodness is? he thought. Not getting the irony of the words, even when you the one putting it out there. How goddamned beautiful can you get? She got no clue, he thought. Or else is she so good she don't give a fuck how much the bad is stacked up like a big cliff, to hell with the clues, and what everyone—even me—knows? Even though she been coming here for almost five years, he thought, she thinks it ain't uphill in every direction.

So where should he practice this purity of language? With the resident molester-turned-preacher on the tier, Reverend Bones, as they call him behind his back and sometimes right to his face? The reverend had said on the stand, as if this were a defense, that every five-year-old boy he knew warmed his very bones. The thought of the boy was enough, he'd written, forget the image. Of course he loved them!

Or maybe he'd hit up Huero for a lesson on decorum, the way the sureño ironed all his homies' shirts and pants every morning was glamorously generous of him, was lily-white beautiful to see, the double-murderer gone unpaid bonafide cleaning lady in a mere thirteen years of institutional emasculation.

Even the cops here tag their skin, he thought, with big colorful claims. Worst mutherfucking gang on the yard. Come deep when it's time to handle theirs, come wrecking fools. Can't be trusted as agents of correction, let alone agents of redemption. One punkass hura named Jeremole has a gun tower on his fat white blob for an arm.

Well, Pika thought, some people got endless brick walls for a view, some got a dope stretch of beach. Gunners with dripping moobs like Jeremole—he gets to see the top of our heads every day. Gets to fantasize what it'd look like to spill em with a single bullet through the skull. Probably walking around with a mutherfucking beer up there, chillin' like the villain he'll say we all are after the federal probe ten years, seven bodies late.

"Well, Sis, you right about that, anyway. I'll be goddamned if I put one bad word in that kid's head."

"Don't cuss, Pika."

"Sissy, listen. You been hurt enough already."

"You, too, Pika."

"No. Listen. Fuck me—sorry bout that. Shit, sorry. But I'm telling you this now, okay? I won't take your visit on Labor Day."

"Benji loves you, Pika. I love you. He wants to come. We'll be here in the evening."

"That's what I'm saying, Sissy. I won't take it. Do I gotta end the visit to make my point?"

He stood and turned his plastic chair around, gripped the rails, and dropped down the way he did bar dips in the yard: all his weight suspended in midair, slow lowering of his legs and feet. He heard her tap the tabletop with a fingernail, and he looked over his shoulder dutifully.

"Come on," she said. "Stop acting silly."

"I'll end it, Sis. All I gotta do is tell the cop I don't want you here."

"Did you like those kipper snacks in your quarterly package?

He spun in his chair, slid forward. "You ain't gonna even discuss it, are you?"

"Kipper snacks or sardines?"

"Shit. Okay. Okay."

"I like sardines, if I had to choose. Especially in tomato sauce."

He smiled. "You a beautiful girl. Goddamn. Sure we related? Shit, Sissy. You a little baller, you know that? I'll take anything you send me, okay?"

She smiled back. "Okay."

"Anymutherfuckingthing."

"Okay, Pika. Get all that cussing out in here."

"I will. Trust me."

"Cause I want to have a clean home, Pika."

"Oh, nah. Nah. Nope."

"Yes. You're gonna move in with us, okay?"

He waited. Still. Always. Goodness was goodness—right?—but at what point did it collide with so much badness it was stupid to throw up as a front? At least be subtle about it. At least work toward the thing on the side, on the sly, on the DL. Did everything have to be so frontal in her pressurized world of keeping goodness alive?

He stared into her unblinking eyes and saw the fiery dispute of his question without a word said.

"You crazy, girl."

"It's what's right, Pika. I won't have you sleeping under a bridge or in some sleazy motel."

"I appreciate that, Sis, but—"

"It'll be okay."

"Look here, Sis."

"Plus, Benji wants you to."

Prison did something to your sense of openness. All you needed, really, was a few years locked up to forever eliminate from your vocabulary the following words: I don't believe that. Do a bit of time and you can't help but believe that when it came to human beings, *anything* was possible—mostly bad shit—because it was right there on the jacket of your cellie, fresh off a lead story for the local news, or over here in a cop's untoward confession on Christmas Eve that meth and not weed was his drug of choice, or in the horror story of a little boy taught by his own mother how to manufacture smack at eight years old, run it at nine, distribute at ten, or even the fact that a double-murderer named Jimmy Cox, hitched to an old law trenched beyond the legal reach of ex-post facto, was about to get out and see the very streets where he'd slit a black prostitute's throat *times two* in the mid- and then late-1990s.

People will do whatever their dirty-sponge brains can imagine. And so why not, he thought—why not move in with Sissy and the boy and her punkass husband he'd walloped on point—move in on principle? Why not live in close quarters with his case? With the very ufa who got him locked up in the first place?

Why not break bread every day with the scum who raped your own sister five years ago?

Hell, he'll feed the gimp mutherfucker himself, stuff a whole loaf of bread down that rapist's throat. Breakfast, lunch, dinner, and any snack time in between.

Yeah, he believed in the possibility there.

Open your mouth, mutherfucker. Go on. Get it all in there.

"Okay, Sissy. Okay. All right. But let me tell you—"

"Not yet please."

"—something. You tell that GI Joe mufucker he better have his shit straight when I get out. He fucking half-steps with me and I'll make him wish he never been born, man. Thinks he's hard cause he went to war? Shit, that shit's a break to me, homie. Least they give you love when you get home."

"*If* you come home, Pika."

"Sissy, you tell him—"

"Please don't get all worked up before you go back in there."

"Just tell him—"

"I don't want you to get in trouble."

"—I'll break his spine again if he even touches you,—"

"Bye now, Pika"—as she leaned toward the door—"I love you—"

"—Sissy."

"—very much."

He watched her stand and nod in the kind of innocent concern that must have been another aspect of goodness he admired in Sissy—that you sensed the disaster was about to happen but were ready to face it, anyway, and even further that beating it, however infrequent and damned near impossible the chance, was still technically a possibility. Seeing this on his sister's face made him nod, too, and take a breath, and try to calm himself in order to calm the only woman who'd ever visited him in almost ten years of cumulative downtime.

She smiled and whispered some kind of three-second prayer, and he looked down at the simple, racial, institutional tags on his forearms that he'd tired of seeing—let alone reading—so long ago, and then back up again at his sister.

"Go to church please," she said.

"Ain't going anywhere near a church. You keep me alive in here, not anyone else."

"I'll pray for you. Remember ora et labora."

"Stop talking that stuff."

"Prayer and labor, Pika."

"Don't know about all that shit, Sis, but just tell Benji he's a straight champ, okay? That uncle gonna take him to a ball game."

"He's too young, Pika."

"Fishing then—"

"Yes! He'd love that!"

He almost said, *Who* would? We talking 'bout the same party here, girl? You mean the kid or the kid's crippled dad? but instead muttered, "Okay then."

She crossed herself again—one last time?—and he looked around for anyone snickering who he'd have no choice but to address after she left. That's how weird the world is, he thought. We both at risk. We both go the distance on two different things—she needs goodness and I need respect—and yet we both been ruined by our needs just the same.

"Stop crossing yourself around me, Sissy. Making me feel guilty and shit."

"Somebody's got to."

"And Sissy?"

"Yeah?"

"I love you, too."

Sissy

May 1, 2006

HE DROVE IN SILENCE AND THIS WASN'T UNNATURAL or odd between them nor was it unhistorical: the precedence of silence had been more or less established the four previous times he'd returned from the war; in fact, each time the silence had actually increased in sustainability, hours now between them without a word, until she couldn't take it any longer and would ask if he was okay, if there was anything she could do for him.

She wore a loose gray sweat top, her clavicle and neckline naked, loose sweat bottom, half-a-decade-old sneakers, her hair down, no makeup. She knew she looked ridiculous in this rag-tag outfit, exactly like the trash Michael's mother said she was, but he'd insisted she hurry and pay no attention to fashion which hadn't ever mattered between them nor even between any other human beings betrothed or engaged or in love, and the way he'd said that in less than a quarter minute's time—fenced-in with finality—made the little hairs on her arms stand up; everything, his empty eyes and monotone suggested, hinged upon efficiency and emotionlessness.

The deep moan of the Hummer as it climbed the hill to his farmhouse still made her feel spoiled and ashamed, all that power beneath her buttocks and legs and feet, and even the leather seats themselves—eternally shiny and new-smelling—shamed her as she thought about whichever dilapidated living room her mother was in, hopefully their own, the square footage smaller than the cab interior.

Which man, she thought, is using my mother tonight to get what he wants, but doesn't need, and won't ever stand by?

After she'd once picked on him for an opinion, Michael had said that her mother gets what she wants, too, that it was a two-way street when you stepped onto that dirt-trampled road, and who cares if it's her mother or the guy who gets run over, who cares which direction the thing happened, who cares who's driving, who cares who fled the scene? The important factor is the road itself, he'd said. That nobody focuses on the ones who'd stayed clean of the dirt in the first place. Ignored, he'd continued, because the users of it like to use the dirt-trampled road—don't they?—and go out there and risk everything they have so that everybody else has to come out and ogle the accident, mourn the tragedy, forensic the scene, clean the bodies off the pavement. All the resources get spent on saving their asses. Your mother's lucky she's still here. I wouldn't be surprised, Sis, if your mother wasn't even your mother. How the hell can an angel like you come out of a devil like that?

They pulled up to his house, traversing the seemingly endless driveway brick by bumpy brick—laying those bricks must have taken a year to complete—and when he stepped on the e-brake for the thousandth time in her presence, she still expected it to creak like the eaves of her own house in a mean Pacific Northwest wind.

She didn't want to think about this and so stated the obvious: "I don't want to go inside your house, Michael." The silence was still there between them, and not knowing what it meant, she said further, "Please, Michael. I know what your mother thinks of me."

"Sometimes what people think is accurate."

"I don't want to see her right now, Michael."

"Sometimes we don't get what we want, do we?"

This was the Michael who scared her. The coldness in his voice like the January ice on Church Street: ungraspable, vast. He could murder the little lives of her insides with one passing look of disgust. The seventy-two-year-old judge in a twenty-two-year-old body. He'd condemned the majority of America who didn't join up on September 12, 2001—"cowards," "traitors," "unworthy of their social security cards"— but of late had swung back around to condemn the few who had—"zealots," "scoundrels," "sheep who thought they were rams." His own place between the two poles of extremity either missed or ignored. The space for safe discourse between them seemed to get smaller and smaller the longer they knew each other.

He held the door open and she walked past him slowly but with as steady a gait as she could, already spying his mother seated there in the monstrous, velvet, gawdy living room chair like a governess from a by-gone age. Sissy tried to catch her attention to nod a modest greeting, but his mother was either immersed in her needlepoint, or else consciously ignoring them, or maybe newly deaf. Sissy stood there, and didn't even rock on her toes. She could hear Michael's heavy breathing, the anger in his head building. Finally his mother reached out without looking up and palmed a remote on the coffee table, aimed it just to the right of Sissy's heart, and hit the button. Mozart's *Requiem*. Michael had played this for Sissy between his first and second tour. So not deaf. His mother returned to the embroidery in her lap, the needle pinned now between her grit teeth.

Despite the music's purpose—to isolate a houseguest, enforce an elit-ist choice on anyone in ear's range, to make the guest feel dirt-low—Sissy loved the morbid sounds, standing there with nervous hands crossed in front of her vulva, as if shielding her procreative capabilities from the cancer-causing X-ray vision of this woman. She smiled humbly, more to herself or to some wig-wearing genius-composer from another cen-tury than to anyone else present, at last looking around for a figurative hand from Michael. He was more focused on his mother than on Sissy, glaring so obsessively she thought the weight of his next blink or breath or God-save-us-word would bring the walls down around them, and so she made a passing, stupidly hopeful glance toward his mother again—*please please please help him stop*—and then down at the floor.

Michael stepped past her with learned, refined, robotic militaristic strides—the way he'd walk even at a fishing hole, even before bed—and stood before his mother, looking down at the top of her head.

"You got a problem, woman?"

His mother aimed the remote at Sissy's breast again, muted the music. She raised her face to her son, waited in the kind of silence he'd far better mastered at least three tours ago, and then pointed the remote and hit the button, Mozart's treatise on death failing yet again to fill the space of the house. His mother's head was weaving back and forth through the air, mimicking the in-and-out motion of her needle.

Michael grabbed Sissy's hand and led her into his room. She looked around. Nothing had changed. How strange to see, given how much he'd shed of himself in less than half a decade.

He molts too much of his skin, she thought. He refuses to own a story. And yet he's being eaten to the core by the stories. Doesn't know how to live with a story.

Terrified, was how she understood the love of her life—terrified of any change. He took in change, she thought, the way the beautiful child we'll have one day—this would happen, she knew, was a guaranteed shoe-in, despite all the problems with communication they seemed to be having—might eat vegetables: wincing, in need of something to wash it down, on the verge of departure from the table of communion.

He was "making his rack" now, Semper Fidelis lingo she'd learned long ago. Methodical STRAC-minded Michael. Quiet but always thinking. When he talked, it meant something.

He closed the windows, he closed the blinds. She sat on the edge of his bunk, watching him cut across the shadows of the room, not quite quickly but not with any trace of hesitation either—without *effort,* was the better way to put it; without the *possibility* of any other course being taken at that moment, the best description, she thought, of his one-way-street mindset—the swiveling, centering, über-fit waist nearly as thin as her own. Something was wrong. Outside the door the hallway clock ticked in an even greater methodical manner, almost sinister in its relentless, secondly insistence that time could be measured in perfection.

"Michael. You shouldn't talk to your mother like that."

"You shut up, Sissy."

"Sorry," she whispered.

"You want to leave?"

"No."

"Then don't assume you understand anything between that woman out there and me."

"But I love you, Michael, and I—"

"Love doesn't give you omniscience, does it?"

"No."

"You think it does. You think you're empowered by some omniscient force from the same fucking desert I just came from."

She was the kind of person who wanted to fix at once what was wrong, wanted to reach out and touch the hurt, the tired, the wounded. She wanted to make it better forever, she believed in that thing she'd seen so little of—*healing*—and the rarity of its occurrence actually strengthened her belief.

You're a healing fiend, Michael had once said, kissing the side of her neck, the thin rim of her ear.

Since that first time almost a year ago, she'd gone to church every Sunday, and while she couldn't exactly articulate what was happening to her soul, she nonetheless took the walk each morning at sunrise. Almost two hours out from town, if she didn't stop. She'd get there and go straight past every parishioner to the bathroom, dry off her pits and her forehead. Michael would say it was a dealer's trick the way the electric cord in the homily always plugged into the socket of her life, that the purpose of moral vagaries was to maximize the number of inroads to your heart, that no one is more easily seduced by the power of a parable than a nineteen-year-old angel embarrassed by the sin of her family history.

But she expected that he wouldn't understand. Something held her body up every time she felt like collapsing, and she was looking for that something, whatever it was, whoever.

Maybe the point, she thought, was that you have a soul. That you even have one.

He wasn't looking at her now, she could see, because the outline of his face was silhouetted against a wall. The darkness had won in the room, it seemed, the darkness came so fast in Amity even to a native of Amity, but she could get up from the bed and turn on a light. She could tell him about the steps she'd taken this last tour to be a good human being. How hard it was to go forward in a real way, and yet not abandon her mother. Every step forward, she'd read somewhere, unsettles the dust of the past. But forget dust, she'd thought. In Amity, Oregon, you have to crawl out of the quicksand to get on your goodness feet.

She watched his mouth move, at last, and got the tone of the words before the words came in and defined her suspicion.

"You fuck around on me, Sissy?"

She gasped and closed her eyes, but didn't move. Mostly because— when she opened her eyes again—he hadn't moved either, nothing but his mouth, which was still again, holding in all the nothingness. What is he but a boy, she thought, an Amity kid battling PTSD (she'd looked up the term on the library computer), damaged from a war whose laws existence reach outcome he seemed to lose control of in his head, but put to order with her as audience like a child building blocks for the captive babysitter?

"I said, you fuck around on me when I's over there?"

Outside the door his mother's tiptoeing trickled across her heart like a thief's footsteps, and then the leaning-in—Sissy could hear it—of her head against the door. Was she on the floor, lying down in her own hallway in the same prostrate abandon in which she'd given birth, all to capture every bit of the drama about to happen with her son?

Sissy stood and went to his side. "Mikey, please. I'm trying to change mys—"

"Sit right there."

She dropped down at the edge of the bed and looked into her lap. She didn't know what else to do but cross herself, and so she did it fast, not wanting him to see this, to destroy this. "I'm so sorry, Michael."

He walked over to the door and squatted down, putting the side of his skull carefully against the wood, a crook earing the lock of the safe, and suddenly head-butted it. The scuttling of his mother's footsteps like mice in the attic. He didn't say anything about it, didn't even twitch. He still was there on all fours, like a monkey at the zoo in its cage. Not even a thought about the door he'd just fissured, she noticed, not even a consoling palm to his skull. Not even an acknowledgment of the mother's returning footsteps.

"Did you get trained?"

She looked up at him with horror.

"I said did you get fucked by this town or not?"

She would do the right thing now. That's what it meant every Sunday getting mocked by her mother at the door, this is what it means to go forward. She nodded, as if in a trance.

"What a piece of shit."

"I'm sorry," she said in a breathy whisper. This breathiness made her start to cry. She'd been saving the breathy whisper all these years for his marriage proposal. *Yes*, she'd planned to whisper. *Of course*. But now that hadn't been saved for their marriage either. Now he had to love her without the few little frills she'd saved to fool him.

"You know what they would do to your skinny little ass over there? Huh?"

What she thought—talking about jail? banishment?—didn't come out of her mouth, as she was panicky at asserting a concrete answer, which he would attack, being so much in the right right now, being exactly where he liked to be. She managed instead: "Where? Where?"

"Iraq, you ignorant tramp."

"Please don't say—"

"You know what happens if you open your legs up like that? Huh? You're one lucky bitch, I swear to God. They won't just kill you. That's not good enough for them. They're gonna make you *suffer*. This one woman—you listen to me. I'm gonna teach you."

"Michael."

"Shut up. You talk too much. Shut up shut up shut the *fuck* up!"

She was whimpering into her palms now, tied to the evil realm of the world not only by what she'd done but what was happening outside the door, his mother loudly positioning herself for the speech they were both about to hear in a tone of condescension thrown at Sissy her whole life, the one she'd been raised by and conditioned in, sad from her whole life, as long as she could remember her first walk through town.

"Now this lady, she got her fucking face—I saw the before and after photos, all right?—this poor fucking lady—*poor lady*—got her whole face toasted with a hot iron. That's right. The thing pressed right into her face. Skin sizzling like a fucking fajita plate—and why? Cause it was 125 degrees out, that's why. Took her fucking burkah off, hijab, whatever that fucking thing is, and some Sharia law asshole saw her do this. Was she lying about why she did it? Was she winking at some dumbass GI? Making blow-job eyes in the dust? Who knows, huh? Who cares? Well, you would. You'd care. You'd lie. But then that's no proof cause you're a liar. That's no proof cause anyone would. Take your fucking clothes off."

"Please, Michael."

"Could see it from forty feet away. The face red. Nose decimated. A piece of fucking raw hamburger. Can you imagine trying to breathe out of that thing? You get closer and you can see the little circles, even, little BBs of scar where the hot air comes outta the iron. Fucking huge chevron from her hairline to her chin. Let's see the plastic surgeons fix that one, let's see em make that face pretty again."

"I'm sorry you had to see that, Mikey. I'm so sorry you—"

"All she did was take her fucking veil off in public. A stupid piece of cloth. Goddamn. Poor lady. One stupid piece of cloth." He stopped. She hoped. He said, "And what's going on back in the Land of the Free?" Oh my God, she thought. My God My God My God. "Huh? Well, since you asked, here's your average two-bit whore in the two-horse-dump town of Amity—"

"Michael."

"—buck-fucking naked, sliding across every bed on her fucking back. You see how it's too much irony to accept? I'm over there watching that shit, and you're over here getting trained by the high school football team?" He stopped. "What a fucking joke. A treacherous cunt."

"I swear to God, Mikey. Was almost a year ago. Haven't been with anyone since that night. I . . . I've . . ." She couldn't find the word. "Repented. I swear to God, Mikey, I'm not like that any—"

"I said shut up." His hand was on her throat, and he held it there. She couldn't breathe, her eyes shutting down on the scene, and for some stupid reason she tried to cross herself instead of—and he let her breathe again, grabbing her right arm, and pinning her down so that she couldn't move.

"Hail Mary, full of—"

"I said shut up with that shit."

She was whimpering again, as a young man of Amity was entering her again, ripping at the clothes she hadn't—this time—taken off of her own free will, as everything she'd been hoping for had been ruined again and again and again, like the sun rising every morning again and again on exactly the kind of life that it rose on.

Michael

May 4, 2006

HE FLICKED THE BATHROOM LIGHT ON like an afterthought, the fact
that he'd been standing there in the dark for the last thirty-six minutes
completely unimportant, a piss drop of time in the ocean-wide toilet of
humankind, and the begging outside the door stopped. Curious, nosy,
self-serving silence. He looked at himself in the mirror, bearded, shirt-
less, pistol to his head, the muzzle at the temple. Pressed in so hard that
the bone pressed back, layer of skin around the steel bunched up like the
dirt rimming brand new piping on the farm.

His pus-rimmed, blood-red eyes were burning with some realization he couldn't quite name, something like what a man becomes when
turning his gun on others, let alone himself. He reached out and flicked
the light off. The begging came back from outside the door and he nearly told her to shut the fuck up if it weren't for the darkness's consum-
mate envelope seal, the way he felt separate from every living thing he'd
ever known, especially the woman, babbling like an anti-Christ, who'd
brought him into the knowing in the first place.

"Miichaaaaaeel. Please. Pl. Pleea. Pleeeeeeeaase. Please open. The
door. Don't know what to do. Don't know. Who to call. Pleeeeaaase.
Can't call the police on you, Miiiiichaaaaaeel. Can't call them, okay?"

He stood there for several minutes before the next thought came. How
phony people were, even in crisis. A few more minutes passed and the
babbling now like the voices one heard underwater. He built himself by
beading on her betrayal. Won't call the cops cause you're *ashamed* of me.
Not because you're trying to *preserve* me. Or *save* me. Noooooooooo.
Won't call cause you're trying to save your*self*.

What I think makes sense, he thought. What I say no one hears but me. And what I'll do will make sense, too.

He flicked the light on again and the pistol was kissing the bridge of his nose this time, right between the squinted eyes. The babbling outside the door stopped. He flicked the light off.

"Miiiiiiiiiichaaaaaaeeeeeeeellllllllllll!"

Seconds later, he flicked it back on again, and found the muzzle deep in his mouth—cocksucker! he thought—the steel cold against his tonsils, gagging him into dry-puking it out in one gut-roiling cough. He aimed the pistol at the dead reflection in the mirror and fired three shots—*Pop! Pop! Pop!*—the glass shattering like hail hitting a rain-puddle full speed.

"Aaaahhhhhhhhhhhhhhhhhh!"

He broke open the locked door and stomped past the body curled like a potato bug into itself, his howling mother in the hall—"Ahhhhhhh!"—only stopping to reach back and rip her trembling hand from her own eyes, make her see the world for once as he knew it.

Pika

September 12, 2010

WHAT DOES IT TAKE, HE THOUGHT, to stay out of this ki'o dump?

He stood from his bunk and took two steps to the steel toilet sprouting out the wall. His cellie, Ioane—head three feet from the head—woke from his slumber and said, "Gonna sit down for a minute, uce?"

"Yep."

Ioane spun so that he was tier-side, feet by Pika's face, nose farthest from the toilet. He lay back, hands behind his head. Pika pulled the sheet curtain, pasted the strips of paper to the thin steel rim, and sat. The steel was always cold, still cold, even through the paper it was freezing cold. "Yeah, yeah, Pika. You go right on, boy. Drop your last stink k'io for these pua'as, man. Fa'amalosi with it, too. Blow it up."

"You know."

"So they ready for you or what, uce?"

"We'll see."

This was his tenth out date going back to his twenty-second birthday, one from a four-year term in Avenal Two-Yard, one from Quentin on a six-month violation, seven covering the saints from the three unsaintly counties of Santa Clara, San Mateo, and San Luis Obispo. Looking back on it, once he even got kicked to the street on the strength, not even a meal in, not even an hour. This before the era of looming cameras and cancer-causing digital fingerprints and the clean, well-lit, modeled-after-Brits, super max, money-making, 5-star facilities now packed with twackers and petty thieves and the homeless—on that night the Sunnyvale Police/Fire Department two-cell jail booking cop/fireman had actually said to Pika, "Get out of here—I don't feel like doing any paperwork—would *you*?" And then, too—it was coming back to him now—another four-nighter in Santa Rita, which—like LA County, run by second-term gangsters on their way to being struck-out third-term gangster lifers (who'd never be given again the de facto commission of running a county jail like the joint)—was a straight shithole: Santa Rita, all in all, might as well have been a prison.

So this was his twelfth out date, counting the loose change under the couch cushions.

On average he'd seen more crazy shit in a week than most people see their whole lives. Oh, he'd done crazy shit, too—was too old and tired to lie about that—but somehow hadn't been disappeared by the system. Not yet. Was still here. Though he came hair-thin close to the precipice of catching a figurative blade to the neck on his knees, his throat hairs tingling magnetically from the descent happening somewhere out there on the planet. He wouldn't ever get a chance to talk about it with anyone, but in '02 he took a trial the distance, got an eleven to one guilty vote on a fifteen-year sentence. One innocent vote away from forty-five hundred straight days behind bars thanks to a chetnik from Serbia who'd thought—mistakenly—that he hadn't done it. The whitewashed ese DA came up to Pika after the hung jury and said, "I'll get that vote on a re-file, Mr. Tamavavae. I know you know that. You don't want there to be a next time we meet in court. I like you. Think you're honest. A little violent, sure, but who hasn't done his fair share of whooping ass? So here's the sweet deal of your life: I get to have my stat and save a little cash for the state, and you get to *keep* said life. De nada, enchilada."

So he did a year in county with no second strike, and a feeling that he'd never earn, no matter what he did, the gift he'd been given that day.

Problem was that wherever he did time—Cali, Oregon; county, prison—and whatever for, he could never cop to the crime a hundred percent, the way so many homies did who successfully made it on the outs. Brainwashed to think they were once the devil, but now were Jesus Christ. He rooted for them, he wanted them to beat the dreadful recidivism rate, but he also knew how much their freedom relied on being dumbed down by the system. Of taking the scraps they threw you, and thinking you were chowing down on filet mignon every night. He could feel them, though—he *understood*. Was all good, was all about the comparative peeks over the cliff: measured against where they'd been, maybe freedom in whatever form was not just filet mignon, but all the gravy with it, too.

But bottom line was he wasn't one of these cats cool with pacifistically pushing an after-hours broom at whatever charity outfit would take him on, silent as a nun, only "yes, sir"-ing and "no, sir"-ing anyone with a necktie in a five-yard vicinity. Fuck that. Oh, he'd *work* those jobs, wasn't too proud to scrub the floor like any good Fa'a Samoa hamo, but not a single second on his knees Lysol-ing the grease out of Antonioni's kitchen did he think that Antonioni—the millionaire restaurateur, the ladies man debonair, Pika's last boss kind enough to kick him down a minimum-wage job—even Spiro Antonioni wasn't any better a man than he was.

It sometimes felt that the more time he spent in "penitence," the further he got from redemption. Not because his strikes were adding up and it was mathematically too much to address, a mountain of contrition impossible to chop down with his hand, but because he was more and more convinced as he aged that he wasn't—even despite the foot-long rapsheet—a half bad mutherfucker. Not half bad intellectually, not half bad spiritually, not half bad morally, especially given the people he knew who'd never done any time behind bars, but straight-up deserved a gang of it.

Wasn't getting on his knees to clean for pennies enough of a shaming? He was cool with that as long as they didn't need a lifelong confession out of him. Why couldn't they be cool, in a balanced return, with his silence? Why'd they have to take his brain and his heart and his nuts, too?

"Live through what I've lived through," he'd mumble in mid-scrub at three in the morning, 'Pac's "Dear Mama" on the old school eighties ghetto blaster he'd found in a dark, tucked-away, forgotten corner of the broom closet, the empty Italian restaurant a pumping heart-enclosure of the world's greatest rapper ever, living, dead, didn't matter. "Walk a mainline for a week, mutherfuckers, and then come talk to me."

"You know, you real lucky, sole."

Pika leaned forward, reached behind him, and flushed once. Twice. Institutional power blasts sucked everything down, damned near your large intestine on top of it all, and let everyone in the block know what you were up to. Is like a nuclear blast, Pika thought, and you be sitting on top it. "Yeah. I know."

"Last visit I got was '08."

"Yeah."

"Folks wrote my muli off, uce."

He wanted to say, They be back, sole, but he knew Ioane. Damn near a saint in here—clean, fewer options to stray, Samoan guilt and regret driving him back to his knees at church; but straight demon out there—all hopped up on ma'a, peeking out the motel blinds at four in the morning, a loaded .38 tucked into the rubber band of his boxers, his mother's jewelry box of family regalia originating in the homeland about to be traded for a teener of methamphetamine. Cris for cris, they called it on the streets. Crystal for crystal. "Yeah."

"She musta come out for you fifty times, man."

"At least."

"Like a true island girl."

Pika waited a bit, thought about the truth of it. Loyal as any Poly, his sister was. Sissy was more down than any of the hoes he'd known from the hood growing up, too. In some ways, she was even harder than they were: once she got a thought in her head and it got approved by her heart, she was like a bullet and the target: beeline, full-speed ahead, right through mass resistance if aimed right.

"Yeah. She a island girl, all right. Crazy Irish island girl."

"Tough as fuck, huh."

"You know."

"And how's the kid?"

"Jus' love his little ass, man. Got a lot of hope riding on that boy."

"Right on, uce."

It went quiet for a bit, and Pika was cool with letting this happen—flushing twice in between for emphasis—because the boy was off limits conversationally. The sad thing about the joint, he thought, is that when it come down to it, I don't trust no man up in here.

Not even this cellie of his for three of the five years he'd been down, and who'd cried to him last year at Christmas about his ten-year sentence for manslaughter, and who was, by far, the best cellie Pika'd ever had in his institutional life. That didn't matter. The boy is what mattered. Getting an out date was what mattered. Keeping what you love locked down in your heart is what mattered. You put it out there on the tier, and it's not just barter material for the hustlers and usurers and players, it's defiled forever.

He talked about Sissy because he had to give em something. You had to share a little shit about your life to get em off your scent. Adults before kids, and pronouns like "she" and "crazy Irish island girl" before names and surnames. Any tracing of anonymity would come right back to him, which he'd handle accordingly.

"So where you stayin, uce?"

"She want me to stay with her."

"All right, all right."

"I ain't trippin' but, you know, don't know if it's the right thing."

"Gotta have some residence for those ufas from parole."

"Yeah, I know. I'm a second-termer, Mr. First Termer."

"You a fool, boy."

"For sho."

"Maybe just hit the streets. No-tell Motel, uce."

"Nah. Through with that shit, uce."

"Or head back to Cali, sole. Blow this place."

"You know the program, uce. Want three years, man, 'fore they cut you loose."

"Nah, nah, you can plead hardship, uce. Trust me. Make some shit up and have your folks sign on in Cali. Transfer the case in a month. These northwest mufuckers be happy to get rid of your brown hamo ass."

Pika thought about the proposition, but returned to the main point from before: 's about the boy, not him. He reached back and flushed again. "Well, I feel you, but I gotta stay, man."

"Nah, it's cool, homie. You love the boy."

Now he felt guilty enough about the earlier thoughts to open it up for a sentence or two, go against what he'd just drawn as a perimeter earlier. This was his problem! He couldn't stay inside the lines they were always telling him to abide. Or else planted in his head. Ioane was a human being, mutherfuckers. I been there! I lived with him 982 days straight. Y'all got me fucked up.

"Yeah, that's right, uce."

"You getchyo money, sole."

"Gotta handle my business once I hit the streets, uce. Done with this shit."

"Right on, uce."

"That's all I been thinking about. He ain't my kid, but he's still my *concern*, you know what I mean, uce?"

"Oh, hell yeah. Feel you, uce. I ain't one of these kefe knucklehead walking the yard. Family is family, homie. Le aiga."

"Ioe, uce. You know. Sorry for not talking about him more. Just special to me."

"I feel you, sole. No worries."

"That kid's got it goin' on upstairs, smart as fuck, man."

"No relation to you then."

"My sister's kid. She real smart, too, just never got a shot. Quit school at sixteen. Always reading a book. She learning Latin, man."

"Fea alu high school?"

"Iloa Amity?"

"Yeah, man. I know it. Small town out by McMinnville."

"Place seem broke as hell. Leai galuega lea, man. No jobs. Mutherfuckin' tweaks on every corner, homie."

"Shit. That ma'a destroy everything. I ain't missing you, baby."

"Well, this town never seen a hamo before. Those palagis gonna think I'm Mexican, uce."

Ioane chuckled. "Órale, vato."

"Nah, hell no."

"Your sister good people, uce?"

Pika waited, thought about it. If she was already good, what would happen when some true bad got thrown into the mix? "Ioe. She raised the boy up herself, uce."

"Our women keep us strong."

Pika flushed the toilet. "No help from anyone."

"You know, uce, you never told me how you ended up here."

"What? Showed you my papers right when we bunked up, uce."

"Nah, nah, not your *case*. In *Oregon*, man."

"Oh."

"Yeah, yeah."

"I was in Cali and my moms and sister was up here. Came through to handle that shit I told you about—"

"Right, right."

"—and got pinched that same day." Pika leaned back and flushed just to make some noise. He didn't like talking about it. He didn't know why it mattered one way or the other. "Never got to see my mom. She died about a year later—"

"When you's in here?"

"Yep. My sister told me at a visit. Trip, man. Never saw her, never met her—if I'd gone straight over to the fale that day, I might not be here, man."

"Cause you went to go see homeboy instead and knuckled him up."

"Right. And then one day this lawyer comes through and tells me she left the fale to me in her will."

"Moms kicked the house down?"

"Yep. And then I kicked it down to my sister. Give her and the kid a place to live."

"Oh, I feel you. That's why she want you to stay with her. All right. So what's wrong then, uce? Whatchu tripping for?"

"I don't like her husband."

"Just ride it out, uce, till you can save up some kupe. Get on your feet, home."

"Let me put it another way." Pika shook his head, wiped once, flushed twice and re-drawered. Then he hiked his pants, leaned over, and hit his hands with soap. "I don't like my case."

"Whatchu mean?"

"Well, that's the fool I crippled, uce."

In the steel mirror before him, Pika watched his bunkie pop up to his elbows. "Hoooo!"

"Lay your shit back down, ufa. Ain't you got some roof to contemplate?"

Ioane was up now, legs over the edge, the drama of the moment too much to bear lying down. "Hoooo!"

"Yeah, that fool's a punk."

"Goddamn. You gonna be back here in a mutherfucking minute, uce."

Pika walked over to the cell door, looked out at the tier, then back down at his cellie, who'd slid over a space and was now patting his bunk. "Nofo 'ia, sole."

Even after all these years, Pika sat only when given permission, institutionally trained as he was. He leaned back against the wall, his heels pressed up against the wall opposite. Ioane leaned back, too.

"Damn, uce. Listen, sole. You better find you a motel in Northeast or something. Eh, I got this uso out in Eugene named Masi, played ball at U of O with Masoli, and that fool'll put you up, man. Let me get on the kelefogi with that uso—"

"Nah, I'm cool."

"—and see what's happening first."

"Fa'afetai lava, uce. Means a lot, man. But I'll be fine."

"Yeah?"

"Hell yeah. I mean, what the fuck's he gonna do, man? Fool's in a mutherfucking wheelchair, uce."

Ioane half smiled, shook his head. "Damn. A wicked world, man."

"You know."

"Well, shit, uce, you ready to go then."

Pika turned to his cellie and they knuckle-bumped. Then he ducked under the low steel rim of the bed and stood. "Iloa oe, sole. You know that."

"Chooo-hooo, Pika. Better send me a fat package, man."

Pika leapt up on his bunk, and then sat there, his back to the wall, eyes on the wall's twin straight ahead. "Shit, send a box of my first k'io on the streets, homie." Ioane laughed, and he smiled. "Fresh out this mutherfucker, I'ma blow all my kupe on twenty Big Macs, homeboy. Run that shit like Konishiki."

"You a fool, Pika!" Pika leaned over the front of his lap, kicked out his legs, and looked down on Ioane. "You and Saleva'a! 585 pounds, uce! Nigga's got rolls for days!"

Pika nodded, smiled, felt guilty again for keeping shit to himself. This the last time, he thought. Last time I look down on my boy like this.

A last knuckle bump, and then they both lay back on their bunks. Ioane said, "Ma ufaaaaa, Piiikaaaa. Well, you stay up out there, man. And stay out this mufucker."

"I will. Tell all the usos much love, okay?"

"I will, sole."

"And you tell those fufus and leo leos on the yard, I ain't missing you, baby."

"All right, boy."

"Sing that shit."

"You know."

Pika reached underneath his mattress and pulled out a photo. Sissy and Benji on a visit, the kid's smile damned near wider than his head. "Manuia po, uce."

"Night, uce."

"Love you, sole."

"Love you, uce. God bless you."

Pika took in the photo and then lifted his mattress and slid it under. He rolled to face the wall, the fatal fetal position you were never supposed to fall asleep in. "I hope, man."

"Yep, yep."

PART II

Today

The Family

October 5, 2010

His people are at the edge of the pool, watching.

The boy's mother stands between the rubber handgrips, nervously nodding at his every stroke across the water's surface. The boy's father sits in the wheelchair, a John Deere hat brim-curled into a half moon, just as attentive, but not nodding, not smiling. Several feet away, the boy's uncle squats against the wall, black beanie pulled down to the brow, chewing on a toothpick, calling out words of delight and instruction through the little temple of his touching hands:

"That's it, Malietoa! Reach for the stars, Shotcaller!"

The boy pops up and down in the water, like a playful seal with a *National Geographic* photographer. The goggles are too small for the boy's head, tied off like a shoelace in the back. His eyes are bulging—you can barely see through the foggy lens of the cheap fiberglass—from the pressure of the rubber band, which pushes his ears down perpendicular to the joyous face, little handles you pull on to make the doll talk. At some point during the past half hour, most of the parents present have watched the boy in wonder, his elation so pure and unadulterated, they are all waiting, more or less, for him to slow down.

The boy goes full speed in everything he does. Right through the house, right across the yard. "Walk!" he hears ten times a day. Jump out of bed, dive into bed, climb up the tree. "Careful!" they say. Sing from the tiny well of his lungs, down a glass of milk in seven breathless gulps. "Easy!" are the words he just won't abide until he's heard them from every party present two or three times, usually too late to matter.

The first week of Tiny Timbers Summer Camp, one blue-haired lady thinks the boy is a bad boy, and they come—each one on different days—to correct her of this error.

"You've got a fundamentally wrong understanding of my son," the father says at a private meeting arranged on his behalf by his wife, "and I'm here to enlighten you on what you've missed."

He is looking up from the chair with more bravado than she has ever seen in her thirty-six years as camp counselor. She sits, not to make it eye-level so much, or even respectful, but to avoid collapse in the face of his judgment. "You've got to pay closer attention to something about my son: he is ready to perform, ma'am, and it's your job to make sure that happens."

The uncle comes on Wednesday morning with a loaf of bread he'd baked the day before at work, nodding and smiling, saying nothing but, "Here you go," and "The little guy? Yeah, he a little baller, in't he? Hard to stay caught up with pure, hard-core, hopeful speed and all that, I feel you."

The boy's mother researches for a word she'd once heard at church, but had never looked up. At the public library, she finds it in a three-thousand-word pocket dictionary, copies down the pronunciation and meaning before she visits.

The boy memorizes the word—joie de vivre—in a little longer than a quarter minute by repeating it twenty-six times. "Joie de vivre! Joie de vivre! Joie de vivre!" He doesn't know another word of French, nor even where the nation of France is on the map—not until this new word, after which he wants to know everything they know, which is very little. Which is perfect. They don't want to give him too much. They're worried about what's on his plate. They want to give him only the stuff that is right, even if it isn't very much. He runs through the house saying to anyone in his five-foot vicinity, "Joy. Day. Veev," and they all laugh, and then he asks it in a question. "Joy day veev?" as if he is offering them cheese on a platter. They laugh and watch and wait.

He's the Boy of Many Names. His father calls him "Top Hat" and "Big Britches" and his uncle calls him "Malietoa" and "Shotcaller." Most of the time his mother calls him "Baby" and "Benji." "You, Benjamin Michael" when she is angry. She isn't angry very often, and so when this happens, it is less episode than epic. The boy, thus, remembers these times. He usually gets the lesson real fast, but he remembers these breakdowns more because—whatever he's learned—he doesn't like to see his mother bothered. The boy's father and the boy's uncle always confirm this at different times, in their own way, away from one another.

"You keep your eye out, Top, for Mom, got it?"

"Yes, sir!"

A few days later, his uncle will rap, "Little man of the hour, little baller shotcaller, little doer of the deed, who lives back in the holler! Got more spunk and seed than your average dirt-farm farmer, hear me out, Malietoa! You're your mama's pit bull, her bodyguard with . . ."

"A card?"

"No."

"A shard."

"Definitely no. How'd you hear of that word?"

"A bard."

"There we go. You're mama's pit bull bard, the A-1 bodyguard, catching every bit of badness running round the yard."

The boy laughs and giggles at the rhymes of his uncle, who is never angry, though the boy knows he's done bad things. He remembers visiting his uncle in prison, the long bus ride over and back, the way the guards would nod kindly, pat him on the top of the head, and then shake their heads at each other.

The boy's father, on the other hand, is always a little angry, but very rarely at the boy. He is quiet, the boy knows, and maybe, the boy always thinks, he cannot talk as good as I can talk, and that makes him embarrassed. The boy wants to talk with his father, but also *not* talk with his father, so that his father does not feel embarrassed.

They all live in Amity a few miles up the road, tucked back by the creek where a single lost car—once a week, once a month—will U-turn at the dead end and disappear forever. On Tuesdays and Thursdays the McMinnville Community Center gives free swimming lessons to underprivileged families across the county, and so they're here from one town down. "Doing it," the boy's uncle says. "Handling it." The boy's mother catches the late afternoon bus out with the boy and meets the boy's father at the pool. He wheels over from the VFW, where he spends the bulk of his days. The boy's uncle, the full-time baker at the Red Fox, right across the street from the VFW, walks over to join them after work.

The boy jumps out of the pool and speed walks toward his people. The water glistens on his skin, funneling off his chin and ears and elbows with each step, his hair slicked back like a "greaser" in his father's favorite book from junior high, *The Outsiders*. He reads to the boy in selected parts, appropriate to his age. Benji doesn't like the "socs" and when his mother asks him why, he says, "They think they're better than Pony Boy, Mom. Not. Cool."

"Good job, Benji!"

He hugs his mother and she lifts him up, squeezing as if she were drying him with her sweater, then carefully sets him down on her husband's lap. The boy hugs his father as hard as he's just been hugged. He receives a kiss on the top of the head, plus, "Job, Tophat." Then he jumps off the wheelchair, stands chest out, chin tucked, heels at a "forty-five" just as he's been taught, and salutes his father, who merely nods and smiles. When the boy turns, his uncle is standing at his side, and they knuckle bump, both of their hands blowing up into fake explosions.

"Psssshhhowww!"

"Powww!"

"Good work out there, Malietoa."

"Thanks, uncle!"

"You're like a fish, little brother," his uncle says, nodding, looking down at the boy, whom he dwarfs. "You swim like a shark on the reef."

"I'm trying to learn to swim like a *SEAL*."

"You're cute as a seal," his mother adds.

"A *Navy* SEAL!"

"Thatta boy," his father says. He wheels between the boy and the boy's uncle, and the uncle nods and walks ahead. He leans back into a crevice of drywall between the counter and the exit, chewing his toothpick, and then squats down.

"Mom?"

"Yes, baby?"

"That's what the Navy SEALs do. I learned that from Dad. They bounce up and down on the bottom of the pool to practice if they don't have their arms and—Mom?"

"Yes."

"That's what I was trying to do right now at the end, okay?"

"Okay, baby."

"Did you see my arms? I had them by my side. They might get tied down."

"Yes, we saw, baby."

"Or cut off."

"That's enough, baby."

"I had them like this." He pushes down and stretches his neck out and looks up at the ceiling and then over at all three of his people. "You see?"

"Good work, Top. Let's get you dried up. We got a bus to catch."

The boy speed walks by all three of them, so fast he's passing the other kids from his class. "Walk!" his mother shouts. The uncle nods at the boy's mother and goes out the front door and squats again, wide V-shaped back pressed against the glass.

The family has a special room just for them: a double-doored closet with all the swimming gear and pool stuff in it. They're separate from the other families, who have to split up and go one way or the other: boys here, girls there. Down to the showers and lockers and toilets. On the first day, the boy overheard the lifeguard say, "No way we wouldn't do this for your husband, Sissy," and so the boy knows the room is for their family to stay together in.

He's lean and spry like other little boys before him, and he's got a little towel wrapped around his waist, copycatting the way his uncle wears his lava lava. He rips it off and tosses it at his father, who's blocking entry to the room, his wheelchair backed against the door, the leather seat wedged under the knob. The boy shakes his head and body like a dog right out the pool, and the water whips off his hair. He's moving fast, and efficiently, especially for a five-year-old boy. He pulls his shorts down to his ankles and jumps out with both feet, holding them out for his mother, naked and shivering, but not for long. She hands him his undies and pants and shirt the way the mailman hands you the mail. She's pushing all his swimming gear into one side of her purse, pulling out the dry stuff from the other side, and handing it to the boy: socks now, shoes. Her husband nods, "Here you go," and then takes the towel he's just folded, and says, "Thanks, Sis. You know I can hold that. I'll just tuck it under the—"

"No, no. I got it." She pulls the towel between the straps of her purse and ties it off.

"Okay."

"Ready, Dad. Ready, Mom."

"Okay. Let's head out, Top. Let's roll."

The boy leads them out the equipment room and through the check-point of the main desk and past the kind, nodding, blue-haired lady running the swimming program and then out the door. His uncle tosses him an orange and the boy says, "Thank. You. Sir," running straight into the gray, relentless Oregon rain, the path to the bus stop cutting right down the middle of the storm.

They yell for him to wait, and the boy's uncle starts to casually jog after him. The boy's mother is pushing the wheelchair, her husband pumping the wheels nonetheless. The boy listens, slows to a speed walk, just like back on the deck of the pool. The boy almost always listens. Pushing himself all the way to the boundary of having to listen. They rely on him for energy, but sometimes they want to preserve the energy, too.

He stops under the dry space made by the long, ageless branches of an evergreen, and turns to his people nearing on the path, and sings a song through the sheets of rain. Some of the words die between them, but they catch: "Long! . . . Remember! Rain coming down! Clouds . . . pourin'! Confusion . . . ground! Good men! Ages! Trying to get a little sun! And . . . wonder. Still the wonder! Who'll stop the rain?" The boy puts his arms out like he's holding a rifle and air-guitars the licks: "Buntdunit-bundunit-doon! Doon-doooon-doon-doon. Duhnuh-nuh-nut-duhnuh-nuhnut-dun. Dunt-dunnnnn!"

They smile and nod and follow.

"I can't wait!" he shouts.

They near and his mother asks, "For what, hon?"

"Dinner! All our family together! All my people at the same table!"

Pika

October 5, 2010

BEEN ON BUSES ALL MY LIFE, HE THINKS, and so this little half-pint deal for handicaps ain't nothing new.

He smiles and winks at the boy, goes right past his sister's husband, says wassup to the tweaker in the corner, and lifts his head at Sissy. She nods back, and then he stretches out across the seat next to him, vacant like 95 percent of the rest of the bus, and closes his eyes.

Back in the day, he and his cousins used to ride the 522 from East Side San Jo all the way out to Palo Alto, killing off two hours of sunlight just like that. They'd fuck around and shoplift merchandise no one would set chase for and basically do nothing of any real value and then jump back on the bus and head home. Seemed like so much of his childhood and youth was spent killing time, euphemism for wasting time, and the irony about that was how all that killing time ended him in places where time ended up killing *you* inside, tick by maddening tick. The seconds like minutes, minutes like hours, the hours like days, right down the hard-time line till death do you part.

Crazy, he thinks, the way life balances out like that. Life ain't fucking around. You wanna waste your life? it be asking. You wanna waste *me*? Okay then. All right. Let me drop you in a nice little place where you can really get what that concept means, homie.

That's what the kid has going on for him: do, do, do. The boy fishes, the boy swims, the boy reads books, the boy plays the flute. The boy is in the Scouts, on a grant from the monastery. The boy doesn't even watch TV, except a show called *Oregon Field Guide*, where some beneficent former park ranger goes around the state pointing out hiking spots and bald eagle nests.

Got no time, Pika thinks, for the boy to fuck around. No time for him to wonder like I used to wonder. Like I still do. Still stupidly do. What's it matter, man? She gone. Been gone since I could know she was gone. Now she's in the ground for good, the long haul.

All the way out.

He opens his eyes and they're passing the town of Whiteson, even more run down than Amity. Probably eighty-two people total, he thinks, eighty-three by tonight if a twacker from Mac wanders through and sets up camp in someone's dumpster.

You think growing up that only brown people like you are poor. Pika looks out for a few seconds at the two wet-dog palagis thumbing it on the side of the road, camouflaged hoodies unused in the rain, not even safely tucked back behind the berm, but making the few cars and this bus arc into oncoming traffic to avoid making roadkill of their shaggy-haired white bodies. He closes his eyes again. Then you come out here, he thinks, look around, and gotta revise your theory. Gots to be honest about it, can't fake the funk. Gotta broaden your understanding of the story.

Like Malcolm back in the day, he thinks, dumping the Black Muslims for a larger vision.

And paid the highest price for it, too, Pika recalls. The last price.

He counts out the six seconds it takes to leave Whiteson behind at fifty-five miles per hour: Tasi. Lua. Kolu. Fa. Lima. Ono. The lives of real people are in there, he thinks. Just like the joint: the nobodies of Whiteson get straight-up forgotten about.

His hordes of Americanized Samoan cousins never sent a letter, never visited, and he knew without asking anyone anything that they were "'shamed" of him. One auntie wrote a three-sentence note telling him to drop the aiga's name, take his palagi mother's name instead. Every now and then when he was maddened by the time, hardened by the hatred, marinating like a tequila worm in his poisonous thoughts at the bottom of the bottle, he almost did. Said, "Fuck it," and filled out the paperwork in the prison law library with some mole named Specs. Didn't shake in his boots, or cry out like a punk, but didn't move either, and before anything could get processed said "Fuck it" again, took the paper back from the rape-o dork, threw it into the garbage can. Would've lit the thing afire if he'd had some fire back in the block. A few FOB cousins and uncles showed up once on a malaga from Western Samoa to spread the word to the American hordes, but they were so stoic and preachy about his time that he'd felt guiltier at the end of the visit than before it, and he'd felt plenty guilty all the way through. He was just grateful that the damned thing was over, and they could go do a fire dance, or dig up an umu, for the Polynesian Club at Oregon State or U of O. He wanted to get back to the yard.

Only Sissy came every weekend, the clinically depressed Pac-Northwest white girl he'd never met in person before her visits. Just the conversations on the phone when she was feeling down. Was like she was making up now for all the times he'd taken her calls on Christmas Eve, on her birthday, two in the morning. Her sad Amity stories about having nowhere to go even on a Daylight Savings Time Saturday, always whispered so as not to wake their mother.

"You got that kinda hope," he'd once said, "that no one can ever check, Sis."

If she stops calling me, he used to think, it won't be cause things are finally right. It's cause she's through with it, she done, got swept out with the tide like her mom.

So it was only Sissy who had a smile on her face through the glass, only Sissy who came correct. Every time, no matter what.

Once, he remembers, the alarm went off right when she'd come in, and the poor thing jumped out her seat and spun around, then right back at him. Scared as shit, and who wouldn't be? Blue lights and "get down!"s and the nearing surrounding terrifying jingling of chains. He'd winked at her to play the drama down, show some experiential coolness in the storm, grace under pressure, or whatever they called it out there in the safe abstraction of freedom, pressed his face to the glass and kissed it, and then dropped to his stomach. Looked up from the floor because he could feel her right there, looming above him in the shatterless glass, and she was covering the O of her mouth with both palms, poor thing, as if he hadn't been on his face once every couple days back in the CDC. She was living his pain, man, she was feeling him for sure.

The next week to prove it she was all ears back—the same time, a little more versed in the weird, unpredictable paranoia of prison, how nothing happened until it happened, and you'd never forget it—and he explained why the visit cops had been needed in the yard, to address with mass correctional force some knucklehead riot between norteños and sureños. How they had to get off their asses of this cush detail and work for once, earn their fat paycheck and fatter pension from the citizens of Oregon. Rush the cells in the block, toss the mattresses, break off the light shades. Risk getting AIDS from a sabotaged pen or razor or sharpened comb under the top bunk bedframe. Line the homies lips and dicks to the wall and search every imaginable bodily orifice for keistered shanks and ballooned heroin and baggied kites detailing in-house hits from the streets on snitches and punks. "Bend. Spread. Cough. Good. Bend. Spread. Cough. Cough! Yep." Then bring interpreters in from downtown Salem to interrogate the eses faking like they don't speak English, brilliant the paisas playing dumb, saying, "Me? No hablo inglés. No know nada. Que quieres, pinche hura?"

And how isn't it nice—today, Sissy, right here—to have the whole damned visit room to ourselves—along with the whites and blacks—since every ese in the yard is in twenty-four-hour lock-down?

He winks at her again, smiles, right past the broken back-reason for being on this bus, and then at the tweaker.

"Howdy."

No teeth, top gum, bottom gum, underbite chin pointing forward like a finger.

"What's happening?" Pika says, looking off at once to stifle talk.

"Uncle Pika."

"Yep yep."

"Ask me how many bus stops left."

"How many, Malietoa?"

"Nine bus tops, Uncle Pika."

"Right, right."

Pika isn't as strong as Sissy, doesn't believe the way she does in goodness. Not even close, actually, not even comparable. In some places he's seen goodness hiding under the covers like a little bitch, pissing its own pants. No. She makes him better, indisputably—she and the kid lift him out of the pit of institutionalization, and now it is up to him to walk, man, to mutherfucking go forward on it.

Even when she was big in the belly she had come in smiling, tilting. And it was like the kid showed up in the world armed with the same disarming smile. Pika hated seeing the kid in there, but he also loved seeing the kid in there. Was afraid that the kid would get hijacked by the memory some day, but also needed that smile there for a wee bit of hope. Now that he thinks about it, the kid spent three Thanksgivings in that visiting room. Three Christmas Eves even.

"Lug your punkass load, sole," he whispers to himself, and then mad dogging the husband, despite everything he's just thought, despite Sissy and the kid angelically shrouding the scene, just running with instinct basically, giving in.

The husband doesn't give in. Doesn't look down, or away, but meets Pika's stare, and says, "Let's hear the mileage, Top."

"Nearing 2.5 miles, Daddy."

"Very good, sir. Dad's going to teach you kilos next. We in America keep track of distance in verified measurements, okay?"

"Okay, Daddy."

"Space you can verify with any other civilized person."

"Okay."

Don't matter about space, Pika thinks, winking at the husband, if you can't get across the space yourself, Gimpy Rape-o Toy Soldier.

Sissy

October 12, 2010

SHE CAN'T EVER TALK ABOUT IT, but she knows what they'd thought at the clinic. She'd learned as far back as childhood how to distinguish the judgment of silence—disapproval without a said word, abhorrence even in the supposed affirmation of a nod. Despite their judgment of where you'd just come from, it was like they were gently guiding you forward out of their sight, right back to the same place they'd just said to your face was no good. Crystal clear message expressed in the eyes, transparent passage purveyed in the brow. That she was dumb, that she was trash, that she was backward. Uneducated redneck, riff-raff hick. A Yamhillbilly from the nazified Tea Party county of Yamhill. Tied to a reproductive bovine code which had brought her to their famously progressive city in the first place.

"Primordial" was their word she'd found later in the dictionary. That she was actually *insane*—she'd heard it in an "Oh my God" from a kind, compassionate nurse practitioner named Allison hearing the details of Benji's conception—not just remaining with but actually planning to *marry* the nameless perpetrator of the deed one day, the party to be ID'd of the crime—presumably—once the child was born, and the certificate would require a signature from the father. That deed which was worse than murder, she'd been told at the clinic, because it killed the insides, and you had to keep on living with what he'd killed.

She couldn't judge them back, she couldn't judge *anyone* back—but sitting there in the company of these city people who seemed so smart, so *informed*, she wanted to have the child nonetheless, and yet not so much have the child *against* them, if that was possible, but to partake in exactly that which she'd been given, her own life: she understood what they'd meant when they'd said she was hurting herself, how every modern woman actually dies a little death with his forced seed inside her, and she admitted knowing next to nothing of philosophy or feminism or urban progressivism, whatever the last might mean, but to her the notion of life had always been about hurt and what one does with the hurt, and to her, even, she sometimes thought that life was a *synonym* for hurt. And that her only failure as a young girl was that she couldn't ever measure when to quit because one quit, essentially, when the hurt was too much. Which meant—if she quit—that she'd forsake her only true friend in childhood: hope. And she wasn't about to do that. She'd lost enough already.

So after she'd walked out the door of their silent judgment and just beyond reach of Allison's kindly, compassionate, dripping pleading to return the next morning after a little more thought, she knew as the bloodthirsty crowd outside called her a killer and a cunt and a pig that she wouldn't ever go back in, anyway. However much of her was dead inside after he'd done it, however much had been taken from her core, whether rape was philosophically worse than murder, or not. She made herself small and squeezed through the sweaty arms pumping horrid alien-human signs and the guilty gates of index fingers—"Excuse me, please, can I, excuse me"—and caught the bus back to Amity.

Every day for the next five months she remembered that impasse at the exit of the clinic, and how the mental discomfort didn't mitigate at all even as her belly grew, as her physical discomfort therefore also grew. On some days she thought of nothing, literally *nothing*, and just lay there on the couch like a hog in the barn, and then she'd come alive to the automated font of sniveling to herself for an hour, bothered by some vague feeling she had about the world, and also of the world inside her. How her mother would come in and call Sissy exactly what she felt like—"You look like a sow on a mud bed"—and even new feelings, new barnyard species—"Just a big useless heifer for a daughter. Mooing all day. Mooching all day. Eating me out of house and home. You never listened to my warnings, did you? I told you to get an operation before so you wouldn't have to worry. First thing I said. That way: could be as stupid as you are with the boys. Then I told you get one *after*. Still didn't listen. Even after I got proven right. Bought you a ticket, even, to that city and what did you do? Stole my money. Never went near it. I'm an idiot. I don't have any peanut butter. Don't have any olives. What else don't I have that you've taken from me?"

When it was finally time she caught the bus twenty miles up the 99 to the Newberg Providence Clinic for insuranceless white trash and undocumented Hispanics out of the fields and drowned herself in the hurt, was blinded by the hurt, alone in it for sixteen and a half hours except for a nurse named Erin and the indifferent doctor pumping her full of generic drugs and artificial compliments. Their words were suspicious to her even while giving birth, almost as if they'd been entertained by her horrible homelife on a horrible sitcom and now felt bad about witnessing the spectacle in the real world.

But what a lovely baby he was! Benjamin Michael! Most gorgeous face in the hospital! The nurse had said this! That doctor—even him, the clinically unkind eyes and silent judgment—reluctantly agreed!

Benji was crying the same as she when they'd met—just couldn't stop herself. Their fluids all mixed in, their tears and blood as one. Holding in her arms what she'd known she could do without anyone's help, or approval, or whatever. Her secret now out: not the baby as secret; but her absolute knowledge that she could do it. This was more than her business now, more than what was purely *hers*. This pulsing red, softly warm embodiment of hope, a real tangible heartbeat of a life saying with each breath of air all the things she couldn't ever say. That maybe no one could say. Or else dared to say.

But from the first minute she'd laid back on the bed with her son, she couldn't bring herself to relax. She was paranoid about the world and its claim. She could hope for herself to sidestep the void, and then live with the consequences of that hope, but here was true reliance, attached already to her leaking breast. And here was the urge to protect. To build in Benji the immune system he'd need to deal with backstory: her own, or her mother's, or Michael's, or the town's, or anyone's.

Everyone's.

She stayed in her friend's basement the first few weeks. Slept on the couch with Benji, suckled him in this cellar, as if she were a mother on the run from baby catchers. Which she was, in a way. She feared her own mother, bottomless fount of flowing pessimism. Never had to drill too deep, always more nastiness in reserve. Frack this, frack that. The baby would get eaten away by the hissing words, like a raisin decomposing in the sun.

But they couldn't keep her mother from knocking gently on the door after the first month of little Benji's life and waiting in silence on the doorstep. Sissy had heard the kindnesses on the porch because she and Benji were underneath it, a musty gray echo chamber to every conversation in a twenty-yard radius. Her mother's gentle tone magnetically brought her up the thin, slanting row of concrete stairs and out the house to witness for herself.

The new mother couldn't make any words, and she held onto her friend's elbow for protection.

"Oh my God," Sissy's mother said, looking upon him. "Oh my God."

This was enough for her. She didn't hand Benji over—no way; no—but she did turn her back and showcase the little plum on her shoulder, something she hadn't intended to do (you won't even *look* upon my child, she'd thought a dozen times a day), bouncing up and down the way she used to in grade school, practicing with the doll in the rocking chair. Then she heard the sobs. Incoherent words bubbling up from her mother's throat like Styrofoam trash leveling on the foam of a spilled wave. She couldn't turn to take in the anemone of her mother's mouth whenever she was in pain, the sensitive ends of Sissy's own arm hairs tingling as if she'd been stung by that same anemone, her whole body on fire.

She wishes now that she had turned around, that she'd looked upon it when she'd had the chance.

A few weeks of this ritual each morning before she finally asked the question. Her friend still standing there, lipping the glass of an Hecho in Mexico Coca-Cola. Her mother put her head down, arm out. "Yes. I would. Thank you very much, Sissy."

She won't recall anything beyond that moment right now. She doesn't want to cry in front of Benjamin Michael for the same reason she didn't want the venom of her mother's negativity. Instead she'll corral the raw concern in her son's heart for herself, this boy that throws all his coins into the river for a wish, or else into the red Salvation Army bowl for someone worse off at Christmas than himself.

She tucks the boy into bed, pulling the covers to his chin. Kisses him on his brow, closes his eyes with a kiss, and then the end of his nose when he opens them up again for more. They can see themselves in the mirror before them, and the boy's mementos: a cardboard cutout of Michael Phelps on the Wheaties box; a wallet-sized picture of Michael and her at the Amity High prom; a Polaroid of Pika, Benji, and her at the OSP visiting room.

"Mama?"

"Yeah, honey?"

"How come Daddy and Uncle Pika hate each other?"

Too fast she says, "They don't, honey," and then, "Honey?"

"Yes, Mama?"

"I don't. Well. Honey?" She touches a nose with a fingertip. "Well."

"They never talk."

"They will someday."

"And sooo. What that means is . . ."

"It's tough to communicate what you feel, baby."

"They keep secrets, huh, Mom?"

The lovely, disarming, missile-aimed charm of a five-year-old's question that matters! "Well, I don't know, baby. Oh, jeez. It's not that easy. Sometimes people—they can't say what they want to say—do you know what I mean, Benjamin?—or even what they should say, and it's for a good reason."

"Well, I've got a secret, Mom."

She's genuinely surprised. With five-year-olds you don't think this, and with a five-year-old like Benji—jetting through his life at full speed—that it must be impossible. But everything is out there, or else— she thinks—is it out there, and I just miss it? "Tell me, baby."

"I'm happy, Mom . . ."

He looks up at her for a confirmation. "Yes."

"But I'm also sad sometimes, too."

She understands this, she bemoans this. The gene passed on. Right down the line into her son's susceptible vision. The eternal battle that goes on hourly, minutely, secondly. One side of the world someone jumps for joy on the bank of the river, while on the other side someone enters it forever with rocks in her pocket. She can't say this, of course, and it's wrong to even think it under the circumstances. She clears her palette by closing her eyes and inhaling deeply.

What is it that brings us together, she thinks, and yet keeps us apart?

"Move over, hon." He curls into a ball as she slides in, and nudges himself into the pit between her chest and underarm. "I don't know, hon. Life is hard sometimes, honey." She brushes his hair and pulls him in to affirm that he's a part of the equation, that his life is hard, too. "But what's really important, baby, is that everyone in this house *loves* you. That's all you gotta remember. They just don't know each other yet, Benji."

"I want everyone to love everyone, Mama. Not just me."

"Well, you keep praying for it, honey, and you just might get it."

"I *do* pray for them."

"And you just might get it."

"Mama?"

"Hmm?"

"Do they hate each—I mean. Are they quiet because of me?"

She puts both hands on either side of his cheeks, looks into his eyes and says, "No. Absolutely not. I don't ever want you thinkin' that, you hear me, baby?"

"Okay."

"If anything, you're the one that keeps a little love in their hearts. You're the one that keeps em human."

"Mama?"

"And you saved Mama, too, you know? You saved me, Benjamin Michael."

"I did?"

"Yep."

"How, Mama?"

"You were born."

"Mama?"

"Listen, honey." She wants to get him off this topic, but he's too smart for that. He doesn't know the word but he understands the meaning of the term coercion. Even at five, he doesn't like it, and wants directness, frontal interactions, questions answered. So she'll stay on topic, but in her own way: "I'm gonna tell you a story, okay?"

"Yeeeeeeeeaaaaaahhhhhhhh!"

"Once there was this little boy named—I don't know: pick a name."

"Benji!"

"Another one."

"Cyrus James Henry."

She thinks about it and nods. "The other three boys in your swim class."

"Mmm-hmm."

"I like that. Okay. So. Cyrus. James. Henry. Can I just call him Cyrus?"

"No."

"C.J.?"

"No."

"Okay. Cyrus James Henry grew up in a tiny two-horse town called Amity."

"That's in Oregon. That's where it rains a lot."

"That's right."

"That's right here."

"Right here, right now. Rains half the year, can't help it one way or another. Sun and rain divided right down the line. Now. This boy named Cyrus James Henry—he went to a swimming hole in the—"

"No swimming hole in Amity!"

"—part of town—you gonna let me tell the story, hon?" He pulls her face into his own, and nods, eyes wide with commitment. "Okay. So this boy Cyrus James Henry—he makes his way out to the swimming hole, okay? Now he loves this place, and how come he loves it? Well, it's a cool, clean hole with no one around—all right?—and he can strip down to his skivvies and jump in. Easy as pie."

"And not get in trouble."

"That's right."

"And not get sunburned."

"That's right, too. Now. There's this big tree over the hole—"

"Like *The Giving Tree*?"

"Honey, you're ruining my story."

"Sorry, Mama."

"'S okay, you little scholar. Now zip the lip." Benji pulls the imaginary thread across his mouth. "Just gotta borrow a little bit from Mr. Silverstein to finish it out, all right with you?" He nods very seriously, as if he's exactly the pretentious scholar she's accusing him of being, and then he presses his left ear to her heart. "And so this tree was sorta like the Giving Tree in one way. It talked."

"Like *The Wizard of Oz*!"

She can't help but smile, wait. He's everything she's not, or ever was. Being a mother, she thinks, frees me. I don't feel envy for something I never had. I feel supremely *pleased*. I feel warmed, I feel taught. What irony! What refreshing, life-sustaining irony!

"You're very smart, young man. Now. Now now now. This tree is Cyrus James Henry's friend, see? Helps the boy understand the world. One day he told Cyrus James Henry where they're both from."

"That would beeeee . . . Amity, Oregon."

"Exactly, honey."

"That's our town."

"So one day Cyrus James Henry said, 'Hey, tree. I got lots of people at my house who love me, but something's wrong with em, tree. Can you tell me what's wrong with em?' And the tree says, 'Sure. That's a easy one, little fella. The world's what's wrong with em, Cyrus James Henry.' 'The world?' says the boy. 'What kind of answer is that?' 'This kind. They each one are carrying the problems of the world in their hearts, see, little boy? And they don't know how to carry em.' And Cyrus James Henry says, 'But that's the people I come from, tree. I wanna help em.'"

Benji jumps into her lap just like she knew—and maybe even hoped—he would and shouts, "I do wanna help em, Mama. I do, I do."

"Shhhhhhh." She's chuckling, tears coming out now, can't help it, kissing him atop his head. "I know you do, and guess what, baby?"

"What, Mama?"

"You *do*."

Michael

October 13, 2010

UP THE RUBBER-LINED RAMP HE ROLLS, coil-tight arms pumping the wheels. The VA built the ramp in a day and a half when he'd gotten back, along with a few volunteers from Habitat for Humanity. Most cooperation he'd seen between hostile political forces in some time, and then in his hometown no less, where work ethic isn't exactly a strong point. Not unless you're out on the farm, or up logging the mountains. Around town you see the same people in the afternoon that you saw in the morning, and will see again at night. At least a fifth of the town, he's guessed before, must be unemployed.

He feels his wind centered somewhere in his six-packed stomach. He'd ascend a hundred ramps for the kid if he had to. Always climbed hills strong as a boy, always eyed the peak of Erratic Rock from the blurry flush of a full-on sprint. When he ran his qualifier for boot camp at Benning, only the little cross country Asian guy from LA beat him, by four seconds, about twenty-five yards. So second in a graduating class of seventy-five. Not bad. Especially since he'd almost killed the Asian guy in the mud with the pogo stick. Could've knocked his head clean off the neck. Surprisingly big-headed Vu Quoc Nguyen, he remembers, from somewhere down in California—that clown damned near climbed the shoulders of his four little Asian friends after he'd won, looking for his tiara crown, arms hoisted like a Vietnamese Rocky, and the top didn't waste any time: "Get down from there, you little primadonna fuck, before I knock your buck-o-five ass down myself!"

Although he was bent over, his own lungs on fire, palms bridging the tops of his kneecaps, "sucking wind and worthless," as the top called it,

Michael had had a laugh attack right there: coughing, nodding, eyes tearing up.

That was warm-up to war, he thinks now. Summation of war: coughing, nodding, eyes tearing up. And then later the internal guilt for even summoning the memory, as if it were a victory: Nguyen, he'd heard somewhere somehow, had stepped square on an IED on patrol in Fallujah, smithereens-blown, done.

The ramp levels on the side of the porch, and he pulls himself in. Leans back so that the front two wheels are airborne. He can hold out like this any time he feels like it, that's how strong his arms and midsection are, despite everything else on his body that's nothing more than dead weight. They say there's blood down in the lower extremities, supposedly, but it doesn't amount in utility to a Lincoln copper. Who the fuck could he save in this chair? Only entity really worth its weight in gold down there is the .45 at his hip. And then the chambered bullets worth their weight in lead. He spins in the chair. Face out now to the wet, foggy, gray Amity, Oregon, morning.

If it's like this tomorrow, he thinks, I'll hitch a ride down to the river with Top and snag a couple cats. Gotta get some chicken livers tonight for bait, check the tackle box for sticky string.

He rolls to the door, reaches out and opens the screen, pins it with his elbow, and holds his position.

"What a coincidence," he mumbles. "Just thinking of bottom-feeding fish, and here's the human version."

The felonious savage of the house has his back turned, just the way Michael likes it. Doesn't bother looking over his shoulder, and it's just fine. Who wants to look at a face like that? Michael thinks. All that eyeliner and mascara he tattooed to his cheek and brow. Polynesian makeup, whatever you want to call it. With felonious idiots, expect something else? Well, what's next? he thinks, Lipstick? Botox?

He sits and waits, evaluating, hating. Been almost two months. Feels like two years.

Oh, sure, the felonious savage is big and strong, just like anybody lucky enough to work out 24-7 behind bars is, building and sustaining muscles while the rest of us are building and sustaining the world, but that doesn't mean a damned thing in the burning sand, does it? Middle Eastern sun will teach you discipline. The dunes pulling you down the hill will have your ass. All that muscle mass will melt away, he thinks, like a goddamned ice cream in a microwave. And then you're just left with your guts.

If you have any.

"Get fired already?"

Finally he turns. "Say what?"

"Say what? What does 'say what' mean, anyway?"

The savage jumps up on the counter and takes a bite of a sandwich and says nothing, looking out the window and then back again. "Still here, bruh? I thought you mighta rolled back where you came from." He winks and acts offended that he doesn't get a wink back. "What's the matter, dog? Wake up on the wrong side of the wheelchair?"

Michael decides to click the safety off and open up on him. "You know I never thought I'd find a bigger illiterate than the trash in this town, but I been wrong before. White trash—"

"'Ey."

"—brown trash. It's all trash. Trash in my house."

"Your house. That's a real good one, gimpie."

"Deed's in my wife's name, is it not? Last I checked, property goes from wife to husband. Not sister to brother."

"Let me tell you something, homeboy." He jumps off the counter, dusts his lap off, smiles. Pulls a chair out from under the table, pushes it toward Michael, and straddles it backward. Ten feet between them, no more. He leans forward, forearms pushed out from underneath like two slabs of ham. "You'd die on a mainline. Don't matter if you can't walk, homeboy. That just make the job easier. They wouldn't let you roll that fucking wheelchair through the gate, you feel me? Shit. On day one, too. Mutherfuckin' cops turn their back on your ass, homie, shout: 'Will someone come over here and hit this punk, already?'"

This piece of shit, Michael thinks. Goddamned felonious savage piece of shit. Gonna eat a meal in this house? Every minute he should be thankful I haven't capped him. "Think I care about that place? I've been to *worse* places. Places you wouldn't *near*. Why? Because you've got no guts."

"Must burn you up, baby, that I put food in this family's mouth."

"I don't owe you anything. Not *you*. No way. You could work for me a hundred years, and I wouldn't owe you a penny. You live, we're even. You die, we're even. Except I'm happy, of course. That's the difference. Joyous if you catch a stray bullet."

"Hey, you know what I think, homes? Been here long enough to know whatchu are. You one of those Tea Party mutherfuckers, aintcha? Yeaaaaahhh. Always yelling don't touch my wallet! Don't touch my money! You think I don't know what's happening up in this mutherfucker? Ya'll flying that Arkansan flag in mutherfuckin' Ore-ee-gone? Don't tread on me. Shit. Tread where I want, fool."

"Yep, you've shown that. Urban rats unleashed north. Bringing your California jungle attitude to this beautiful state."

"You identity crisised mutherfuckers—"

"Ruining Oregon with every U-Haul up the 5."

"—ain't gonna bite shit. Know that."

"And even if I were a shitheel Tea Partier—"

"Mufuckin' garter snake."

"—I'd still be a better man than you."

"If you could walk, you couldn't walk no mainline. So who's better, huh? They'd slit your throat on day one, homie. Your own people. Yeah, even a Nazi got standards, don't he?"

"I've got a clean rap sheet. Which means I don't have one. How about you?"

"You got a *rapist* sheet is what you got. Like talking down to women, dontchu? Let me tell you something: you so much as raise your voice at my sister, and I'll put you in the fucking ground, homie."

The giggling comes first, bubbling up in Michael's throat like seltzer water in a glass, and he's breaking down inside at the absurdity of it all, the gun pulled up out of his beltline and stuck out in front of the chair, offering its wares and purpose like a handshake from a businessman. The sights beaded right between this felonious savage's arrogant eyes, the facial tattoos guiding his hand like signs on a freeway, saying, Here. Right here. Aim here. Put the bullet right here.

"Who will put who in what ground?"

The felonious savage slowly stands, and turns, takes a step backward. He's giving me his back, Michael thinks, shoving the gun into flesh with all the strength of a half-man's body, the muzzle already burrowed into muscles around the spine. For a nick of time they're stuck like that in perfect counterbalance, all that weight coming down the line, all that weight coming up it. He pushes out just as the felonious savage pulls himself up, still not turning toward Michael, and then walks out the door and down the steps, the gun trained on his heart from behind.

The safety's off, his hand's steady, this war hero is 100 percent ready for the slightest misstep, that quarter-revolution of the next attack on whatever you'd call these remains.

Sissy

October 13, 2010

SOMETIMES HER NIGHTS ARE SO RESTLESS she'll take to the kitchen in the early morning, as she's doing now on the crook's tiptoe, to study her Latin, or read the scriptures, or else just sit in the darkness before the light of day brings her life to bear, and wait for it. Whatever she does, she avoids at this hour the *Register* that Pika sometimes brings home for her from the bakery. It's tiring and disconcerting and a monumental drain on your energy to see mug shots of your neighbors—whatever they've done this week—on the front page of the local paper at 2:26 in the morning.

You wouldn't think, she thinks, that a hundred-thousand-dollar bail and twenty-three charges from distribution to larceny to child endangerment could be mundane. But then just based on that, she thinks, you wouldn't think we'd ever get this far, either.

Lucky, she thinks further, there's more to base our lives on than the *Register's* unquestionably evil *Snatched* column of the week's Yamhill County arrestees.

She turns on the reading lamp cornered under the shelves and hears tin-on-tin scraping and thinks, raccoon, but then sees the wide-shouldered shadow from the moon's glare on their porch. She's relieved to see Pika there hunched over his lid-peeled can of corned beef, as her sympathies surge to the pity and mercy and compassion no one who knows her has ever doubted, not even her mother.

Michael said once, "She's jealous of your goodness, Sis. There's nothing else to it. She wants you down there in the pit where the two of you can rot together. Thought she could wreck you, make you a carbon copy of misery. She can't understand why you haven't been broken yet by life."

"I've been broken, Michael," was all that she'd said then, horrified at the casual way Michael had talked about a human being rotting, be it herself, or her mother, or one of the regulars in *Snatched*.

She comes out on the porch and he turns his head and smiles softly, his most charming feature, she thinks, especially with how big he is. He scoots to his left to give her space, and she takes it. Her grayish nightgown has no fancy insignia, but it's warm tonight in the cold wind, it's always warm. Her mother gave it to her on Christmas Eve, 1999, gift-wrapped as if it had been bought at a department store and not a garage sale.

"It's quiet, huh?"

He looks over his shoulder, winks. "Morning. Noon. Night."

They're the last house on the street, and from there, it's the woods. Then the creek. Then the base of the Eola Hills, up and over the top. She knows the isolation of this part of Amity as well as anyone. Only her mother knew it better.

"Way different than what you're used to, huh, Pika?"

"Well, it's peaceful. But almost too peaceful, you know what I mean? No one ever comes up this road."

"Uh-uh."

"No one ever comes up any of these roads seem like."

"You all right, Pika?"

"Oh, yeah, yeah. It's all good. You know."

"Whatchu thinking about—mind if I ask?"

"Ah, nothing, really. Just disappearing from life for a minute, you know what I mean? Getting my late-night jones on here. Pisupo—"

"That's corned beef?"

"—and canned spaghetti—Yep, yep."

"Sorry the microwave's down, big brother."

"Nah nah nah, it's way cool. I learned to eat cold out the can by the age of ten. Got to the joint, and mufuckers were selling em on the tier for twenty coffee shots."

"A lot of caffeine."

"Lotta lonely nights."

He offers her a bite. "Pisupo's every Samoan's guilty pleasure."

She takes a spoonful, passes it back. "Us Irish, too."

"Right, right. It's a British thing. We came, we saw, we left corned beef with the natives."

She smiles, nods. "They brought good things, too."

"That's true. They passed around penicillin. Told us Samoans to stop eating our dead enemies after battle."

"Well, that's definitely good."

"Oh, and they brought cricket bats, too." He shivers as if he's cold, says, "But nah, nah, that wasn't cool."

"Why's that, Pika?"

"Because they'd crack the kids with em. Was an upgrade on discipline."

"Mean a downgrade."

He looks over at her, squints. "Right. Used to be divots of coconuts, you know what I'm saying? Good thing they didn't hand out guns."

"Pika?"

"Yep, yep."

"You feel okay here?"

"Oh, yeah, yeah. Hell, yeah. Everything's cool as can be, little sister."

"I know you'd say that even when it's not."

"Yeah. Well. You right there. Old code I can't ever get rid of. Doesn't take too much imagination to figure out where it started. Or why. Somehow gotta figure out how to live with shit. And the only way you do that in there is to never complain about shit. But then: I'm good this time. For real. Yep. Here with my sis and her little boy, chilling on the porch at two in the morning, pounding a can of pisupo: got no chains on my legs, got no regrets."

"Okay."

"You cold?"

"A little bit. Gonna go back inside." She uses his shoulder as a post to push up on and only sees now that he's barefoot, in a T-shirt and a thin lava lava: yellow tuberose on a blue backdrop glimmering in the moonlight. "You must be freezing, Pika."

"Nah, I'm cool. I warm up with my belly full. Got all kinds of acid reflux gas pumping through my pipes right now."

"Pika?"

"Yeah?"

"You won't do anything, right?"

"What?"

"Sure everything's okay here?"

"Shit. Of course. Stop worrying, all right?"

"Okay."

"I already lost enough time to that mufucker, you know what I'm saying? I don't need to say one word to that fool."

"I guess you guys are just naturally quiet around one another."

He looks up, and is smiling wider than she is. "That's a real good one right there."

"I thought you'd like that, Pika."

"A little joke from the lady of the house. And on a full moon, too. Can you hear the crickets laughing back in the creek? Damn, man. They like that one right there."

Pika

October 14, 2010

WHAT TRIPS HIM OUT MOST IS HOW these hang-dog Northwesterners walk around in the rain without umbrellas. Just leave em at home on the rack. Or else don't waste the dollar at the Dollar Tree, buy a four-pack of Kit Kats instead, buy a ten-gallon bag of Hawaiian Funyons.

Now he pulls his hoodie up and over his head, down low over the brow, covering the tags just like he's been doing since the day, rain or no rain, and thinks, Sometimes they don't even use their hoodies on their lumberjack flannels, man. Let em sit on their shoulders like a muther-fucking kitten. So what happens? They turn into human sponges, that's what. Mop up the water with the hair on their heads, the lumberjack beards on their faces. Get home and gotta throw every article of clothing in the dryer, if they've got one, or else just hang it out there on the line and hope for twenty-four hours of sunshine.

The rain the rain the rain.

That's the story, that's the deal. Two-thirds of the year, minimum.

Don't come up here to Ore-ee-gone, he thinks, if you fear water from a cloud. Can't handle being rained on? This is not the state for you. Not the state of mind you want to be in. When he and Ioane could hear but not see the rain pelting the bank-safe walls and rooftop of D Block, his cellie used to say that they were getting pissed on by the deity for their sins. That it wasn't raining at that moment anywhere else in the whole state. It happened a lot. He felt plenty guilty about plenty of shit he'd pulled in his life, but Pika couldn't bring himself back then to believe the punitive side of Ioane's prophecy, and this shit right here, he thinks, unable to see the markers across the 99, wiping the rain off his face every five seconds despite the hoodie, pulling the baker's bib from his chest and stomach to air bubble off his skin, is the mutherfucking proof.

Look at this, he thinks. Lookie here.

A sureño emerges of the grayness, low to the ground, sure and slow through the shadows as if he were walking the Flea Market in East San Jo, his blue LA hat and blue LA shirt stuck to his brown LA skin. Look at this. Even the eses don't cover their asses in this shit. Even the eses around here act like straight-up hicks. Something more to it I'm missing. Something out of whack in either them, or in me, man.

Well, he thinks, meeting the southerner in the eyes and institutionally holding it, I'm wacked. And y'all *know* this, dontchu? So that eliminates that part of the equation. Maybe what it is is we're both wacked, but in different ways. We're both fools.

All fools.

He's waiting for the ese to say something about his outfit, as if they hadn't both of them worn the same kind of two-dollar threads back in the block, as if the whole thing matters out here in freedom, posted up at the Mac bustop in this weekly biblical flood.

"Hey, homes."

"What's happening?"

The ese nods. After a few seconds float away in the rushing gutter puddles, says, "Where'd you do your time at, ese?"

"OSP, man."

"South Fork, homes."

"What's that?"

"Fire camp."

Pika decides to give him some repetition—"fire camp"—and nothing else, not because there's any special shame in getting a short-term prison sentence for sixth-offense jaywalking—once you catch a beef, Pika thinks, all of it's shame, man, all of it needs head-on, deep-down addressing, all of it is uphill re-emerging from the pit—but because it's the jaywalker who likes to play hard 24-7. County jails are full of hardcore, jaywalking, pug dogs barking out their bars like murderous pit bulls.

"You a southerner, homie?"

"Samoan, youngster."

"Oh, all right. You a oso."

This clarification not really necessary, but why not? Educate. Kill some time. "It's uso."

"Oso?"

"No. Uuu. So."

"Ohhhhh. Uuusooo."

"Right."

"So it's not oso."

"What's that?"

"That's a big bear, homie. That's what we call big-ass eses like you. Oso."

"Well. Y'all say whatchu want, man. I ain't trippin'. And we'll say what we want, you feel me?"

"Simón, ese. Simón. Uuu. Sooo. Uso."

He's nervous already, Pika thinks. Mutherfuckers in the joint always dangerous when they're nervous, even Chinese lap dogs with smashed-in faces. Fucking tweaker faces looking like the bottom of a bound foot. This little light-in-the-muli, south-of-the-border, Chihuahua maile talking like he's a lifer. Kick rocks, man. Walk. Split, you fucking displaced thirteener. Go drop your grenade in some other lame's lap. Earn your life sentence with some other sucker.

Delivered between the shivers from the cold, or else the cranka he just slammed, the southerner finally says: "You from Mac, homie?"

"What?"

"What'd you do, homeboy?"

"What?"

"What'd you get locked up for?"

Pika smiles, shakes his head. *When? Where? Which time?* It ain't fun to me, it ain't a mutherfucking stripe on my baker's coat and it ain't single digits, youngster.

Plus the kid broke the old rule on the yard. Guess they don't got it down there in the camp. Don't ever ask another man his case unless he's a cop or a snitch or a child molester. Why? Because you might become his *new* case, that's why. What? the question insinuates. You saying I need to PC-up, fool? Saying I look like a cop or a snitch or a child molester? Trying to regulate on this g? Can't trust you. You spreading shit on the yard, mutherfucker. Come here: let me show you something.

"You ain't from Mac, eh. Yeah, I can tell."

"Oh, you can tell I ain't from Ore-ee-gone, huh?"

"Nah, nah, nah. Just talking, homie. Whatchu doing here?"

"Trying to get to tomorrow, what else?"

"Ain't seen you around, eh. That's all I mean, you know what I mean?"

"Amity's my homekick, Mr. Torpedo."

"Got a couple homeboys in Amity. You know Sit Low Apartments?" Pika barely nods. "You know Sleepy?" Pika barely shakes his head no. "You don't know Sleepy?"

"Nah."

The ese looks at Pika with straight accusation: where you living, uso, at a fat cottage on the winery's edge? "Well, you should check him out some time, homie. He got it goin' on over there. Tell him Flaco sent you, eh."

"I'm cool, youngster."

"Sleep got action out there, man. Wait. Nah, he gets out—"

"Told you I'm cool."

"—of county en Noviembre. That vato's running it up in Amity, homeboy."

Can't give him anything else, Pika decides, or else it opens up the deal. Then you gotta play it. Just like before getting sworn in at the stand. When your dumptruck pee-pee tells you to keep your mouth shut. Fucking pee-pee's. Public pretenders either fresh outta law school zit-chinned guppies, or dusty old ladies who couldn't make the leap to private practice.

And so you get up there in the box, all locked-down about your life, hands crossed on your lap, hair combed, and look like a mutherfucking liar to the jury, anyway. Cause you gotta open your mouth to talk, where the teeth are still capped in silver, you gotta show a profile of your face to the whole room, the ink on the cheek still there green-on-brown, and right about the time you're ready to disappear to a thirteen-to-fifteen-year sentence just so you can breathe again, the DA's pulling in a five foot by eight foot blown-up poster of your San Quentin ID card.

"I ask of you goodly jurors: Is this the same man," the DA's drawn-out, cheeseball pauses learned from some dumb Lifetime® drama, "that you see here today?" His index finger swiveling now from the posterboard to the stand, which he leans on heavily, only inches from your fist, looking up and away at the ceiling.

Fucking circus of a trial, Pika thinks. Public lured into the sideshow tent by the court's ringleader-jester: check out this law-breaking freak, everyone! Betchu didn't know human beings could do *this*! Betchu didn't know they looked like *this*!

Least if you take a risk and open up about it, he thinks, one or two of those jurors who been through it themselves and somehow snuck past incognito the DA's surface interrogations—one or two just might believe you're a *real* human being, man, who's been through it, too, in your own way, and that you are the way you are for a reason.

Gimme the time. Go ahead: break me off. Regulate on my ass, and send me upstate on the next silver bullet outta town. Wrap the chains around my waist and wrists and ankles: run that institutional ivy! Thread it! I won't break down. Won't shout. I won't research in the law library some dot-your-i-out by law technicality, some cross-your-t-key to freedom. Won't play Malcolm or Mussolini on the stump, trying to rile up the masses and ride the momentum of the cause out the gates. Won't do a Houdini, either, twist into a pretzel for a fast break on a loading truck in a laundry bag of dirty drawers.

But just keep your ears open—all I ask, that's the deal—if I ever feel like telling you what kinda ruthless diss life can throw your way, okay?

Still, Pika says nothing. Standing strong, without crossing personal space, without intruding, thinking on this thing judiciously. Been a minute or two since I seen a legit street hood. But won't judge this fool, and yet. Nah. Can't do it. Can't give him access to me either. Hit up some social worker, youngster ese, if what you want's a little charity this evening. You might be the kinda cat, I can see, who turns an entry vein into an exit wound. Got too much to protect right now. Got the kid. And Sissy. More than just me now, straight-up. But then always was more than just me, once I really think about it. Just more obvious now. Just more apparent in real-time, not the dreamland of freedom we're always seeing on the ceiling from our bunks, tuning out on all the shouters and haters and incarcerators.

Shoutin' hatin' masturbatin' incarcerators. Pika smiles. Won't share that rap with the kid. Won't even share it with his mother.

They wait there in the muddy-ditch-turned-bustop in a strange but familiar feeling-out silence that makes Pika more immovable than he already is. They watch at the rain striking the ground in a thousand simultaneous bursts per second, descending rushing flowing through holes you never know are there until the water itself goes down em, and yet barely a minute passes. Just like in the cell, man. That's the hell of it: posting up with a mutherfucker you don't want posted there. On the yard. In the tank. At chow. Look over at the visit, and there he is, next table down, nodding at your old lady's tits. A second like a minute in the joint. Minute like an hour. Hour like a day. Same hustling mutherfuckers, over and over and over, pointing up at the slow-mo clock.

Gotta do it myself. He knows this. Can't make a deaf man love Ray Charles. Can't make Ray Charles love a sunset. Who's a miracle worker in this redneck trap? Shit, he thinks. I'm barely walking these slick streets legal. Barely breathing on the free air. Gotta happen by the old school way. Separation on foot. Take off, push distance, make tracks. Pika bends at the waist and leans forward, pulls the hoodie down across his face, squeegees it the way you wring out a towel, re-drapes it around his head, and then starts the long walk home in the rain.

Polynesian hang-dog from Ore-ee-gone.

"Take it easy, youngster."

"I catcha later, oso."

Oso.

Slow-learnin' flunkee punk-ass, Pika thinks.

Benji

October 19, 2010

THE BOY LIKES TO WATCH HIS FATHER SHAVE. One pump of lather and the wild slap spread on one side, one pump of lather and the wild slap spread on the other. Like whipped cream, like foam in the ocean. Then you cut into the creamy foam with the blue cutter. That's when the bushy hair comes off. That's when his daddy rinses the blue cutter and scrapes at his blowfish face again.

The boy squeezes himself smaller now, little human basketball in the closet, propped on a pair of old steel-toes to get front row. This the third time watching his daddy shave, the first time in a while. His father's beard is thick with growth, like the big silver-backed gorilla in the big book on the table about the Portland Zoo, where his people promise they will go for his sixth birthday. All his people together, at once. His daddy's beard is like those people Daddy went over there to fight in the war. But not that much hair, actually. Not *that* ugly.

The boy can see through the crack and he can be his daddy's friend the way he wants to be but doesn't yet know. He will learn how, the boy knows. My daddy will learn how. The boy can't wait to grow up. The first thing he will do is battle against the alone-tears of his father. He sees other things from the closet. He closed his own eyes when his daddy was crying that day and didn't open them again until he heard the wheels of the chair roll out the door. What daddy needs, the boy thinks, is a buddy. I'm gonna be his best buddy. I'm gonna make him laugh. He can't dance, but I can dance *for* him. I can make him sit up high in the chair. Mama said she danced with him at the prom! I can make him remember. I can make Daddy never forget.

The boy will work on all the things the rest of the people who already tried but don't know how to work on because they're dumb and so failed and that's why it didn't happen, and he will share all his secrets in order to be a good buddy to his daddy, and will keep nothing to himself. That's their deal.

"Try not to keep too much inside, little fella," his daddy once told him. "Trust me. You don't wanna go that route. Take it from one of the worst internalizers around. Anyway, not natural in you, Top. Just remember: you can share with me anytime for any reason, okay? And if not me— not around for some reason, or you're embarrassed, or whatever it is— you go find mama. She's a part of the deal, too. Between the two of us, we gotchu covered, Top. We're not exactly geezers, but we got a lot of life added up."

"Thank you," he hears from the other room. His mom. He loves his mom differently, but the same. One million, and then some. That's their call-sign. That's the only math he needs to know, she always tells him. But go ahead, she'll say next. Go ahead and learn you some more math when it's time, hon. Learn you every star out there you can, honey.

And once he heard her also say: *while* you can.

I have to learn while I can, he thinks.

"Thanks for what, Sis?"

"I know you're not happy about this, Michael."

"Just something else I've got no say about, that's all."

"But there's a lot you don't know about him, Michael. I think if you—"

"What else I need to know except what's right there on his face?"

"No." The boy knows his mother is thinking of what to say. The boy shifts on his heels because he doesn't like when his mama doesn't know what to say. It's too close to his mama being sad. And sometimes it's the same thing at the same time. "There's more to him. Just like there's more to you. He only looks mean."

"Looks? I'm talking about what's on the *skin* of his face, Sissy."

"Will you listen?"

"It's no use, Sis, but I'll listen just the same."

"Thank you."

"Well, go on, please. Just put it in me already."

"Don't talk like that, Michael."

"I meant the knife, Sissy. Jesus. You're mixing us up now, too? I'm not a felonious pig like that lawbreaking—well, okay, go, go, will ya, just go on with it."

"He gave me all the money, Michael."

"What money?"

"The money we been *living* on the last four years." Oh, no, the boy thinks. Daddy doesn't know about the money we been living on the last four years. He thinks we live for free. I can tell. His eyebrows are making the rainbow shape like when he said at the movie theatre that we should go home because of the cuss words from the cartoon fish, and they're stuck there. His eyes are too big if he doesn't blink, the boy thinks. He wants to go close his daddy's eyes like the shutters on a rainy day. "That's right, Michael. The money we'll be living on for a long time, God willing."

"So he stole—"

"No! No. Please. He didn't steal anything."

"So that's what he meant the other day. Goddamn."

"What?"

"Never mind. Sissy, listen. I can get a check from the VA, if I just—"

"How?"

"—go and talk with a psych."

His mama doesn't believe him. The boy knows this. When he lies and she knows that he's lying she looks at the boy like this. She's pointing at the wheelchair.

"That happened *here*, Michael."

"Says who? *You*? That tattooed *lady* from the circus?"

"You already told me you couldn't get more than 30 percent, Michael, because it's in your head."

"Damn." He's quiet. The quiet means he's listening.

"I'm sorry, Michael. I want to help. I always will."

His daddy nods. Then he whispers so the boy has to put the side of his head out of the closet door, low by the floor where no one, not even Daddy in his chair, looks. "Okay. I'm sorry, too. Thank you."

His mama waits to say thank you back and the boy shifts. He can tell when adults are being adults. He can tell this is an adult time, and not for him. All of a sudden like the way the rain in Oregon just starts without any warning, he presses his hands against his ears to be good, but Mama comes over and stands next to Daddy, and he can still hear all the words, anyway.

"You know Mama hated me. That's okay. Took me a long time to understand who she was hating. But, anyway, she went and done it, Mikey, to prove how much she hated me."

"But I thought she came around at the end. Why would she—"

"She *did*, Michael."

"Well, what are you saying then?"

"She gave him everything, Mikey, that's the money I'm talking about, and—"

"That's so selfish."

"—then he gave *me* everything, see? And it wasn't selfish, Michael. She forgot. I know that."

"Forgot what, Sis?"

"She just didn't have enough time at the end to change her mind, that's all. Sick for two weeks, and that was it."

"I know."

"She was in too much pain to think about the will. Well, I forgive her. But with or without the money—I don't *care*. Rest in peace, Mama."

The boy crosses himself like his mama outside in the room is crossing herself but not his daddy, but he doesn't really feel that way because no one can hate his mama—not even that lady, her *own* mama. That's wrong! he thinks, and he stands to come out and hug his mama, but his daddy says, "Well, I don't forgive *him*."

"But we have to try to—"

"He's lower than an al-Qaeda operative." Those are the people with the beards, the boy thinks, nodding, squinting. Those are the *ugly* ones. "At least they have loyalty to the tribe. Wouldn't hesitate one split, Sissy. If you weren't around, the coup de grace happens in an eyeblink."

"Let's not talk like that please."

"Like *what*? Like what I really *feel*? Do you think he feels any differently about me?"

"He didn't keep a penny for himself, Michael."

"And he *shouldn't*."

"Okay, okay. But that's not the point. Maybe none of us should. But you just said my mama was selfish for keeping it from me, right?"

There's that lady again, the boy thinks. His daddy doesn't talk. Talk, Daddy! Tell her that that lady shouldn't hate anyone, especially our queen! "Go on."

"Right, Michael?"

"I already know what you're gonna say so don't even bother."

"Well, why isn't he *generous* for doing the opposite, Michael, huh?"

"See? Knew it."

"He's also done what he's supposed to do. He's trying, anyway. Everyone is, I think. He has good in him. And he loves Ben—"

"Yeah, what a hero."

"No, I'm not saying it's the same thing as what you did over there, but I just want you to see that he's trying, that's all."

"Well, you just tell him to keep his distance from me."

"We live in the same house, Michael."

"You know what I mean, Sis. My *business*. You keep that civilian disengaged from my affairs."

"I will. I have."

"Thank you."

"And he does, doesn't he?"

"Well. Yes. He does."

"Well. You're *welcome*."

They turn the light off. The boy waits in the darkness. Now if he closes his eyes, it's the same as keeping them open. Darkness on the outside, darkness on the inside. He keeps them open. He will come out soon. He knows the way out. The boy doesn't understand that he doesn't understand, but he waits for a while in the darkness just the same, listening breathlessly for the answer he can't find in his little boy brain.

Benji

October 20, 2010

THEY GET OFF THE BUS ON 1ST AND EVANS, and the boy splits the difference, his father on the left, his uncle on the right. His people take up the whole walk. Other pedestrians make big loops around them and if Mama were here, the boy thinks, they'd make even bigger loops. Benji is skipping, excited to meet his father's admirers at the VFW. This is downtown McMinnville, Mama's favorite place to walk. Mama told him to listen first today, talk second, that's the rule. He's going to obey, he said to her, the way soldiers obey orders. "Yes, ma'am!" Uncle Pika has to work at the bakery, and that meeeeeeeaaaanns, the boy teases himself, that he's gonna bring me a bialy tonight.

Three of his daddy's friends are already waiting where the ramp starts at the VFW.

"See ya later, Uncle Pika!"

"All'ight, champ."

The boy sees his daddy's friends look meanly at his uncle, and what this means to him is that he doesn't like them. My uncle Pika works hard for our family at the bakery, he thinks. Don't you know that? That's what Mama always tells me because that's the truth. Mama doesn't lie to me. He brings home leftover bread every night. And that's why he's walking across the street right now. He has to work.

They roll on, stop before the VFW.

"How goes it, men?"

The boy straightens up, acts like a little soldier. Everyone is saying, "Mikey," and shaking his dad's hand.

"Good, good, Mikey." This is the fat one. How can he be a soldier if he's so fat? He looks like that sumo wrestler Uncle Pika showed him at the Amity Library. Cone. E. She. Key. That was his name. He was from Hawai'i. He beat all the champions in Japan. He's a champion. "How you been?"

"Good."

"This your boy, huh?"

"Yep." His dad rubs his head, pulls him in, and kisses the top of his head. He bounces back up after his daddy releases him. "Say hi, son."

"Hi."

"What's your name, buddy?"

He puffs up, and looks the sumo in the face. "Benjamin."

"Well, Benjamin. I'm Laird. That's Chuck. And Simon." Benji turns his head to each, and nods, but says nothing. This is serious, and I don't like you for the way you looked at my uncle. "You know your dad here, he's a real hero in this town." Benji nods, but doesn't smile like he wants to deep down. This is serious. Chuck and Simon also nod. "We're gonna get a plaque up for him in the square. Right next to Ben Franklin."

"Or a park or something."

"A park?" Benji asks.

"They're just playing with you, son."

"No, we're not!" says Chuck.

"Sure ain't," says Laird.

"These things just take a little time," Chuck says. "You know how the military is. They got their own clock they use."

"We already put in the paperwork at the last city council."

"Well, just the same. We'll be all right without a park, won't we, Top? Anyway, how about giving my son a tour, huh, fellas?"

"Sure, sure. Come on."

Laird takes the boy's hand, but he rips it out at once and catches up to his father. They go up the ramp together, as Laird, Chuck, and whatever the other guy's name is take the steps.

In the anteroom, Michael parks his wheelchair. "Go on, Top. They'll show you around."

He does what his daddy says, but he's not happy about it. Laird smells real bad, the boy thinks, like rotten cream cheese. And that guy whose name I forgot, he's the opposite of Cone. E. She. Key. He's skinnier than me and I'm only fifty pounds. That's what Mama told me. Uncle Pika, too.

"This over here, Benjamin—these are all the World War I soldiers from the valley. Pretty long list, huh?" Benji nods but not with his whole head. Just his eyes and his eyebrows. This is serious. "This town has a long history of bravery, that's for sure. Your dad is the latest member."

"Sure is," adds Chuck.

"And this over here is the banquet hall." Cone. E. She. Key looks down at Benji and winks the way his Uncle Pika does. Except not really. Uncle Pika winks like a buddy. "I like this place the best, little fella."

"This is where you eat."

All three laugh. "He's got you, boy," says Chuck.

"We have a Christmas dinner here every year. You come along with your daddy, all right?"

"That's right," says Laird. "I play Santa Cl—"

"Hey!"

"Oh, sorry. Stupid. We got Santa and everything. So you make a wish for Christmas, all right?"

"I don't do that anymore."

"How come?" Chuck asks.

"Cause the last time I asked Santa if he could get my daddy some new legs, and he didn't."

Laird looks at Chuck, who shakes his head. "Well, we're gonna help your dad out just the same, buddy."

Michael

October 24, 2010

HE CAN'T STAND GOING TO CHURCH, be it with these IHS Catholics or the LDS Mormons of his childhood, and so he waits outside for the hour with a pen, folded paper, and a stamped envelope in his chest pocket. He gently strokes the feral cat tiptoeing at the base of the right wheel, pressing into it in plastic contortions, the calico fur on needlepoint end from the intimacy.

Domesticated enough, my little friend, to not bite the hand that pets you, Michael thinks.

Which is usually the way it goes with human beings, too. Don't smash the heart that loves you. A golden rule: beware thy line-crossing feet. He can't talk about why he won't enter the church, or entertain in conversation with Sissy the idea of God, or even the notion that anyone would need an ancient entity to feel good about their lives, but even this starved thought of blasphemy right here, the one that war made and signed off on, is infinitely smaller than his love for Sissy.

Which grew over the years, even as he shrank. Which got bigger here back home, even as he'd held her picture over there in war, a pilgrim with his relic pasted to the heart in his chest.

He can't talk about it but he can think about it all right and out here in Southern Amity where no one lives but seven devout chocolate-making monks and too many colonies of wild birds to name and the majestic bald eagles with their eight-foot-by-eight foot nests on the telephone poles and the irritating soon-to-be-hunted-with-bow-and-arrow turkeys, what else does one think on but God?

Everyone in the world salivating and commiserating and murdering, he thinks, over their mythology. But it's all tied in, he thinks further. You extract one aspect of the story, and the whole thing gets stuck there in the mud, a tank without tracks. War is like that, he thinks. The eight-year-old child playing Jenga with your worldview. Oh, that doesn't bother you? That preventable death in the oily sand doesn't bring you down? How you knew that human being only seconds ago, had started calling him "brother" over the last few months, but now will be sending him home to Nebraska in a flag-draped bag, if, that is, you can safely retrieve his body? No? How about this then? Let's air-drop a village entire through the gates of hell, women and children, too. No. Let's up the ante, actually: women and children *first*. How about we pull five Jenga sticks out at the same time, see you stand on that single-leg crutch like a flamingo? Here. Let's take that crutch from you, too, see if you can levitate like a Jedi master.

Hah.

Was hardest for Michael to get along with the Force-induced Christians on his team, mostly from the South and Midwest, the ones who officially kept themselves clean with scriptural wipes they never read. But he'd read it. Actually loved the dream of the New Testament, much respect for the gospels, all the revolutionary Semitic peaceniks talking up Christ's turned cheek to the Roman guards in a garden of Jerusalem: boy, he couldn't think of *anything* more foreign in composition to war, more absurd in the land of the dead! Land of the fled and the fleeing! Which, now that he thinks about it, is probably why he liked Matthew Mark Luke and John so much. Took his mind off the place he was in, even though he was officially in the land of constant reference. Or damned proximal, at least, right down the road. Sure as hell felt like the wrath of the deity was nearby, where whole peoples were being felled like the cornstalks back in Amity, where the golden idols were liquidated into black gold, their architects prime to get struck down by either lightning in the sky or an F-18.

The Bible in battle was like a philosophical sci-fi book, far-out extraterrestrial rhetoric from another universe.

That was the first tour and the second. By the third and fourth and disastrous fifth he'd softened on religion, couldn't hold the line. He still couldn't stand the warmongering evangelicals, the ones who equated their own wanton lust to kill with fulfillment of Old Testament prophecy, as tunnel-visioned about their mission as Likud-party Zionists, but by now he'd figured out something about the human condition: it was in a sorry state. Not only that. Of the humans contributing to the human condition, Americans were in the *sorriest* state.

We Americans are lost, he'd thought so many times over there it became a mantra, and yet here we are leading the goddamned world.

He was starting to hate the very people he was charged and paid to defend. The ones who waved the same flag, who claimed the same team. Didn't take long to entertain the accusation in his own head of self-hatred. One was what one was, after all, and he was one of them. One of us. Certain elements of self that not only wouldn't ever change, but *can't* change.

Then he got back and heard all this nonsense about American exceptionalism, a term he'd misunderstood for several months. You mean exceptional as in *great*? He looked around: it didn't square. This is the land where bug-eyed tweakers and the morbidly obese compete for space in the town square. Where far-right big-shots call for a war their sons and daughters don't go anywhere near, where tree-huggers kill the Amity logging industry while sitting in a Bridge City coffee shop playing bluegrass on a toxic-wired I-phone soon to be "obsolete" at the calendar year's end, and thus sent en masse with a million other "units" to an indigent Filipino village. Little brown Melanesians doing their laundry in a swamp of keyboard and laptop runoff, and you're peaceably back at the hipster café saving six seconds per minute on downloads about saving the trees.

More like decadence, he'd thought. Like mass societal deterioration.

So if what you mean is that we are *exceptions*, you're right. Let's call it American *exception*ism then. Living how no else in the world lives: *that's* an exception. No consequence to any choice, no price for any action: *definitely* an exception. Most people in the world live by needs, but we coast through life by our wants. Most people in the world have a buffer zone of coexistence called mutual respect, called universal morality, meaning merely that no one would forsake a moral tenet no matter what, which is to say, he'd thought, that they *do*, in fact, view that particular moral tenet as universal. Meanwhile, we piss on prophets and presidents and whole civilizations in mid-yawn, and mock anyone using the word moral in a conversation.

As soldiers called to their country's duty, as men and women protecting their children, as human beings with their metaphysical cultural moral beliefs, what honest American warrior wouldn't respect more than his own breth- and sistren citizens the very people he was killing in their name? Killing in his own name? Who was tougher, who was better, who earned their time on this planet? Who was the underdog? Who was fucked, and yet kept on? Wasn't he the troop with a fat blue Camelbak manufactured in Michigan and Dasani water to fill up the air-bubble's middle and top-notch weaponry with the night lit up green by infrared scopes clear as video games you grew up on? Who was it that really lived on the land, who lived from it, and therefore—in and of the dirt already—didn't need anyone "driving their dicks into the dirt" in the first place?

You go to war, you learn to assess suffering, he thinks, calibrate it like you do anything. Well, he was pulled out of that place—*wasn't he?*— came home to a peacetime nation within its borders, the ones his fellow citizens ahistorically think are inviolate. But the last he checked, he lived in Amity, Oregon. Born, grew up in, probably perish in. Was he supposed to be a patriot about it and lie in his heart, say his mind and half-functioning body were really over there, insult an ancient people who were stuck ad eternum? Should he sit on the doggy-duty perch in the doggy-doo parade and wave in his VFW beret like a homemade smalltown Miss America? Think, or else say out loud, that a hundred dead Iraqis were mathematically the same as a maimed American? Come on. Supposed to say that what he saw over there was actually *not* what he saw, but the *opposite*?

His own hypocrisy was everywhere in the war, and then he came back home and there was more of it. Not even lessened by the effort, but grown as if a Pacific Northwestern crop like hops or hazelnuts or barley, hypocrisy weed-wild in this part of the country, but probably any part when it came down to it, a characteristic by-product driving force element of the American Age.

And so it's only natural, he thinks now, the cat jumping into his lap, rolling its furry head along the hardness of his knees, that I became a lifelong member of the Hypocrite's Fraternity. In love with the woman I hurt irreparably, whose soul I burnt like a pyre to the ground: that's a hypocrite; that's a phony.

He sits there understanding perfectly why he's staying put and not going in. He won't bring down her true faith, which is good in the end, he thinks, which is maybe all we have in the end, which he wonders if he himself will ever have again, if he ever did truly have it. Now, tomorrow, whenever the end will visit him, he wonders if he will have the faith to face it. If he stayed with the ideas of goodness in the book and didn't stray toward his countryperson's perverse embodiment of the book, he started to think that maybe the book wasn't half bad. He'll sit on the idea, just like he sits on everything else.

So he's waiting there and not going in but yet not leaving. He wants to be good like she is. That's it. He wants to stand up and say something. He wants to stand up. But even if he'd never been crippled for his crime, even if the idea of consummation was not the physical absurdity he knew it to be, they could never lovemake again, he knew, and this was right. Absolutely. It wasn't Sissy being punitive, an injudicious measure he couldn't understand, but instead a way to keep dead that which he, and the war, had killed. If the humanly urge to be touched and loved had been murdered in one by the other, then it was justly killed in two by the same. Celibacy, like the abstinent life of these monks, had been made not by God, but by wretched man himself, and he, still, always, was man all right.

He might sit there in regret and shame, but what else does that mean, he thinks, except that I'd be better in a do-over revisit of the crime-in-question? Which is the same, he thinks, as this judgment I have of America.

I judged and raped America, he thinks. I judged and raped my own thoughts of America. I hurt the woman I love.

They come out of the church now, all twenty-three parishioners, one by one, crossing themselves at the stone fountain, and she and Benji are last out the door, having stayed behind to say some medieval prayer to (of all the million wingéd angels they could pray to:) St. *Michael*, protector of valiant causes. The boy now darts toward him, stops just short of collision, his excited eyes on the calico he calls Marty.

"How's Marty doing, Dad?"

"Good, Top."

"Marty. Where'd you get this scratch at, Marty? Look, Dad."

"I see."

"Dad?"

"Yes?"

"He's scratched by the mouth, see?"

"Yep."

He'd actually seen the scratch first thing this morning, he realizes upon his son's innocent, ardent, present-tense interrogation, the kind he's used to and loves and gets goose bumps on his arms from damned near every time, but the cat's wound didn't quite register then. Or else it registered, but didn't matter. That was it: the latter scenario. Iodine-wound is what it's called in the front. You break the bottle, cotton swab the wound, wrap it up stained, drive on. The cat is still alive, was Michael's immediate quarter-of-a-second judgment, and could still be pet and loved on, and that was enough to ignore the scratch, and wherever it came from, whyever. So it wasn't quite that the scratch didn't matter; it's that another thing—impending death, for instance—mattered *more*. Always, in fact, matters more. Remove that reference point from the world, he thinks, and everything collapses.

You made it out of the pit, little fella, he might've said out loud. Escaped it. Be grateful for that.

And one didn't need much of an imagination to appreciate the late-night feline war-zone that must happen around here. That scratch is the same as the cat saying back, Hello, mister. I'm alive. See? Now pet me.

Inevitability in this life: a concept best divined by us lowlander handicaps, he thinks. We don't have much else. But we know, don't we? That every turn is rife with spilling disaster.

"You gonna eat with us in the cloister, Daddy?"

"No."

"That's okay, Dad. But remember."

"I know, Top. I remember."

"If you change your mind, juuuust . . ."

"I know. I'll just ring the doorbell."

"Yeah. And Dad? The monks don't mind answering the door."

"You told me that."

"It says that on the door, Dad. As long as you're polite."

"Okay."

"Mom said they're built to suffer, and that's not suffering, right?"

"I guess not."

"I've got to tell Mom something, okay?"

"Yep."

"Mom!"

She doesn't look over from her conversation with his elderly peer of the lowlands. Elevation: eye level. The eighty-year-old wheelchaired lady covered with colorful lei-like rosaries for the arm and wrist could be her grandmother. Enjoy this, he thinks. Please. Ignore me. Take a break from me. You deserve it. Get from her whatever you can. Focus on another cripple for a minute. For an hour! "Dad's not gonna eat lunch with the monks!"

She nods at their son, and he says to the boy, "Let Mom talk, okay, Top?"

"Yes, sir!"

"And maybe try to yell a little less."

"Yes, sir," he whispers. "Dad?"

"Yes?"

"You're actually right. There's a rule: see?" The boy is pointing at the request for silence and respect on the grounds, and he says, "Yep."

"I'll be back, Dad, okay?"

"Yep. Be careful. And stay away from the pond."

"Yes, sir," the boy whispers, and then he sprints off.

The crowd is passing him now. Several parishioners patting his shoulder. Somehow Sissy lifts the John Deere cap and kisses the top of his head without losing the bead of her conversation with the withered lady, his wife momentarily erect between the two chairs, a shadowy silhouette on the walk like a skyward middle finger. Then the black hand on the ground breaks as they move on, and Michael is half a thing once again, the ring and pinkie finger knuckled in on itself. He sits. Watches the rest of the hand leave him. The old lady is shouting louder than his son had and Sissy is enthralled, he can see, by the words about universal goodness. He loves her for the forward-lean at the waist, the same angle employed to teach their son to walk years ago, the same angle given him ten times a day. The way she's lowering herself not to make it even with the lady so much, as if that were possible, but to merely show that she's listening closely, nodding within the old lady's line of vision.

"Jesus summoned all the children on the mount to his side!" shouts the lady. "And said! 'Be like them.'"

He doesn't think about the parable's lesson with any real depth because, to him, it's a pretty screwed up world if you have to go backward on life to find true goodness, but this deceiving inroad to contemplation is enough of a cul-de-sac to force a conclusion that, well, it is *indeed* a screwed up world, isn't it?

We've made a mess of the word adult.

Graduate to what?

Mature to what?

Look forward to what?

But then on the other hand, the dreadful "yet": the Cambodians and Polpot made the children little gods for a decade, his recall of history providing a two-million-dead anomaly, and look how that turned out.

He wishes he'd never seen the film *The Killing Fields*, and while he's at it, read *The Rape of Nanking*, and you can burn that book given him by Laird about the Armenians in Turkey, 1915, a million-man march to the caves, driven across desert to melt into little piles of Christian bones. He wishes he'd never seen a dozen families a day clearing out en masse to Syria and Lebanon in fear of his foreign presence, or else of their neighbor al-Qaeda's.

He's confused again and alone again, and to make things worse, his son is tugging on the sleeve of the lead monk here from Manila, the one that gives his son nothing short of brilliant avuncular presents every Christmas, the kind that proves he's listening when Benji talks or else to Sissy when she's praising Benji as only a mother really can. He's nodding very kindly now, "Yes, yes," to Benji's urgent pleas. His son points one last time at his father for emphasis, and then flees so as to remove himself from whatever is about to happen in the mysteriously ruined adult world.

This monk, Michael thinks, touching his .45 at his waist's side with his thumb, an old tick just to check that things are still safe, he thinks he can change me. Thinks he can eradicate the nickel-plated hatred in my heart.

"Here's some pork adobo and pancit bihon for you, Michael. If you don't like it, I will find you something else."

The monk walks off, gray robe flowing. He sees his son in the field, peeking around the unwavering trunk of an evergreen like a goblin. Checking on his father then, making sure he's fed. He corrects himself: an angel in the field, that's an angel.

He pulls out the paper he's brought, the pen, the envelope addressed to Mr. Ernie Terrell of Tuskegee, Alabama, and writes:

Thank you, Lt., for sending me home and saving my life.

Then he digs in, rubbing his belly for the boy.

Sissy

October 25, 2010

SHE DROPS MICHAEL'S LETTER TO HIS LIEUTENANT into the slot, and then watches her brother. He's bear-hugging the two boxes of canned goods to be sent off to their respective prisons, one that she'd visited regularly here in Oregon, the other that she'd heard about during those visits. Compare and contrast south and north, source and reference brown prison with white one. Benji's legs are wrapped around either side of Pika's tree-trunk neck, the little feet tucked under his armpits like two hands in the mittens. She's used to being the one carrying the child and pushing the chair and so it's no small letdown when her peaceful stare out the Amity Post Office door is shattered by the arrival of that same cruel woman, the one she sees every nine or ten months in town, but can't turn around on, but can't command, "Get away from us. Go away." At the grocery store. On the street. The lady who passes her own son in the chair and holds her breath, as if his damaged spine could be passed along airborne. That she'd be crippled, too, a polio victim, if she took in even a smidgen of the bad air he daily blows out. She doesn't know what to tell Benji about the lady, or if she should say anything at all.

Sissy might talk to her today except that she sees the new evaluation: Michael's mother in her tweed sweater and woolen scarf calculating the unfathomable presence of brown-skinned, tattoo-faced Pika in the post office, and then: no. Oh, no. Recognition. Realization. She squints at Sissy, and Sissy knows the accusation she's making: here you are shacked up with the man who lamed my son! Was he fucking you then, too? What kind of ruthless new-age swinger are you, you white-trash whore!

She turns to leave and what can Sissy actually say to make it good, be minimally understood? To reduce the hatred? To destroy the newly believed stories in this lady's head?

She doesn't know, and she fears, maybe can't ever know.

"Oh," she says, watching her walk off. "Will you—" and then nothing.

"Life is fragile and ironical and uncontrollable, Sis," Pika had said at a visit once. And then: "A straight trip."

He puts the boxes on the OCD-organized counter, and steps back to toss Benji over his head and off to the side. One package southward to Tut in the CDC, the other to Ioane right up the street in OSP. Then he steps forward again to an ogling Mrs. Raymond who's been here, it says, since 1979, but is seeing something for the first time, Sissy imagines: a half-breed Samoan with Maori tattoos on his face who could well be right off the lot of the circus.

"Hello, ma'am."

"Hi there. How can I help you?"

Sissy smiles, grabs Benji's hand and pulls him over to push his face between her clavicle and chest, and watches Pika do his magic. With the right parties, she thinks, he's a charmer. He gives back twice the kindness to a kindness thrown his way, that's his trick. And his problem, she thinks, is that he gives back twice the meanness to a meanness thrown his way.

"Thank you, ma'am, for all your help. You have a nice day, okay?"

"Thank you. I will. You, too, now."

She takes his arm and says, "Wanna go to the park, Pika?"

"Yeaaaaaaahhhhhhhh!"

"I was talking to Pika, Benjamin."

"How can I say no now, Malietoa? Let's. Yup yup. U'o kakou."

They pass the empty Ashes Café and the antique store with all the Oregon pioneer regalia in the window. Two eye-shadowed tweakers, both bearded, both in camouflage shirt and pants, camouflage hat, approach. She grabs Benji's hand.

"Don't sweat shit, Sis," Pika says.

The one closest them nervously nods within a few yards, even bows. "Hey, Pika," he says.

"Whatup."

"You know them?" she whispers, two seconds later. She lets the boy detach and speed walk ahead.

"See em at the bus stop."

"They were so scared, Pika. Was it because you're big? Or brown?"

"I just look the part, that's all."

The three of them cross the interwoven tracks and a pile of rusted rails, unused her whole life near as she can remember, and then the boy asks, "Can I run now, Mom?"

"Yeah, hon. Just stay off the road, okay?"

"'Kay."

He's off in a mad dash again to the same playground he's loved long before he could conceptualize the place enough to ask if they might visit again and go play on it in the same identical fashion as the day before. As the year before. Which he does nearly every day, certainly every time they pass it on foot, whether the sand is drenched in little pools or not.

They both sit on the bench, and watch him zigzag over the woodchips, around the downed branches, long-jumping the small piles of sandwich wrappers and abandoned Circle K Froster cups.

"You know who that was, Pika?"

"Where?"

"In the post office."

"Yeah. She in there every time. Cool as fuck. I call her Mrs. Mayberry in my mind."

"Not her. The other lady."

"The one that left?"

"Pika. That was Michael's mother."

"Damn! I knew something was up. No wonder she was looking all crazy and shit. Oh, shit. She the one that called the cops on me back in '06! Can still hear that crazy bitch now! She had—"

"Pika."

"Yep, yep. You don't need all those details. Well. Never know what's sitting right around the corner. It's a crazy world, that's for sure."

"I know what you mean, Pika. I do. I mean, our own mother—she came around at the end, you know, and she only had a few weeks with Benji. And it's so sad because of—well, you know—the way I knew her—"

"And the way I *didn't* know her."

"Yes. That, too."

"It's like two different ways of saying the same damned thing."

"It was all so sad and hard being her daughter, Pika, and then she just loves Benji the way she did. Automatically, as if she were his mother, and not me. I used to watch—"

"Mom!"

"Yeah, Baby!"

"Watch this!"

The boy leans back in a wind-up, and then runs as fast as he can to the sandlot edge, looking immediately over at them once the race in his head is done.

"Good job, Baby!"

He raises both hands like a medalist, and then sprints off again.

"And so I wondered, Pika, about her heart, you know? How she squared it. It was almost like she'd been saving a life's worth of love for that beautiful boy."

"Yeah."

"I mean, she had more hope in her eyes than I'd ever seen, I swear to you, Pika, and then—one morning, raining like cats and dogs, of course—she's gone."

"Wish I could've been there for you, Sis."

"She knew she was dying."

"Why didn't she change that will out, man? That was some of the coldest shit I ever seen when she kicked everything down to me."

"Well, I have a theory, Pika."

"Okay."

"Think she was so happy about Benji and all toward the end that she *forgot*. I really believe that. She literally *forgot* about 99.9 percent of my life with her. Or else she just *allowed* herself to forget."

"Who'd want to remember that shit? Crazy."

"Or beautiful."

"All right right."

She can't help herself. "So that's why I wish I could do more for Michael—"

"Did more than enough for him."

"—with his mother. Can't you just listen, Pika?"

"Yes. I can, Sis. I will."

The boy is building a castle with the wood chips and it won't stay up and so he calls out, "Use the sand instead, sole!"

The boy puts his finger up like a green light just went off in his head, but which really comes from a Kung Fu movie they've watched together where Bruce Lee says, "You will miss that heavenly glory," a joke between them, and drops to a knee, and gets to construction at once.

"Go ahead, Sis. I'll hear you out."

"Well, it's just that it's been going on for so long, Pika."

"Yeah?"

"She's held this silly boycott for four years now."

"Since I went in?"

"Yes!"

"So four and a half then."

"Four and a half years she won't talk to Michael or me. No phone call, no card, no letter."

"Must be hard in this town."

"And I've seen her I don't know how many times—downtown Amity, downtown Mac, once I even saw her at church, Pika—"

"Thought she was LDS."

"They kicked her out."

"Right."

"So maybe, I thought, she's trying mine out, you know, to see if we were less pious—"

"Good luck there."

"Well, I intended to be less pious—okay?—and so I went over to her pew and she stood right when I slid in. Raised her nose like I was one of those untouchables in India. She didn't even let me get a word out before she walked off."

"Probably did it on purpose, Sis. Lured you over and all just to fuck up your program."

"I've always wanted, you know, to lighten Michael's load, and—"

"Hope that fool feels the same way."

"And another time—oh, never mind: the stories are all the same with her. But here she's got all this time, you know, to be with the people she should love, if she does at all anymore, and look what she does with it. Squanders every minute. Every hour. That's why when you talk about how prison changes your sense of time, I always think, You're lucky. You won't ever waste a minute."

"Lucky me, that's me."

"You know what I mean, Pika."

"Nah. I do. Just playing around. Wasting a second or two."

"You're trying to keep it light so I won't feel sad."

"Yeah, that, too. There's something else, though."

"What, Pika?"

"Well, there might be something else is all I'm saying, Sis."

"With the mother?"

"Yeah."

"No."

"Okay, if you say so."

"She's always been like that."

"Well, you never know, do you? A lot of people keep shit to themselves, you know what I'm saying? Especially the big shit."

"Well—"

"And maybe that mutherfuck—excuse me. Well, that. You know. Maybe *he* did something to her you don't know about. I mean, she doesn't know about a lot from your end, too, right?"

Sissy puts her hand over her mouth. "Oh God, Pika. I'm such a fool."

"You always say that, Sis—take it easy."

"Can I tell you something, Pika?"

"You know that."

"Sometimes I used to see my face in the faces of others, Pika."

"What do you mean?"

"Faces like yours. Half-brothers and half-sisters all through the valley. Some even in Amity. Older than me, older than you, even. I'd see it in the eyes, or else the way they'd stand. Something ineffable."

"What's that dug-up Latin bone mean?"

"That I can't describe it perfectly."

"Oh. That's me. Ineffable mf-er. The insider. The ineffable life on the inside."

"You're so smart with sounds, Pika."

"From too much time in the hole, rapping to myself 161 hours a week. And to anyone else my vent hit, I guess. Poor ineffable mf-ers. I probably took a year off their lives from sleep deprivation. Used to run it into the early a.m., sis. Like a moonlighter."

She rolls her eyes and he laughs out once and then pats her arm.

"You find any, Sis?"

"Well, I found *one*."

"Me, too. That be you. That be the girl of the hour. Straight Northwestern rain-dog champeen from Amity, Ore-ee-gone."

She grabs his hand. "I was mean to our mother in my heart. Mean in my mind. I thought the worst of her. Hated her. You already know all of this—and I feel so ashamed, Pika, it's like I was talking to you on the phone just yesterday."

"You don't have to feel shame, Sis. Definitely not with me. And most definitely not with any other ineffable mf-er you kick it with."

"And you know, Pika, I used to think you were eventually going to tell me that the whole thing was a lie—that you *weren't* my brother—that my mother had made the whole thing up. That's how little I trusted her. I didn't even trust our own conversations, Pika."

"Tu vida loca is what the esas in the hood say."

"And I was ready to tell you, 'It's okay.' We can still be brother and sister, can't we? Does it matter that we don't have half of the same blood?"

"That's crazy."

"I used to have these terrible dreams, Pika, about mother dropping all my siblings in the toilet when I was asleep. I'd wake and they'd be gone forever. She'd drowned them all. And when I had Benji, you know, I never had a dream like that again."

"Well. I don't really know ki'o about this life—you know what I'm saying, little sister?—but my view is you done good in the neighborhood. Overall, the professor gives you an A."

"Pika," she whispers.

"Just take a look at that kid out in the yard." The boy is swinging across the links of the monkey bars, skipping every other one like kids twice his age with arms twice as long do, risking the terrifying fall down below. "See that right there? What else need be said, feel me? You done good, girl. That's real talk."

Sissy

October 29, 2010

SHE WANDERS THROUGH THE ROOM straightening out parts of it already straightened, actually already *immaculate*, and remembers how once at church little Benji told the monks that their clean, unflashy, twelfth-century, ash-gray robes were the same as his home. All seven of them asked, "How?" and he'd said, "Mama says, 'No one has to *live* poor. Keep it tidy, keep it clean.'" She'd hoped he'd stop there, but he said next, "You never change your clothes, Mr. Monks. But! You're never dirty either. See, Mama? See!" They'd all laughed and she felt proud and embarrassed at the same time, as if somewhere in the statement vanity and covetousness secretly ruled, wondering how she might relay a lesson to him more cleanly in the future, or else with a caveat about time and place. And yet she'd said nothing. Just reached down and shouldered her son, tucked his head between her right ear and the strap of her purse, kissed the top of his head, and let him drop onto the grass to pet the cats, carry them around the same way she carries him.

Poor is a state of mind, she thinks. We don't got a lot, but what we got, we take care of.

Sissy knows what she's doing. She's in love with her men. When they gather like this in her room, talking about guy's stuff, she wants to know what they're saying, even as she can't possibly interrupt, which would ruin exactly what it is she's drawn to. So she drifts in and out, hearing everything without a comment of her own, thinking about the words and what she might say differently, unashamedly ready to learn, if she can, without letting on to anyone around that she's learning.

That's as close, she thinks, as I'll get to lying to these boys of mine.

"You an undercover cop," Pika once chided her, after he'd spied her spying on them in the yard. "Leo leo with the binocs. Come on over, teinetoa, and throw this pigskin around, girl!"

"Dad," Benji says. "Can you show me?"

"No."

She sprays the cloud of Windex on the window, makes plum-sized circles with the crumpled rag, thinking on her mother for a fleeting moment and then purposely stopping. Forcing herself to stop. Her mother who never cleaned a window in her life, at least never her own.

When she took over this house, Sissy spent a whole week cleaning the moss off not just the windows, but even cabinet corners, tabletops, light fixtures. Somewhere she'd read an article about air quality in Oregon homes built before 1949, and so within an hour, she was up on the roof with a butterknife and a Hefty bag, scraping every twelve-by-twelve tile clean. The moss rolled into fuzzy green softballs. She'd thought, If I fall through a hole of roof-rot, at least I'll land in my own bed.

"Why not, Dad?"

"Too young."

"Dad."

"In fact, *way* too young."

"That's what I knew you were gonna say."

"Then why'd you ask then?"

"I guess cause I want it."

"For what?"

"Shoot a turkey for Thanksgiving."

She wants to say, I got one already from St. Vincent de Paul, honey, but waits. "No need, Top. Mama's got a frozen bird for us, okay?"

"Nooooo, Dad. I wanna learn."

"Okay, look. Listen up, 'kay?"

"Yes, sir, Dad!"

"Okay, little buddy. You ready for some real Dad and Son Time?"

"Yes."

"I will teach you—"

"Yeah!"

"—a very long time from now."

"Uuuhhhhhh—"

"What I want you to remember, Benji—"

"—uuuhhhhh."

"—is that guns are meant for one thing: to cause hurt. Do you understand what I'm saying?"

"Yeeesssss."

"That's it."

"Dad?"

"Sorry to say it like this, Top, but that's it."

"But why we got em then, Dad?"

She can see in the bathroom mirror Michael unable to answer the question, looking up and over to where she's standing. He wants me to help. You can do it, she thinks, spraying the glass for the fourth time. Only you can do it. Someone hurts you, and so you hurt back in the fear of greater hurt. Or else you mind-read: he's here to hurt me, he's here to take what isn't his, and he can't have it. She drops to her knees and dips the sponge in the bucket of suds and puts her elbow into scrubbing the floor.

"I wish we didn't need em, Benji. I wish there weren't one gun in the world. That's called the Soldier's Code. No one wishes for peace more than the soldier."

See, she thinks. You can. You are. "Did they teach you that in the Marines, Dad?"

"No. War taught me that."

They're quiet now because anytime Michael mentions war Benji's smart enough to know it's a serious thing to mention even though, as a five-year-old American boy in love with his life, he has no clue at all what to ponder. This is just how she wants it, really—open to his precocious, little boy personality to learn learn learn, soaking the sponge in his cranium with stories, but also then respectful and proportionate to his little boy age, letting the sponge soak in the right, untoxic liquids. Meanwhile, she scrubs and scrubs and scrubs at the dirt she can't really see, which isn't there any longer, anyway, except in microscopic swaths she'd missed yesterday, and the day before that. She'll find it tomorrow, she knows, she'll cross paths with the filth hidden in this house she grew up in.

How much time she's spent in her mother's own home scrubbing the floor!

Every time she thinks of late, That's it, no more, she feels the bones of her legs and arms get lead-heavy, the gravity of the earth increasing or intensifying or else just finally working the way it should have always worked on her insides, pulling her down, down to her knees. Sometimes she scrubs so much the lines on her palms turn bleach white, the lines of her fingers the same, pink and iridescent like the PowerBait Michael rolls into balls of playdough to catch farmed trout at Sheridan ponds. Her prints are probably gone. On her palms and knees both. She's young and won't complain about it, but sometimes her eyes burn from the cleaning.

"Dad?"

"Yeah."

"My friends' dads all say you're a hero."

You are, she thinks. That doesn't change. You are.

"Well, that's nice of em, but they wouldn't know one way or another. I wantchu to listen to me, okay?"

"Okay."

"Wish that I could teach you how to throw a Frisbee or something, Top, and we'd be happy with that. But truth is sometimes we need a gun. We hope as little as possible. We hope not for long, you understand? We hope never."

"Do you need one, Dad?"

"Well, I may yet."

"Well, maybe I can help you."

She focuses on these cracked and broken tiles from another century, thinking, See. See.

"You're just like your mama. Heart of gold. You run and hit the sack now, okay? I love you."

She stands, walks over to the closet, pulls out the candles, so old the wicks have grown into the wax like ingrown hairs, and lines them, one by one, along the family photos on the chest of drawers that's older and less sturdy than the house.

Those of us who try, we're smart. We know things. And those of us who try to be *good*, she dares to push the thought, we can beat what we know.

"I love you, too. And I *will* help you one day, Dad."

She opens a drawer and pulls out her robe.

"Go kiss your mama, Top."

Benji salutes and is dismissed by Michael and she waits by the bed without giving away that she's heard the directive and especially their private guy's club discussion. When she pulls him in she can see above their son's unending affection that Michael's sitting there happy for once with the small paternal platter he's just offered, and that's good, she thinks, so *good*, that his role tonight as dad was not absurd or strained. Now Benji's whispering into her ear as she taps him goodnight on the butt, nodding at his urgent, manic, toe-bouncing pleas, kissing his clean-smelling little boy forehead. He skips off into the hallway and then stops. She's up and into the bathroom, the door three-quarters closed, changing.

"I love you!"

"Love you, too, Top."

"Love you, baby," she whispers to herself, letting them have it. She emerges from the bathroom in the same robe her mother gave her on Christmas, '99, and perches at the edge of the bed. "He wanted me to tell you you're the best."

And back to the impossible, the look he gives her says, but she's grateful for what comes next: lifted eyebrows, held there, his patented sign of immediate guilt. She loves more than anything in their marriage not the guilt itself but the idiosyncratic kindnesses that usually follow this look. And then also that only she can read it. That he's a part of the salmon struggle of their upriver life together, that he won't concede to the past.

When Michael's mother had abandoned him after the beating, Sissy didn't wonder what she knew. She didn't really care about why. Once again she felt the peril of looking down on another human being. There she was on the tiny toadstool of a throne: she could judge that ice-cold lady who'd birthed in Michael the easy absolutism, she could judge her own tweaker mother who'd never come home before three in the morning, she could judge Michael who'd wrecked her insides to highlight, and thus destroy, her seething need. If the judgment train would stay there with these people, or else switch tracks and disappear from Amity forever, she might've lived with herself more easily. But she knew, bound by a monstrous impulse to condemn, where the train stopped next. Half-pregnant, terrified of the future, she'd caught the bus to the Portland VA, spied Michael asleep on his bed aside the chair, and decided she'd try. When he'd cried into her lap, she'd decided that trying, whether it worked out or not, was right.

"Tell him I love him when he wakes up, okay?"

See. She knew it. He sees. "He'll be in here."

"Well, just in case he sleeps in a little, I guess."

"You two are beautiful together, you know that?"

"I hope so."

"I got a surprise tonight, Michael."

She didn't know it until the end of her watching them. In rare moments like this, something returns, softly, to her. She was surprised by it, too. But also not surprised, not *now* she's not surprised, breathing heavy in what isn't the past until you think on it.

"Surprise can be bad, Sis."

"Nope. Not tonight."

She walks over to the bridge of the door, presses in on the handle's brass button of their rare and therefore awkward privacy, and looks mischievously over her shoulder. An old joke from her cheerleader days at Amity High. Called at one time between them before Benji came, "The Coca-Cola Coquette Look." He smiles, shakes his head. Then she lights her candles, all four of them, one by one. He's still shaking his head, but she turns off the light just the same, and disrobes. Her feet are his focus, he won't look upon her nakedness, even as it moves along the wall in shadow and passes him like a wraith, even as she drags her hand across his shoulder. Standing now behind the chair with wheels, either brilliant in her tingling rushing surging womanly blood, or else the irreparable dupe again to hope.

"No," she barely hears.

"I say yes."

"Sissy."

"You're the bravest man I've ever known. You're the only man I've ever loved."

She takes a step to his side and kisses him on the wet lashes of both closed eyes, and moves down to the stubbled cheek, where she inhales his scent. At last to the thicker stubble of his neck, where she breathes him in again. She identifies self-hatred the way a dog spots another dog.

"Now I'm gonna love you, Michael, whether you like it or not."

"This is real hard for me."

"Let me do all the work, okay?"

He whispers, "That's what I mean, Sis. That's exactly it."

"Oh, Michael." She stops, stands upright, and then rushes across the room for the robe on the just-disinfected floor. Wraps herself up, ties it off, says, "I'm so stupid."

She's afraid of freezing right where she's standing. Frowning at the old self-hatred she'd mastered by her early teens. Teachers and priests and counselors always agreed on one thing—that nobody's perfect—but that didn't mean she didn't perfectly hate herself, did it? Nor that she can't recognize it in another. She walks slowly toward the chair, to keep the blood moving—she comes to him again.

"No you're not. You're good, Sissy, that's all. So damned good."

"Just was excited to see you like that, you know?" She takes a knee, takes his hand. "*Am* excited."

"I don't even know how that's possible."

She raises herself to kiss Michael on his cheek again, where—since every time feels like the last time with him—she's bending over now to prolong it, pushing in on the sallow flesh with her nose, trying to awaken this half-man into half-husband.

"Well, it is, Michael. Do I look like I'm faking anything, handsome?"

He's about to whisper into his clavicle again. "You really move me, Sis. Goddamn. I don't know what to—"

"Shhhhhh."

"I'm so sorry about everything, Sissy. I feel like I started the bad luck in th—"

"Shhhhh."

She's face-to-face now with her husband, actually invigorated, cannot blink, and he's buried his head the way their son gets kisses before bed or school. Except that Benji doesn't tremble, Benji doesn't sweat. She reaches out for the lock on the wheel and clicks it the same time she's pulling herself into this dead zone of his incapacity. Personal space invaded. The perpetual last frontier for her husband, she thinks, don't cross this final line of this handicap I've earned, and therefore can't whine about, and have to die in, as he wedges his softly crying eyes between her chest. "I know you're sorry."

"Mmmmm."

"Sometimes I think our whole life is built on sorries. Let's not say sorry tonight."

"Thank you."

"You let me say thank you, too, Michael."

She forces her mouth on his and tongues the sealed lips, brings her hands up and traces with her fingers what she's just kissed. The lips slowly miraculously part and she goes in without even a tick of hesitation, pulling his head into hers, their tongues finding each other. His eyes are closed, she sees from the candles' oscillating glow, and she remembers how they used to call French-kissing "getting lost together"—she remembers this just before going over into their shared darkness, losing herself, and thinking, he's found again, only I could find him. Only me.

See?

"Give me your hand, baby."

She sets it atop her hip. This is real, she's saying. This is mine. Yours to relearn. He's leaning back in the chair, child on the roller coaster, the hand she didn't grab covering his mouth in disbelief of the ride. She unwraps the robe, and slides her naked waist across his palm, and holds it there. Your upper half is not paralyzed, she almost says, but lets him feel her instead, lets him rub her skin.

She bends down and puts her own hand on his crotch, and he's sprouting.

"What's this?"

"That's what's left of me."

"Never seen you like this."

"Never been loved on like this."

She fiddles with his pants at once, unleashes his sprung cock, turns so that her ass is inches from his face, and mounts him, slowly working her way down, all the air out of her chest, and then his own wind matching her compression, blown one upon the other again and again—life's tweaking alteration of a familiar rhythm.

"I like making never happen," she moans.

Pika

November 2, 2010

HE SEES THEM FIRST. WHERE THEY'RE STANDING, HOW. Leaning on the rail of the VFW handicap-access ramp. Old Rape-o's crew of military riff-raff kiss asses. The ones that red-carpet him in and out on that equalizer of a wheelchair, probably drop down to their knees inside closed doors to clean his boots, or else lick his boots, give a good tug on gimpy's limp cock.

I don't care if you wore a government uniform, mutherfucker, he thinks, nodding at the one in the middle. Need a triple-x to fit that fat ass into fatigues.

Coming forward, he sees other townies, too. Different versions of the same thing: he can't relate to these people. Four yuppies sampling a red in the Terra Vina Wines floor room as he passes the glass show window. Red velvet walls, weirdo new-age art, chocolate truffles from the Amity monks on display. Three collared shirts—pink, peach, mauve, one black high-cut skirt—all clean-skinned, slightly tanned, splish-splashing the wine in little orbits under their noses. He sees all this in a second's time. The woman double takes his face, and he smiles. He's off work, what the hell. If she's a fat cat up there on Second Street, it'll probably be the last tattooed face she'll see in a while.

This stupid-ass pe'a on my grill, he thinks, gritting his teeth, inhaling, not even turning to his reflection in the next window, disgusted with his own history, what he chose to do, what he did. Says fuck you in there, but ends up fucking me out here.

He sees them again. Haven't moved. Fat white guy watching him hawkishly, and the silence of two other men looking off, and quiet. As if they're posing for a painting.

In the pen the line that gets thrown around all the time is seeing without seeing. He can do this. Not some ninja or super-human cartoon character crap, but using the peripherals like the mammals that we barely still are used to do, processing threat nonstop, wondering what this person is doing right here, that group of eses there, and doing it all without offense to another party: looking out but not at, looking for but not on. No disrespect, never that, but no weakness either. I'm not staring you or anyone else down, but I sure as hell ain't looking down or away either. Anticipating threat, constituting it in equal or greater measure.

His phone rings and he takes the call, stops and posts up, still processing. "Whatup, Sis."

"Can you bring a pizza home for dinner?" he hears.

"Oh, yeah. Caught me just—who's that?"

"Pepperoni, Uncle Pika!"

"You got it, Malietoa."

"Don't forget the parmesan!"

"Won't, you know that."

"I love parmesan!"

"What am I, Shotcaller, a blind man? You think I forgot your Halloween outfit, or what?"

"Kraft Parmesan cheese, Uncle Pika."

"Should've been a parmesan vacuum cleaner, or something."

"I want to be a parmesan anteater next year, Uncle Pika."

"Right, right."

"Here's Mama, okay!"

"Thanks so much, Pika."

"All good."

"How was the bakery?"

He sees something he doesn't like, the heavyset cat finally nodding at him (He don't know shit about me, he thinks. You staring me down, ne'er-miss-a-meal punkass?), but starts walking forward now, anyway, toward the building, and says, "Let me get backatcha, Sis, okay?"

"Something wrong, Pika?"

"Nah, nah."

"Okay, Pika."

"I'll hollatcha in a minute."

He flips his phone shut, the clapping sound louder back here near the brick alley, which he cuts down to be alone, where no problems you don't create yourself ever happen, where those white boys' eyes can't watch him.

Sissy would be proud of me, he thinks.

As he goes deeper into the alley, the old familiar urban smell envelops him. All alleys are the same, he thinks, hiding the operation's grease and guts for the A1 presentation on the other side of the building. Alleyways are like our insides. Alleyways stink.

The mistake those punkasses make, he thinks, looking back over his shoulder and turning all the way around, the avalanche of their footsteps rolling down on him now, is not waiting here in the alley to ambush me. Getting dirty from the onset. Already seen this whole scene in my head, mutherfuckers! Already *lived* it! And with worse killers than you punkasses! That's your bad, and you will pay—

By the time they're on him, *he's on them*: good to go—one shot: Bang! First dropped. Clean. He rushes right to the biggest fattest one who was staring him down from the stoop, feeling the inner institutional animal awaken now, which means nothing other than you care about one thing only, ending another animal before *you're* ended, and he gets his footing beneath him and flips the fat fuck around on the brick wall, pins him there, right palm clutched on his Adam's apple, left palm pushing up under the underarm, and a head butt—poomp. Pika expects to get hit from the side, from behind, but it doesn't happen. Fat boy doesn't drop, but the nose is burst like a grape in the microwave from Pika's hammer-like forehead and the eye is already swelling blue and he bends over as Pika looks at the back of the other upright tweaker-looking mufucker fleeing, blood pooling in the dipping bowl of fat boy's beggarly, doughy, trembling hands.

Pika looks down at Mr. TKO'd, thinks, Let's go, and starts off fast, three steps, but slows—No cameras here, man. Chill. Don't run. Ain't Downtown San Jo, six thousand ants per square block, fifty-two witnesses on the scene, overhead pinprick-sized cameras spying your action at the urinal. No one saw this. I got a bleeding cut on my head from butting that fat fuck, which is good, self-defense good. He presses the wound with his hand, rips off his apron and rolls it into a rag. Pressure to effected area. Got a TB shot in the joint, he thinks: even better. This Andy Griffith land, 2010, uce—and so he speed-walks straight out the other end of the alley, calmly, and up the street.

But then, more qualification: this *is* the county where you got pinched in '06. Don't forget, better scoot from downtown, skip the pizza, et cetera. You still the same wrong color, uce, with a rap sheet to match, labyrinthian notches of paint and ridged slabs of scar on your face—definitely on their radar.

So he listens for sirens the first five minutes, knowing that if he gets had, it'll be early on. They'll come screaming like wild birds.

He walks for half an hour and then finally stops, the long six-mile haul to Amity yet ahead of him. Looks back, turns all the way around. Beautiful lights of Hotel Oregon's rooftop, Downtown McMinnville straight-up deceiving me, conning this con: you wait an hour for the bus, ten-minute ride home, but sitting on display at the scene of the crime like a gift to be wrapped for John Law.

Ioane Law.

Time to walk.

"U'o kakou, uce."

Takes however long on foot, but you're publicly hidden on the side of the empty farmroad, so better. Once again: he's good. Boots in the deep dirt of the berm crunching a path of footsteps he'll never look down to see, alive and kicking and A-okay, he's at the edge of a century-old moss-invaded barn. His homies up here, his Oregonian usos: the other mammals wary of entering the sagging invitation to be penned in for the night, cows and sheep and even long-necked alpacas chewing on their hay-bale-Wheaties to prolong the near-dead day. A black Arabian with a blanket draping its middle like a saddle for a giant sticks its head over the wire, and he rubs the sloped dish of its nose. "What's happening, big dog? You lonely, too?" he asks before walking on.

Yeah, he thinks, getting his head back now, nostrils inhaling the clean discharge of the countless evergreens skirting and climbing the hills— he's always doing this up here in Ore-ee-gone: breathing in deep like a mufucking mystic. Yeah. Nodding now at the quaint storybook surroundings he never saw as a boy to believe in as a boy. He presses into his new wound.

Cool place. Yep yep. Starting to grow on me a little bit.

Michael

November 4, 2010

Up the newly built-in-his-honor vfw ramp he goes, John Deere hat like a sealant around his baby-blonde high-and-tight, loaded .45 holstered at his waist. The cops in Mac and Amity let him carry like this. County sheriff, too. Got voted in on the promise of protecting veterans, "especially those," he'd assured Michael, "who can protect themselves." Firm redneck handshakes and short nods from National Guardsmen and recitations of chest-candy service medal citations collectively equal the turning of the authorities' backs in this valley. He never says anything. They ramble on about why they never went—asthma, bad knees, online education—and he lets them.

Forget me, he thinks. But that's as it should be. Who else in this decadent gutless nation of narcissists should we tip our hats to but a vet?

Not me, he thinks again. But one of the Nam guys. One of the last few WWII guys. They saw worse shit than anyone I knew. Saw worse shit than damned near anybody who's ever lived.

Since his little boyhood at the Yamhill Valley parades, he was aware of the respect the community threw its vets. When he got back the first time, he used to put flowers on the WWI memorial in front of the courthouse. Didn't really know much about that war except that it claimed three-hundred times the men his own war had yet claimed, and that number terrified him. Didn't know any of the names except for Tapia, who was the great-grandfather of his childhood buddy, and a man named McClintock Thompson, who was the great-grandfather of a little league teammate. Once in a while he'll still do this, place a box of impatiens at the base of the bronze statue of a soldier sprinting through razor-wired no-man's land, if Michael can roll up there quickly enough to not be noticed.

Today he's got business. Very focused. Intensely zoned-in on the next moment. Head turning toward the square footage to be wheeled through, head guiding him like a submarine's telescope. Of late, he's felt alive around the house, even when Mr. Face Paint comes around, and that surprises him. He's learning to ignore what he detests. He's learning to live with his crippler. His confidence in his marriage singlehandedly enhanced by a woman he never deserved, even before he became what he is, and the candles she somehow had the love to light.

Regardless of it. Despite. Overlooking.

It's easier at the house where he can teach the boy how to cast for a trout with a rooster-tail, how to lace shoes with your eyes closed, how to do pull-ups from a dead-dog hang. He can usually find a way to be useful to Benji, which is his last line of defense against suicide. Okay. That's the truth: there it is. If everyone left him—Sissy, the vets at the hall—he'd still have the boy, who'd never leave him, he knows, can see. He doesn't yet know how to say this, to let the boy see that he sees, but he's patient. Who in this chair hasn't mastered the elusive concept of patience for life's 99.99 percent?

The ambulatory.

The problem was in public. No, it was still the same every time he crossed a city limit, every time he came into a group of walkers. That was where your uselessness stood out. Where old geezers on death's doorstep stopped to open and hold a door for you, where young children would point and look up at their parent, mouths begging for an answer of how, why, when.

"Laird," he says, pulling into the high foyer, American flag hanging unwrinkled at the ceiling's apex. Along the baseboard, hundreds of unit patches of service: the Screaming Eagles of the 101st Airborne Division to the horsehead of the 1st Calv to the bulldog of his own Marine Division to one he doesn't recognize: a taro leaf, or tobacco leaf its insignia.

"Oh, hey, Mikey." Michael doesn't miss him cover his eye, look down, sniff. "Where's your boy? Had a great time showing him around."

"You sure spend a lot of time here."

"Yeah, well." He's holding a leaflet, looks down at it, says, "Let me put this up real quick, okay, Mikey?"

"Yep."

He can't help himself, Michael thinks. He's already about to vomit out the confession. If only interrogations with the enemy were as easy as getting the truth out of this slob. There'd be no war. No secrets to kill anyone over.

"Catch the Civil War yesterday, Mikey?"

He wants to make Laird turn his face and so he says nothing. Waits. Lips sealed tighter than his heart. Then, in a flash, he gets just enough of an angle to catch the black eye, confirm what Michael had already been told.

"No."

"Ducks, man. They're too strong now. Make the fucking Beavers look like a Pop Warner team. Used to be an even game, you know? Athletical-ly, I mean. Used to be the smart guys against regular guys like us. Who else you gonna root for? Orange and black attack." He pauses. Pretender, Michael thinks. Won't even turn to look me in the eye. Waiting for me to get bored, roll on. "Used to be even."

"You rednecks just love your football games, dontchu?"

He turns excitedly, forgetting the eye, forgetting his own piddling strategy. Tool, Michael thinks. American hang-around who'd break under unenhanced interrogation. Waterboard? Just steal a meal from this slob, force the tool to fast for a few hours, and he'll give you ev-erything you ask for, and more. Some things never change, he thinks, remembering how they'd first met when he could still get around on foot, wage an immediate threat with a single look in his eye, one lone word. "Oh, yeah, Mikey. It's great, you know, to go down to McMenamin's and—"

"The new opiate of the masses."

"What's that mean, Mikey?"

"You even go to Oregon State?"

"No. "

"No."

"But my sister's boyfriend did. You know, I graduated from Mac High and then I sort of drifted around—"

"No dog in the fight then."

"—before I joined the Army. But when I was a kid, we always rooted for the Beavs."

Michael is unimpressed. He lets his silence sink in. Sheep are a dime-a-dozen in this state, whether you can sheer them for the wool, or not. More militant armies turn out these days at your average college football game than on an old school plain of rival generals. So more than just an opiate. Something like the dumbed-down, arm-pumping brownshirts at Nuremburg. Run with that ball! Maim for that ball! Murder for it! Gathered there at the last official vestige where slobs like this guy get to pretend that they're not pure bull cannon fodder. Pawned flesh on the front lines to make the enemy waste ammunition.

Look at him, Michael thinks. Trying to cover that bruise now. At least if it was legitimate, you could walk around in public unashamed. Could lift the burkah and show your battered face to the world. Yeah, that's what I did, and here's what happened. But he's all self-conscious. This guy who's my peer. My countryman. My brother.

Goddamn!

I'd've never gone over there in the first place if I knew I'd be the feeding-tube for this narrative glutton. Just ten of him is enough to justify the U-turn.

Hell, just one Laird Hangaround birthed of native soil should make the civilization reshuffle the deck.

"You run into an angry duck, or what, Laird?"

"What, Mikey?"

"You look like you been in a civil war yourself. Just barely made it out."

"Oh, this old shit?" He points at the shiner, seemingly bigger now that his whole countenance is framed on display for Michael. Points at it, shrugs, rolls his eyes. "Well, I had worse sneezes, Mikey."

"Well, I guess the guy can fight, anyway."

"Who?"

"Laird."

"Yes, Mikey?"

"Where's Chuck and Simon?"

"Went muddin', I think. Out in some cow pasture in Perrydale. You know Chuck. He's a nut."

"I don't know Chuck."

"I just mean he's into that tear-nature-up shit. Four-bangin' tires on his truck higher than a skyscraper. I'm a little more reserved. Huh, huh. They'll probably be here after lunch, Mikey."

"What happened to your eye, Laird?"

"Ah, it's fucking nothing, man. Fucking chickens. I strung the rooster up to teach those birds a goddamned lesson. Cause—"

"Laird."

"Yeah, Mikey?"

He squares himself on the chair, squints for clarity, looks Laird up and down. "You did one tour over there, right?"

"Yeah, yeah."

"Fixing up what again?"

"Oh, the hum-v's."

"And what about Chuck and Simon?"

Laird puffs his chest up and Michael recognizes it as the unmitigated bullshit that it is. Necessary at boot camp, maybe, when shaving the sheep. Not necessary after you've been in the shit. Not even close to the real story that they're supposedly preparing you for.

"I also did the brass's cars. You know, the colonels and such?" Michael holds his silence and hears someone walk in, feels him walk past, not even a nod at Laird.

"'Lo, Michael," the man says, going on into an office. Maybe a retired colonel.

"'Lo."

Laird's deflating, his story's sinking. His head drops, he's sunk. They prepare your body, Michael thinks. But not your mind. "Chuck and Simon? Oh, well, Chuck was with me at boot camp. Somehow we got the same MOS."

But then nothing can prepare your mind, he adds, in his own back-from-the-brink brain. Once rubbed out in flashback flashes, but building itself again, little by little. New brain cells already spoiling with cynicism. "Car-fixer."

"Yeah. That's right. Light-Wheel Vehicle Mechanic."

"Uh-huh."

"And I met Simon here. Never really got around to talking credentials. Not yet. Nah. I guess I don't know about Simon."

"I do."

"Oh, okay."

Always twitching, he thinks. Sketchy, shady eyes. "He was a psych."

"Simon was? Really? Wow, I had no—"

"How else you think he gets his opiates?"

"His meds, you mean?"

"Hey, Laird."

"Yeah, Mikey?"

"You been in the shit?" Laird shakes his head no, but Michael would bet the answer varies according to the asker: "Of course!" to a civilian; "No way," to a legitimate combat vet. "You know that we're not the same, right?"

"Yeah, yeah, Mikey. Of course."

"Despite all this membership shit."

"No, Mikey, you're a fucking hero, you know? We know that. Five tours. Force Recon. Shit, they sent your medals back here and put em up in Shelley's grocer! Right behind the cash register. Yeah. The whole damned town came in to see your decorations, even Principal Polk. If Amity had a parade, they'da honored you, Mikey. Maybe here in Mac on Fourth of July? We'll get the committee to—"

"I don't need a goddamned honor, Laird."

"Oh, yeah. Okay."

"You all think cause you wore a uniform you're a hero?"

He resists for just a second. "No, Mikey. No."

"It's called Veterans Day for a reason, Laird."

Now he nods, as if being instructed. A new understanding of himself. "I know."

"It ain't called Armed Forces Day."

Suddenly nodding vigorously, as in a drug-induced trance of optimism. "I know. I know."

"It ain't called Mechanics Day."

"I know it's not, Mikey."

Finally Laird looks down. Where his eyes belong, observes Michael. And now you will look at me, you dripping pork barrel commodity. Indigestible fat of the system. Extraneous lard of the MIC. "Laird."

His eyebrows raise automatically, stuck there in the pathetic obsequiousness of the kiss-ass. "Yes, Mikey?"

"You tell Chuck and Simon I don't need anyone fighting my battles for me. Especially some goddamned redneck mechanic and a tweaker palm reader."

"They just love you, Mikey, that's all, and—"

"Love's got nothing to do with it. The real sign of hero-worship is going up there in the front. Giving your life for another man."

"I know, Mikey."

"Earn your VFW badge."

"You know, Mikey—"

"Earn your entrance to this place."

"—been meaning to talk to you about something. You know, well, I been thinking bout joining up Infantry, Mikey."

"Whatta you telling me about it for? You wanna slit your wrist, go cut the artery and bleed out in silence. Laird."

"Yes, Mikey?"

"You tell em what I said."

"Okay."

"You guys pull crap like that and it upsets my wife. And that upsets me. You understand?"

"Sorry, Mikey."

He spins on his back wheel, one half of a revolution, pats his .45 visibly snared in the waistband to ensure security, chin tucked, chest out, a few last words, more to himself than to anyone else: "Got more tours than all you dickheads combined. Don't need your goddamned protection."

Pika

November 4, 2010

WHAT'S FUNNY, HE THINKS NOW, a little tired after work, hugging his knees on the bus stop curb, looking out every few seconds for the lights of the hourly line back to Amity, is how I got girl cousins in Samoa— little fifteen-year-olds—who woulda straight wrecked that fat *palagi* who'd tried to jump me out with his cowardly homeboys.

"That all you got?" Pika might've said back in the day. "That's it? This country's in trouble."

Everyone thinks you don't mess with Samoan men. Shit. The women's the one. Better whatchyour ass you piss off a Samoan girl. And if there's more than two of em on the scene, forget it, man: just kick rocks at once. Make tracks. Nod real hard and solid so it seem like you agree with everything she's telling you, say absolutely nothing, then turn around and walk away—and make sure you're ducking the hooks they be throwing at the back of your head while you're at it.

He chuckles, looks up the empty road, the berm rushing with runoff from yesterday's all-day rain.

Now that he thinks about his head being hit, and Samoan girls the ones hitting it—he recalls his cousin, Tuna, who'd stabbed him once with a steak knife back in '93. He hasn't thought on her for a few years, mostly because it was one of a hundred crazy incidents of violence in his life, and if you think on one, you pull up the other ninety-nine, like a trotline he saw on a documentary about fishing in the Deep South. At some point, maybe when you hit fifty, you think, Why think on *any* of em? That way, you go straight through life without OD'ing on fault and pain and your own big mouth. Not so much amnesia, he thinks. Not denial neither. Is just tucking the story into a pocket of your brain, safe-kept for function, allowing the story to go on, the bundle of wounds sitting right there beside the daily flow of thoughts like an ash pit on a riverbend.

But, still. Memories get triggered just the same—that's *also* life—the riverbend gets flooded by something foreign and unbelonging: key words, faces, places.

Tuna had told him to do some work around the fale—even though he'd already done *all* the work, *always* did all the work—and he'd told her do your own galuega. Stop trying to pass it off on me just because I'm younger, look at my fingers, they're raw red from washing dishes, this America, you forget? and she'd leapt the table between them like a 325-pound monkey, called him a "lazy uluvale palagi," and stuck the knife straight into the side of his skull. She'd been eating pisupo, and so he had to scrape off the corned beef later. He was fourteen, she was twenty, and that brother of hers, his cousin—the one who'd jumped him from behind and was strangling him on the floor, as she was stabbing him—he was almost thirty.

But there were far worse stabbings in the family, now that the trot-line was being pulled out the water, there were hardcore beat-downs. One uncle got stabbed in the heart. He'd laughed, drunk, and told his betrothed ko'alua, "Why'd you do that, you fool?" and then knocked her out, the knife still stuck in his chest when the EMT got there, taking her first into the cab's interior because they thought she was dead, him second because he was still yelling at her. Another time a cousin in San Mateo got thrown through the window at the 7-11. By his own grand-mother. She'd winged him like he was Red Rover on his way over or something, and then she came into the store through the customer beep of the front door, got down on her knees and plugged his nose up with her handkerchief, both of them shrouded by the dull sparkle of newly shattered glass. The cops stomped right through the bed of shards, and dragged her away, despite her grandson's refusal at their sharp elbows to press charges.

They might've taken my cousin away, too, Pika thinks, if they under-stood Samoan. Or else just the bad words he was calling them.

Every cop in Cali knows, he thinks further, nodding to himself. They know how the usos get down. We got our MO and they got theirs.

When the authorities get called and hamos are involved, half the department shows up to the address cited. Post deep on the sidewalk, looking up the street, mace out, sticks out, safeties off. Cop with stripes calling even more authorities before knocking on the door. That doesn't matter. Nobody stops when they hear the sirens. The sirens only make the chaos worse.

Few of these Amity palagis can imagine it, Pika thinks, shaking his head, spitting out into the street, wincing at the unresolvability of your own retrieved narrative, even now, twenty years later. Nope. Of getting slapped and bitten and knocked down by your own sibling, but even fewer would believe their own eyes when the authorities arrive: that same "victim" jumping to his feet to defend the "suspect" when they try to cuff him and drag him out the door. So. *Both* guys get cuffed: five cops on one uso times two: "suspect" and "victim" who became "second suspect" when the familial lines of a former world got crossed in this present one.

By the age of twenty, he'd seen a variation of this Polynesian story a dozen times. Immediate family, extended family, cousins, friends. Sometimes he didn't see it because he was making it. No longer observer, but *participant*: singular-minded wrecker of familial neighborhood societal grace. Used to be a point of pride in him. Distinctive cultural trait, a figurative crest to say, See. We're not like you. We go the distance on violence. Noses and jaws and ribs will be broken, not bruises or raspberries, but contusions and keloids.

"Get scars," he whispers, spitting again for no reason but that the street is still empty, still the opposite of the bumper-to-bumper, elbow-to-elbow streets he grew up in. "Give scars."

Then he got to the joint, and this pride was more or less his *life*: first week on the yard was the hardcore harbinger: he fought norteños from Sacra and King City, smashing one out on the tier, head-butting another at the pull-up bars, and the hamos were there backing his action 100 percent—six usos leveraged against forty eses waiting but not really wanting to jump, even though he knew none of em from the streets, not a single sole. That was loyalty, man, that was old school.

And he did his time right. Tut helped him out, Tut let him in. By the time he got out, he was feeling so down for the cause he almost forgot the way the amber tint of his half-breed skin shone under the tags on his face. Thanks to Tut, he spoke better Samoan than he did going in. He looked for ways to keep growing in his culture. He sent care packages to the usos on the yard, stuffed the boxes with SPAM, deviled ham, sardines in soybean oil, kipper snacks, and gufe'e from Jackson Street in Japantown, the fish dried and stringed and salted like jerky from the ocean. He joined a Poly dance crew on the peninsula to learn siva, even a little fire dance, too. Umu'd pua'a at a lu'au in EPA and told anyone in his brood that Hawaiians had died as a culture because they weren't warriors in their fatus like Samoans. Those chumps got overrun not by the guns and ships but their own aloha spirit lethargy. This pissed off plenty of local boys, but they were mostly Japanese-blood and Filipino-blood and Portuguese-blood and Puerto Rican-blood mix plates with barely one thirty-second Hawaiian in them, anyway, which proved his point. What? You gonna jump on a one thirty-second claim, we gonna get down over the *state* you were born in like a Montanan taking on a South Dakotan— or why not just cut up some ahi sashimi and make us all some ono poke, rich-ass windward-side Kam-grad Nakamitsu?

At the library he found Margaret Mead's book about hamos, and when he tried to get something a little more updated, he found a study done by the University of Hawai'i about the "crab in the bucket theory." How the tribe will pull down anyone trying to crawl out and be better. How the crabs will maul any crab with a defect.

Another series of memories got triggered—he couldn't keep em wrapped and tied-down in the pit—self-shame taken off the shelf by some academic studying the tribal code of Samoans, the hands-down biggest crabs in the world.

Now the northwestern Oregon mist thins like his memories, and the sound of predictable footsteps are slow, gangster slow. Ese Flaco—he's right on time, Pika thinks, for my dissertation on race—emerging of the air-water like a cleaned bean in the bowl. About as ironical as it gets: all these Pac Northwesterners think I'm an ese. They think I'm *with* this fool. Órale, vato! just like Ioane'd said back at OSP. Pika doesn't get up, if only to defy the misunderstanding, keep something clear in his mind.

He stays right there on the curb, looking out for a bus, he thinks, that may never come.

"Órale. What's goin' on, eh? How you doin', big oso?"

"'Bout to catch my Cadillac back home."

"Just get off work?"

Pika shakes his head. What's this bib mean to you, man? You think I like wearing this shit? "You got a job?" he says instead.

"Simón, eh. Oh, yeah. I got all kinds of jobs."

Truth was at this kid's age, Pika'd been mauled a few times, he'd been yanked back into the bucket by the crabs. They'd said denigrating shit behind his back plenty of times, once or twice to his face before the big fight came, these same cousins and siblings and usos had called him "Palagi With Attitude" when NWA hit the charts in '89.

Pee-Dub: short for PWA.

This ese right here, Pika thinks, would love the name I always hated.

They were looking down on me the same as this fool—with straight pure-blood piety, Pika thinks now, gritting his teeth, spitting between his legs, not caring if a flash of wash brushes the ese's face. And sometimes they had hardcore racial hatred, man, over shit I had no say about—DNA, and where your mother you never met came from—or else the shit you *did* have say about—the tags on your face, the shame of having done time—but could never correct. Can't amend the constitution of what you've done, that's what this dumb ese just don't get. You brought down the name that took you in, Ingrate Son of that Wily-eyed White Trash Scum. You, that one afakasi sole who couldn't do what he was told to do.

Living in the most diverse place in the world, he thinks, more truth was that not just his mother's white blood but every blood on the planet called out to him all day long from outside the bucket, and not in some dumbass Kumbaya way either, and on days where the curiosity was killing Pika the cat inside his head would think, Fuck it, man, and he'd waver. I wanna get to know something else, too. Wanna learn, open up. Been locked down by the state, mouth duct-taped by the kidnapper-system, brain on freeze from canine laws in the kennel, and I've got suspicions, man. That there's more to this thing than whatchy'all are telling me. Or else whatchu doing here, man, in a land where the very contract you keep with others is mutual cultural dilution?

He frowns. He thinks on it. It's not good.

More truth was that at fourteen, I was already tired of taking orders. Stay here, sit here, stick around, do this, clean this. Pika! Sau'ia! Fea kelefogi? Yeah! That one right there. In your hand, yeah! Hang it up right there and bring right that one here to me, yeah! Nofo'a ia.

Then do a five-spot in the joint where every mutherfucker in uniform is giving orders like your missing mother, whipping ass like your Samoan father, and you ruined, man. You done.

I ain't some FOB sheep!

The answer to everything, even when it doesn't make sense. Something reflexive inside me now, he thinks, like the knee with the hammer: Fuck you. I ain't some sucker doing your bidding on the cheap, man. Who are *you*? You nothing to me, man. This ain't rebellion. This calling it how I see it. How it *is*. Ain't you the same mutherfucker I caught jacking off to "amazon woman" porn last week on the toilet? Walked in on you in the falevau, and you'd flushed real loud like you were shitting, threw your I-phone and the virtual big-tittied amazon woman into the trash, and told me to cut? And now you gonna tell me what's what? *You*? Oh yeah. Sure. Only *now* when it benefits you we're gonna go back and run some third-world shit that you don't even *live* by over here? Try to put that on *me*. Well, whatchu doing here, man— just answer me one time, that's it—in the land where *everyone*—Samoans, Vietnamese, Lebanese, all your neighbors, *any* of em—be watering down their blood by the minute.

And it ain't don't, is it? It's *can't*. You too stupid to know it's *can't*. We all *can't* live by the tribal laws of our forebears. Ever notice it's always the quarter breeds who bark about race the loudest? They wanna go back on time, wanna be their great grandpops on their daddy's side, like them millennial rockabillies in the Bay who were born in 1983, about thirty years after the era they're in love with. Come on, man. You faking it. And you, my FOB uso, you standing out, uce. *Can't* walk around this country with a bone in the nose, you in the back of the bus in your i'e faikana wrapped around the waist—because once you settle in to this deal right here, the story's not just altered, uso, it's straight-up gone, man. You just don't know the difference between the beginning of the end and the end of the end, that's all. But your grandkids will. One generation, two, three at the most: the indigenous blood gets pissed away, and you can't go back.

That's what it means to be an American.

Doesn't feel right, he thinks. Doesn't feel good. I'm in a town where the wilderness of pure true anonymity is right there at the doorstep. I've got two people I'm banking on 100 percent, and one of em ain't even old enough to play Little League. And neither one knows anything about me and my gone forever culture.

He'd stepped out of his state because she'd called like a blessing, Sissy crying out accusations of the worst order, saying some serious shit about a white boy she loved. The one she was gonna marry—the only one—from way back at the outset of their conversations.

This a real shout from outside the bucket, microphone, full amps.

May have never known who I am, or what I am, he was thinking, but I know clarity when I see it: crazy life putting a broom to the variables, mathematical reduction of the options, just like in the joint. I got no choice here—none at all—but to get up and sweep the deck.

So he took off in the stolen Datsun right away, drove the 5 north through the state, straight up the Siskiyous to cross the border into Oregon in a rapid drop the first time ever, and was sleeping that same night on a concrete ledge in a Yamhill County holding tank.

"Shit," he whispers. "That's life."

He blinks out of the recall because the ese's still here, blowing breath clouds into the mist, trying to make rings even: oooooooooo. The silence between them is so heavy, Pika decides to stand—but slowly, no worries—and carry the heaviness that way.

"So what's your name again, big oso?"

"Flaco," Pika says. "What's yours?"

"Damn, you got a good memory, homes."

"I stay off that ma'a. Keep my brain strong, homie."

"Ma?"

"We call it rock. Short for rock-head. Y'all eses call it cranka."

"Oh, fuck yeah, eh. Now we talking."

"White boys call it cris. Dope. You know what I'm talking about."

"Viva la cranka!"

Ese Flaco bobbing his head now like he's doing doowop on a circa

'50's Brooklyn streetcorner, and then pretends that he's smoking it from a spoon, eyes closed. This the whole breadth of Ese Flaco's imagination. Can't see Pika staring him down, shaking his head, wanting to slap him back into reality. This ese can't feel me. Don't know me.

"Eh, homes, you wanna get in some dirt, eh? I got this homeboy out there in Amity—"

"I already told you—"

"—and this fool's spread—"

"—what's what—hey, man."

"—too wide, eh. Needs a mano from a hamo. You like that rhyme, eh? You like that cross-over? Shit, eh, I got more rhymes, too. Hamos are good people. Hamos love me, homes."

Pika thinks, If I wanted any money, I'd just knock you down and take the wallet outchyour pocket, but shakes his head, and goes straight to Malietoa: all those hopes of the boy's for his people. "What happened to me? I'm a hamo."

"So that fool's moving on all the hueros in town. See? Check out these punkass putos."

Pika looks out and up, and sees before he hears: a gray monster truck packed with hicks accelerates ten yards from the bench, country music twang dwarfed by the engine's grumbling. He puts his nose into his sleeve to cover from the exhaust.

"Oh, it's like that, huh?" Flaco walks to the center of the street, shouting up it like he's been left behind in the apocalypse. "Well, I'll see you putos again! El Ese Flaco! Clicked-up trece rider walking on your pinche graves, eh! El loco trigger southside, you mark-ass buster mutherfuckers! No duermes, buey! Me entiendes! No duermes!"

He's throwing signs and slamming them off his hip. Pika shakes his head, but the ese sees nothing. Finally he walks back curbside, still rapping: "Too many fucking white people, eh. Manufacturing in their fucking barns, and shit. Send those white putos back where they came from. Órale."

"You don't like white people?"

"Fuck no, eh!"

"Guess you miserable 'round here then. Defacto Western Europe. The last outpost."

"We came to claim this town, homie. Take the trash out. La basura en la basura. Dump that shit in the dump, homes."

"You sound like Malcolm X."

"Fuck that mayate, too, eh."

"Now you sound confused."

"That fucking monkey, eh."

Life is crazy. Mayate means cockroach. Southerners say mutherfuck blacks in the joint, actually ride with whites. How strange it must seem, Pika thinks, to that change-the-world caseworker on day one, the first hour, first minute. The first second thinking for the first time ever, This world's too much. I can't do shit to change it for the better.

And me? Pika thinks. What's my luck? I gotta keep running into this loose-lipped, hare-brained, ese foot soldier finding ways to hate on everyone.

Is that what life really is at the core? Pika thinks, hating this ese to the bone, wishing he would drop dead in the mud, some taco truck haina come to claim his ass in a tricked-out Lincoln lowrider, dump him in the ditch for good. Identity's nothing more than who you hate? Where your sights are aimed? All the arrows pointing out from the cave. How come I felt most in line with identity, Pika thinks, in the place where hatred rules? Walking the yard like a lion pissing on his little corner of the Serenghetti. Growling at everything, anybody. That place fucked me, man. Did me in. Crossed up my insides. Only Sissy knows how lost I am. Everyone else thinks, He knows what he is (and we don't like it! they always add). Got no doubt about the world. Cause he talks straight. Doesn't stutter.

Appraising Ese Flaco, he thinks, This ese is straight miracle worker shit.

He takes a step back to let him know it's cool, pats his shoulder firmly but kindly, the way it's done in the joint, and shoots it: "Yeah, Flaco, some people say Samoans come from Africa. West-siders, homie. Down around Ghana, dog. You know that?"

Flaco shakes his head no.

"Samoan monkeys, homie. You know, oooohhh-ooooohhh-ahhh-ahhh-ahhh. Though I think we hamos are probably silver-back apes, know what I'm sayin'?"

Ese Flaco's subdued for once, maybe even careful. "You just clowning now."

The ese starts to walk off and Pika shrugs, takes his bus stop throne again, curbside the road, mud on his heels.

Least I don't have to foot the six miles in this crazy Northwestern mist. Can't see anything ahead of you, going forward on faith and instinct, one cautious step at a time.

Sissy's Almighty maybe not pissing on me, but blowing his nose minimum.

Sissy

November 4, 2010

HIS KNEES PRESS TOGETHER EASILY because of thighs and calves nearly atrophied to the bone. She wrestles his legs out of the locked chair. Her own long legs are braced beneath her hips, bearing the dead weight of his upper body until the foot of the bed relieves her, and he can pop himself upward and over on his own, let himself fall down from momentum. She's already pulled back the clean sheets and so he can do everything else without her: covering himself, propping up his pillows, settling in.

She drops to her knees at his side of the bed and doesn't check if he closes his eyes, just the same as she never asks if he believes or not, and whispers a prayer not just for him or for the both of them or for Benji or Pika or their family as an integrated unit but for everyone in the world, all the billions of people she'll never meet in Amity, Oregon. She crosses herself and stands and he nods and then locks his eyes on the ceiling, never revealing to her in half a decade's time a single thought about this antiquated theological ritual they've engaged in every night, no matter what. If he rolls his eyes back, he'll find the crucifix affixed by a single nail above the bed, aimed like a dagger for his heart.

She tucks herself in and then untucks herself at once and sits cross-legged on her side of the bed, shoulders against the wall, backside flattening the edge of a pillow. He looks over and nods kindly.

"You know what Benji told me today, Michael?"

"Hmmm?"

"Something like, 'Even though Daddy's quiet, he's got a lot to say.'" He says nothing, perfect confirmation of what their son asserted, and she goes on: "He knows who you are."

"I need to talk more."

"We were walking by the football field when he said it, Michael, and I flashed back to those years when we were so young."

"Yeah."

"I still remember watching you when I was cheering. I used to think, Doesn't that boy right there ever talk, or what? I even thought you were partly deaf, Michael."

"I was partly dumb, that made up for it."

"I thought I'd figured out the secret affliction, Michael, that no one else spent any time trying to get about you. And when I saw you down at the creek fishing like that, all alone, I watched you, Michael, for about four or five minutes—"

"I know."

"—and I fell in love with you before we'd even said hello, Michael."

"You came down. I gave you the trout I caught."

"Was a small-mouth bass."

He chuckles, shakes his head. "You're right. God."

"I remember I talked about the game and how great you were and you just kept shaking your head no—"

"I was okay. Capable."

"—and then I said my mother was crazy—I couldn't help it—and I didn't know who my father was. You listened just like I knew you would, Michael."

"Yeah."

"Hoped you would, anyway."

"Yeah."

"And what's really crazy—if you think about it, Michael—was that we came from the same kind of family—you know?—even though you lived uphill. Was like the money didn't matter when it came to happiness."

"Well."

"I don't think we knew what to do with ourselves, did we?"

"No."

"I mean, you didn't know your dad any better than I did—"

"Pretty much."

"—and your mom's crazy as my mom was."

He blows out some air. "Close call there."

"But when you really talked for the first time, Michael, I was shocked."

"Because I didn't grumble or growl."

"You were so *smart*!"

"No."

"I used to skip class—remember?—just so we could go watch the History Channel at your house. You knew so much about the world. Anything that wasn't Amity—you knew about it."

"I didn't know a thing about the world, Sis."

"But that was wrong, too." She's shaking her head, ready to correct the history. "Because one day you shared all those stories about *Amity*—remember that?"

"I guess. Yeah. I read a couple of books in the library. Heard stories at the church."

"Were talking about the dead logging industry in this valley."

"You member the stories, Sis? Always a tragedy at the chainsaw. How many guys had missing digits, you think?"

"I'd say one in ten, at least."

"And now it's missing teeth. Nothing for the young men around here to do with their lives—"

"So true, Michael."

"—and that explains video games and meth—"

"Or you joining up!"

"The wineries bring the yuppies from California to Mac. Our stories get swallowed."

"At least we don't live in *that* town—right?"

"Scrubbing the floors of a techie transplant—"

"Yes, Michael!"

"—from Napa Valley—"

"You predicted it would happen."

"—who's really from New Delhi."

She's peering at the wall in front of her, as if it were a movie screen playing in real time every scene of their lives she's mentioning. He's looking over at her with a smile, she can see in the mirror's reflection near the bathroom door, and this encourages her to go on, to keep filling the space of his silence. "I used to imagine the dots on the map to get to a place like New Delhi. Think of all those exotic places they came from just to end up here in the Yamhill. The direction was backward."

"Maybe we're as exotic as they are."

She smiles. "You know what, Michael?"

"What?"

"Back then, I would've worked those jobs for us."

"I know that. I mean, I know that now."

"I would have done anything to get us out of Amity."

"Hmmm."

"And Michael?"

"Yeah?"

"I know the war made you *more* quiet. That's the irony. I noticed it the first time you came back. I read all those books about Vietnam veterans—"

"You did?"

"—to see. Yes. I did. During your first tour." She takes his hands in hers, and nods. "I did. I didn't want you to feel alone, Michael."

"Thank you."

"And I read all these horrible stories about them coming back, you know, and I kept thinking, By God. It's not going to be like this for Michael. I'll die before I let that happen. They're going to have to get through me first. Spit on me before they spit on him. I wanted to be your personal pit bull, Michael."

He smiles. "You're funny, Sis."

"Silly thoughts, I know—"

"No, they're not."

"—but that's the truth of what I kept thinking about."

"Ah, Sis."

"And I never got a chance to prove it."

He looks at her, and then back up at the ceiling. Whispers: "Because I—"

"You kept going back, Michael. Five times. Be here a few weeks, a little tease, and then gone. By the third time, no one knew how much I hated this town. I couldn't hold it in. Want to know something, Michael?"

"Yes."

"I dreamed of it going up in flames, Michael. Like Mt. Angel. Like Rome. Everything and everyone in it."

"I'm sorry, Sis."

"Michael."

"Yes?"

"I want you to know that you can talk to me about anything."

He nods, and winces, and nods again. "That's what I tell Benji, you know?"

"I love that you tell him that. I'm not jealous."

"I know you're not."

"I'm actually *happy*. When I see the two of you together, Michael, I feel a strange sense of *relief*, you know? I'm apart, and can't be a true part of your conversations—"

"You're the heart of *all* our conversations, Sis."

"I don't mean like that. I just mean. Well, you and I are different, but we're also the same. No! We have the same *goal* with Benji, that's what I mean. That's identical."

"That's right."

"Benji told me once that teachers and doctors are the same. I was about to explain the difference to him, as if he didn't see that, and he said, 'They both help children.'" Michael smiles and nods. "That's what we are, Michael: we both love that boy truly."

"Can I tell you something, Sis?"

"Of course."

"Well," he whispers. "It's not that the medal is a sham, okay? The medal means something. And if that medal doesn't mean something, nothing does. Courage matters. But it doesn't mean enough to get Scanlan back home safely."

"But I thought he made it home, Michael. You dragged him back from the fire."

"And it's not just Scanlan. It's an old man—his eyes. He was selling lamb or something. A vendor."

"An Iraqi?"

"They beat him with the butt of their guns, and he looked up and spit blood on their boots. Wow, I thought. What courage. What absolute guts. I respect that man. He's probably dead. Definitely dead. I love him. I didn't know how to reconcile that man with my life there, or even with the damage I've done here. All of it came to me in one moment. I closed my own eyes—I ran out to get Scanlan, you see, mostly because I couldn't stand seeing it anymore."

"Did you want to die?"

"I think I did. I think I didn't know the difference back then between life and death."

She whispers, too. "I think I know what you mean, Michael."

"Too easy," he says, not whispering this time, "to get all messed up in my head."

"Yes."

"I wish I never went to that stupid war."

"Well, maybe—"

"Take that pink-cheeked cherry picture of me in dress formals at Amity Market. Toss it right in the can, man. Take that stupid parade, too. Go ahead. You know those flames in your dreams you were talking about? Yeah. Go ahead and burn the monster truck they're gonna hoist me up on like some old man at the Rose Parade. Burn that down to the ground, Sissy. Half the guys at the VFW—I can't stand. And I'm not gonna wave to anyone, you know that? I'm not going to go out there and pretend like everything's great so all those idiots don't have to think about anyone's life but their own."

"Michael."

"This is a 365-days-a-year commitment, Sis. You know?"

"Yes. I do know."

"War's like that, too. No one in this country understands this any-more. The whole thing is burning at their feet, anyway. We started it. I'll just throw the gas on it. Which is what we started it over in the first place. Just piss on it. Might as well torch the goddamned thing—you know, Sis?—expedite things."

"Please don't smile, Michael."

"I don't know what else to do, Sis. Can't do anything else. Nothing else works for me. Shit. Nothing else—"

"I know, Michael."

"—works *on* me."

"But Michael."

"Yeah, Sis?"

"Benji talks about that parade all the time. He tells—"

"He does?"

"—his swim instructor—yes. He does."

Michael blows air out the way their son blows out the candles, peering over the edge of the cake. "Really?"

"Yes."

"Gotta open my eyes."

"You're doing fine, Michael."

"Pay more attention."

"No one can mention war or the Army or tanks or planes or parades without him saying, 'My dad this, my dad that.' He's so proud of you."

"Ah, shit. Shit."

"You deserve to be the featured veteran, Michael. No one has seen more war in this town than you."

He closes his eyes, opens them, nods. "That's not necessarily a credit to a man's sensibilities."

"Michael."

"Yeah."

"Michael. Look at me."

He does, barely. "You make our family proud."

"Shit."

"Michael. We support you 100 percent. Especially Benji. Especially me. Okay?"

Now he grunts, "Huh," and she knows it's not at her, but at the "family" absentee she won't mention because she can't lie to his face. Only yesterday Michael had called him He Who Painted his Face Instead of the Cave Wall, and then said sorry, making it clear that the apology was to her, and not to him. Still, not even now before sleep, she won't dignify human hopelessness. She will listen to it, but not endorse it.

"Shit. All right, Sis. What the hell. Fuck it. I'll sit on that stupid red, white, and blue monster truck. All right. I'm sorry about it all, Sis—I really am—but I'll do it, okay? Shit."

Benji

November 5, 2010

HE'S RUNNING AGAIN. DARTING RIGHT THROUGH the middle of the yard like a wild turkey and looking up and over his shoulder with the elastic turkey neck of a child in search of the Nerf: there it is! Sailing!

"Look up!"

But the ball's too far. He won't catch it this time, but he chases it down full speed, anyway. Runs back to his uncle full speed, too, and waits for the new route on his uncle's hand. His uncle always says, "Malietoa. Full-speed is your only gear, you little manu you," and these words make him smile.

But he has a question. He has to stop jumping in place to ask the question. He grabs his uncle's hand where the plays are drawn to help ask the question, and pulls down while looking up. The hand will remind him what to say since the question is about the hand.

"Uncle Pika?"

"Yeah, sole?"

"Did you get into a fight?"

Uncle Pika doesn't answer, but he's breathing in real deep, the boy thinks, so that means I hurt him by asking the question. That means he got hurt in the fight. That means I've got to know who this person is that hurt my uncle's hand. That means I have to ask the question again.

"Uncle Pika! Who did it?"

He looks down and rubs the boy's head and says, "You go long, Champ. Alu alu."

The boy sprints off and he can see his mother watching from the window and so waves as she waves back and hears, "Stay on your route!" and returns to the straight line of a bomb. The straight far-out route, which is the bomb. Which is the one he never catches. He turns while still running and puts his arms out like Frankenstein and the ball hits right between his two elbows and then bounces out.

"Ohhhhh!"

This makes him walk. He almost had it right. It's different if the ball's far out and away from you. But if the ball touches you, that means you almost had it. That means you didn't do your job.

"Hustle up, Malietoa! You'll get it. Don't worry. That ball's got too much sponge in it, that's all."

He jogs back to the huddle.

"You all right, sole?"

"Uncle Pika?"

"Yeah?"

"I think you beat em up."

He's twirling the ball to himself. Then he squats down, picks at the grass. "How'd you know, Champ?"

"I saw your hands, Uncle Pika."

"Yeah?" The boy nods. Uncle Pika says with trickiness in his eyes, "How'd you know I didn't hurt em at work?"

"Those aren't burn marks, Uncle Pika!"

His uncle chuckles, shakes his head, knocks on the top of Benji's skull. "Man. You on it, aintcha? Know a few places where the authorities could use a smart little PI like you. Forget search and seizure. They just throw you in with the dogs to sniff the place out."

"Uncle Pika?"

"Yeah, yeah?"

"I don't want you to fight."

His uncle smiles, nods. "Don't worry, man. There's no one around here to fight."

"I don't want you to get into trouble again."

"Awwww, man. Malo lava, little uso. That's some good stuff right there, you know that? My father would've loved you. You'da softened him up some. Where were you twenty years ago, huh?"

"You promise?"

His uncle rubs his head and pulls him in. "Dontchu worry about anything, all right?"

"Okay."

"You gon' be a better man than me, Benji Laikiki. That's all that matters, you feel me?"

"Uncle Pika?"

"Yeah."

"Can we keep playing?"

"Oh, yeah, yeah. Of course. You know that." The boy is jumping in place again, shaking out his arms. "Go on now. This is the one where we connect." The boy is already sprinting off. "Go deep this time, little uce! I wanna test my fire power."

Sissy

November 11, 2010

SHE LOVES WALKING DOWNTOWN MAC with her son, the pre-parade crowd layered from the edge of Third Street back to the storefronts. Casa Bella, Third Street Books, McMenamin's. She loves to see people happy. Doesn't matter who they are, where they come from, if she sees them again. Mac is a good town, she thinks, because it knows how to give good parades. That's the sign, an omen of welcome from the city council. Homecoming, Alien Days, Drag the Gut, Turkey Trot, Christmas and today: Veterans.

Plus the lights. They're up there now, dotting the thin strip of sky like stars in heaven. A few years ago, someone in the town suggested they run Christmas lights from the 99 all the way out to Ford Street. For four days at sunrise, the firemen close off a section of Third Street, climb onto their lifts, and rise above their fellow McMinnvilleans and wine country tourists, weaving and threading the line until sundown. Ten thousand lights, easy, from November to February.

In Amity, she thinks, we have Daffodil Days in February. The height of rain season.

Benji's pulling her along faster than she'd like to go because she wants to marinate in the social cohesion, but thinks, I should see him, too. Today's not his day. Make sure he's okay. She brushes by a group of biker vets in beards and black leather, says, "Benji. We've still got fifteen minutes before the parade starts—let's go see Uncle Pika."

"Okay, Mama."

They weave through the crowd at 3rd and Evans, and make their way to the Hotel Oregon, a former bus depot turned three-bar watering hole—basement, floor level, rooftop. Her mother used to drink there, usually for free.

"There's Daddy, Mama!"

"Yes, hon."

He's up there on the stoop, shaking hands with the older vets from Vietnam, his John Deere hat so low over his brow she can't find his eyes. So many American flags it's dizzying to look at. She knows he's doing work right now, that social cohesion means nothing to him, that he'd rather be home dropping a line into the shallows of the South Yamhill. They're all around him, even those followers of his who'd never gone over but act like they did.

"He's very busy. Let's leave him alone, hon. Come on."

Inside the Red Fox Bakery, Pika is sliding trays of bagels into the steel slots of a roller, and when he sees them at the door, he lifts his eyebrows, signals one for give me one minute, and unties his apron as he walks over.

"Good folk today in the Red Fox. Hey, ya'll. Come for some bread? We got day-olds of that nine grain stuff you like. I'll take my break."

"Hi, Uncle Pika!"

"What's going on, little sole?"

They sit at the table closest to the counter, the most inward part of the bakery, furthest from the street. "Can I go see, Mama?"

"Yes, hon." The boy speed walks over to the window and presses his face and palms to the glass. He's holding the day-old out behind him so it doesn't touch the window. "How's work going, Pika?"

"A job, you know."

"So what are you doing now?"

"Like my job detail?" Sissy nods. "Well, I bake."

"You'll climb the ladder."

"Ain't no ladder around here."

The phone rings behind the counter and he says, "Hold up." She can barely hear him talking, so deceivingly soft-spoken. He writes down the order, nodding into the speaker, as if the customer were right there in the store. Everything in the Red Fox is maroon—the walls, the antique photos of Mac circa 1908, the formica counter top.

He's back and she says, "I'm proud of you, Pika."

"Okay."

"You're lucky to have a job in this economy, huh?"

"Well, that's right. And better than working a penny an hour for the leo leos."

"Leo leos?"

"Cops. That's what they paid you in the joint."

"Oh, my God! Penny an hour! That's criminal!"

"No. That be me, Sis. *I* was the criminal."

"That's a funny word."

"Leo leo?"

"Yeah."

"Know where it comes from?"

"Well, leo is lion in Latin, and did the Jesuits ever make it to the South Pacific because I read—"

"Got nothing to do with the Catholic Church, Sis."

"Oh, okay."

"It's from the siren. You know:" Pika twirls his finger in a circle. "Whoa-whoa-whoa. Leo leo leo."

"That's hilarious, Pika!"

"Yeah, well. I could tell you worse. Some fool I knew got named Falevau."

"What's that?"

"Bathroom."

"Bathroom?"

"Yeah, the mom gave birth to him in the tub so they named the poor sole Bathroom. Fe'a Falevau? Where's Bathroom? Who? Bathroom? Yeah! Where you at, Bathroom? In the bathroom! Sole! Hey! Bathroom's in the bathroom!"

Sissy lets out a loud laugh, and then covers her mouth when Benji looks back at her. "I'm sorry. That's horrible. Worse than that Johnny Cash song. Poor boy."

"You're cool, Sis. Every sole has a good time like that."

"I think you like your job."

"You funny, too, Sis. Stay on it no matter what. I *don't* like it. Feel me? I. Don't. All the rich people come down off the hill and tell you what's what."

"Second Street?"

"Yeah."

"I'm sorry, Pika. Didn't even think about that."

"Nah, nah, nah. It ain't nothing to get worried about. Ninety percent of the people in this country work jobs they can't stand. But I can stand it. Just saying that, though, don't mean I *like* it, you feel me? Cause what I *do* like is that it gets food into y'all."

"Well, I like that, too. But is something the matter, big brother?"

"Say what?"

"I can tell something's wrong. Come on. You can tell me."

"Nah, nah. You trippin'."

"Let me see your knuckles."

He gently pushes her hand away. "Whatchu talking about?"

"Come on, Pika. I know all about it."

She pulls his hand into her chest and he growls like a polar bear—"arrrrrrr"—as she examines its astrology, lightly tracing stars and moons and suns across the dried blood of the knuckles. Benji's munching on his day-old, looks back at them, and he winks at the boy.

"I'm sorry, Sis."

"I know you weren't looking for trouble, Pika."

"Nah. Not this time."

"Then I'm sorry, Pika."

"I'm cool with it if you are."

"What cowards."

"Any time I wreck shop and don't get the cops called on me I count myself lucky."

She shakes her head. "I still don't get you men sometimes."

"Try living with em, sister. About nine hundred of em."

"So you were just thinking about prison then?"

He whispers, "Keep it down, man."

"Like that tattoo on your face doesn't give you away, huh?"

"Yeah, well." He waits, looks at her, nods. "Some of em just think I'm a Maori warrior."

"You're funny."

"I mean, I don't know." He smiles at her, nods again. "It's all good. Just thinkin', that's all."

"A first."

He winks at her. "Yeah, something like that."

"Well, if we could talk over a phone in a visiting room, we can talk now."

"That's right."

"I know what you're thinking."

"Oh, yeah?"

"I think you're worried about us."

"Well, yeah. Always."

"You thinking about Mom?"

Pika's eyes widen and he grits his teeth, nods. "That's a part of it, you know? I mean, hopefully this don't sound disrespectful, you know what I'm sayin', cause she birthed me, you know what I mean, but she wasn't ever *my* mother."

"That might've been a blessing."

"And then I come up here in '06, you know, and I get hemmed up my first day in Oregon and all that—first *hour*—and never see her. Then turns out she's dead a year later. I'd do another year locked up just to meet her for a day."

"I'm sorry, Pika."

"She kicks me down the house, and that's cool, I ain't complainin', she tried righting the ship, but now I'm sorta stuck, you know what I mean?"

"You miss California."

"Well, yeah. But, nah. Guess I just miss the day, you know what I mean? Back when there was clarity. Miss the people who *knew* me back then. Who I could hit up without worrying if they got my back or not."

"We have your back, Pika."

"I know you do. I don't mean it that way. I didn't grow up with you, that's all I'm saying."

"Yes."

"No one knows me out here."

"You gave a lot up for Benji and me. We love you for that."

"I ain't trippin', but life is crazy, that's all. I mean, here I am cooking French baguettes in this mufucking bakery, and only a year ago I was slinging handball on the wall with the homies, life and death on my mind."

"I think about life and death all the time, too."

"You a special one, though. Guess it's just different. I feel like I mighta lost myself somewhere, you know what I mean?"

She thinks déjà vu but doesn't hold the thought to herself because that would bring into the conversation Michael's identical bedtime confessions from a week ago. She says, "I do," and nothing more.

"I don't even speak a word of Samoan anymore, Sis."

"You can speak it around me, if you want."

"Nah, ain't the same thing."

"How come?"

"Cause you can't say shit back."

She laughs out loud again, and then covers her mouth at once. "That's true."

"They think I'm Mexican here."

"They just don't know any better, Pika."

"Oh, I ain't trippin'. Been mistaken for an ese before. The biggest Mexicano in the valley! Órale!"

"You're funny, Pika."

"Also got Punjabi. Lebanese, Brazilian. I never expect anyone to get my shit right. Especially not in this state."

"They don't get me right either, Pika."

"Yeah. Maybe no one ever does."

"Did somebody say something to you, Pika?"

"Nah. Heard this conversation, that's all."

"Oh, God. What'd they say?"

"Just were talking about how brown people are ruining this town. You know. Stuff like that."

"In *front* of you?"

"Nah, nah. Hell, no. Am I in custody? Was in the back on my break. You can hear everything in there."

"Jerks."

He chuckles. "Actually, was two uppity old ladies."

"How embarrassing."

"First, was gonna say something—I got up, and then I sat back down. I kept thinking, Why you wanna say something now, homeboy? Didn't say anything when there were a hundred Nazis walking the yard. Punkass skinheads were mutherfucking heil Hitlering right there at the pull-up bars—you know what I'm saying?—and you were throwing dice against the wall. Cool with it, and all that."

She reaches out and touches his arm. "Oh, Pika."

Pika looks over at the boy, face pasted to the glass, empty-handed. "I don't want to cause any problems for y'all."

"You never do, and never will."

"Okay."

"I wonder what it is, Pika. Never really thought of it before. Mom used to talk about Mexicans so meanly, you know?"

"You know, Sis, I see these little-dicked mufuckers driving their monster trucks through town. Fucking Confederate flag in Oregon? Shit, the only beggars I seen around here are white people. We call that le'ai aisi."

"What's that word, Pika?"

"Means don't beg."

"Samoans are workers, huh, Pika?"

"Yeah. Well. The kids are workers." He chuckles again, shrugs. "Samoan adults are smart like that."

"What do you mean?"

"Oh, you know. Hierarchy. They assign all the work downwards. Just like in the joint. That's why you sometimes see Samoan kids getting so crazy in this country. They look around at their friends in the hood doing no work, and say, 'What the hell am I doing here? Why am I cleaning this house every day? I don't need to listen to my mom. My dad. Listen to nobody.' Next thing you know the blue and red lights are loc'd up on the lawn."

"Is that what happened to you, Pika?"

"But I used to love doing the koga'i."

"Kong. Ah. Ee?"

"That's pretty good, sis. Yeah. Koga'i's this big ceremony, you know, after le aufaipese a ekalesia."

"I'm not even gonna try that one."

"It's youth choir practice after church."

"So then what's Kong. Ah. Ee?"

"Basically the elders, you know, the older folk—"

"Mmmhuh."

"—gathering to eat, usually in a big hall, or something. All these old-timers'd throw their fala on the ground and drop down on their giant mulis—baaammmm!"

"Fala?"

He smiles and she won't look at her watch to cut off his story. When the parade starts, Benji will come tugging at her sleeve. The boy's a better clock than the stars has been her experience. "Mats. Fine mats. Sit right there on the floor—barefoot, in their lava lavas—and talk for hours."

"About what?"

"Anything they can think of. Church business. Family business. Money. Especially money. All the blowhards jocking to make their family look richer, better than everyone else. It's good and bad both. Like just about anything, I guess."

"Sounds neat to me."

"Only thing they do more than talk there is eat. We umu three or four pigs the night before."

"Is umu cook?"

"Umu's the hole we bury em in. All night long we cook em, all the usos."

"That long?"

"Takes an hour to dig the hole, five or six hours for the fire. That's about right. Then you get ten hours for the pig—yeah. Dig em up in one hour, strip it in thirty minutes—bang! You ready to go serve em to the elders."

"What about you guys?"

"We eat last."

"What?"

"Nah, nah, Sis. We eat while we cook. Sometimes drink. I always stash the best meat—the face—and annihilate it later. I like eating it with kimchi and rice. But the elders are funny. Putting it down, man! Telling you: huge plates of food. Yelling at the kids—"

"Show me."

"'Sole! Sau i'a! Ese kamaiki lea. Yeah! Bring me that food right there right over here!' The kids running around full-speed so dad can stuff himself with pua'a and fa'i. I'm talking mounds, sis. Mufuckers put it down at the koga'i."

"That doesn't sound healthy."

"It ain't. But it's Poly history, you know what I mean? The most full-bodied women are the most desired in Samoa, you know that?"

"Why?"

"Oh, well. Says you're well-fed, taken care of. Hawai'i was like that, too, back in the day. Skinny girls like you, Sis—shit, they throw you to the dogs."

She slaps him on the shoulder and he laughs. "Pika!"

He tickles her ribcage and then sits back up. "Not enough meat on them bones."

"Pika!"

"Then guess what?"

"Hmm?"

"Those old g's lay back right there on the floor—sleep. Yeah. They're out." He's chuckling again, and she can see him now—younger, more hair, thicker eyebrows, less cynicism—trying all day long to prove to these people that he's one of them. "The kids gotta be quiet when they're cleaning. Take all the plates in the dark, tiptoe through the kitchen. Ain't that funny? They don't move one foot in four hours. Talk, eat, sleep."

"But they work hard, too, huh, Pika?'

"Yeah, they do. Work immigrant hard, you know what I'm saying?"

"Yeah."

"I'm just telling stories. The koga'i's one day a month, max."

"It's a break from work then. A reward."

He nods. "I miss those days."

She pats his hand. "You're the only Samoan I've ever known, Pika, but I think I love them."

"Could be the only one you *ever* meet, Sis."

"No."

"Oh, yeah. 'S the way things go in America. I know what time it is. All the stories get washed out to sea, man."

"That's morbid, Pika."

"The people get washed out, Sis. Disappear. Like ghosts in the rain."

"Don't talk like that, Pika."

He pats her hand back, smiles, winks, looks down at the table, stands. "Okay. I ain't trippin'. Just feelin' it out here sometimes."

"Can't you name one thing you like about Oregon, Pika?"

"You mean other than the horses, and alpacas, and cows and shit?"

"You left out," she says, "a more populous mammal."

"The tweaker?"

"You also left out the rain."

Outside behind the parade of men, women, and children drowning in the same three colors of the flag, he can see the leaves of the poplar trees. He's been watching them change in stages, branch by branch, the last few days. When they turn from yellow to brown, he's noticed, they come down in waves to die.

"You can tell the season up here. Back in Cali, the bay, they killed the seasons. Socal is even worse."

"Sounds a little dreadful."

"Yep yep. That part of it is, I think. Concrete takes out everything on the map but graffiti art. And it's mufucking permanent."

"We're still on morbid, sounds like."

"Morbid be the sweet sadness. Like the sweet science. Mankind boxing naturekind's kindly ears."

"That's better, big bro."

"Placation nation. I can find it before you say patience. This patient patient's heading back to the breadboard to get a little bread. And I do mean little, little sis."

"Not bad."

"Gonna let you and the kid get back to the parade."

"I love you."

"You, too, Sis." He gives his best maitre d' bow, says in a deep formal voice: "Now, if you and Malietoa'll pardon me, ma'am, I gotta go burn some mutherfuckin' bread for the Second Streeters."

Pika

November 18, 2010

JUST ABOUT THE TIME HE RISKS THINKING, cool to be alone out here at the bus stop, looking down at the photo of Sissy and the boy on either arm in the OSP visiting room, El Señor Reliable appears right on time: the Ball-Breaking Big Baller Firecamp Flaco. Where's your Mactown taco truck, ese? Where's your made-in-China flea market Dodgers cap, nigga?

He'd understood the risk of turning off the radar for a minute. You pull out the old pic from the cell, the one that kept your heart pumping out some hope, you dream it up here in dreamland, dream it up anywhere, and the heartless predatory world's got its eye on what's left of your ticker.

Before I head on home again, whether by bus or on these feet, Pika thinks, I can't let him see what I'm feeling, what I'm thinking. If I step into this ese's personal space, a face-to-face encounter ain't gonna go well, and I know this.

Won't some mutherfucker out there let him *know* already, let him *feel* me: leave a nigga be, man!

Can't you see I'm programming! Walk up on another sucker! Let me live, dog! Let me do my little weebit thing without drama!

"Whatchu looking at there, oso?"

Shit, Pika thinks. Shit.

He's tweaking on me right now. Even his shadow on the ground is shaking. Fingers twittering like an epileptic about to drop into the fit, head tick-tocking back and forth like a movie scene with three or four clips missing in the middle.

I'm here! No! Over there! Back here again! Can't keep still! Oh, well! Hit me up another vein! Try this bloodline 'tween my toes! Go on! Gimme some! Gimme that!

Pika waits. He considers the ground between his feet in some strange dreamland hope that the twacked out ese will walk on, but deep down knows differently. The ese is looking over his shoulder now, but no one's up the street. No one's ever up the street. All this jerking paranoia Pika observes in less than five seconds' time.

Spun on ma'a. Gone on rock. Look at the tracks on his arms. This scab-ass convict's all scabbed out.

Goddamn.

How the fuck did this kinda shit follow me up here to so-called God's country?

The ese leans across the bench where Pika's sitting, sprawled out as if he were on the hood of a cop car, and sees the black-and-white photo in his lap. Pika turns his head toward Flaco, almost daring him to say anything about what he sees (You think I'm soft for getting nostalgic on this picture, you bitch-made crankster twack? Least I ain't dipped into your world yet. Least I'm cool giving hope an honest shot, mutherfucker), feeling himself losing control, the vision reddening. Losing sight of his mission of the boy and Sissy and the house and the future and all that crazy shit.

Flaco points at the Kodak photo and says, "This is in the joint, eh? That's OSP, man!"

Pika doesn't answer, doesn't nod.

The spun ese peers and squints for what seems like hours compared to his previous spasms and then suddenly he's back in form, the pierced eyebrows shooting straight up and held there, puppeteered into paralysis. "'Ey, man! Oh, shit. Nah! No!" He starts into some kind of insane skeleton dance, the fingertips of both hands stuck to his temples like self-administered electric shock pads, eeking out every other revolution, "No! No!"

Pika stands, not watching, looking off, pocketing the photo, protecting it. Not surprised, really, but not liking any more than any other time he's had to watch some fool tweak freak out. Finally he grabs Flaco, who acts like the contact is a jolt from the treatment: "What, man? Wassup?"

"No, eh. No no. Ah, no. Oh, no."

"You got something to say, man?"

"Es tu haina? No! That's not your *girl*, is it?"

Pika shakes his head no, just barely.

"Right right right. Oh, good good. That's real good." He smacks Pika's arm. "Shit, oso! You had me scared, eh! Thought I was Sancho for a minute, homie!"

"Fuck you talking about, man?"

"She sucked me off back in the day, oso! Oh, hell yeah! Pinche whole town in one night, homeboy! Straight-up face-shot that ho like a porno shoot! Shit, eh, that kid right there's probably *my* kid, homie. Hijo de Amidad. Daddy put some ese in your mother, little boy, 'cept you too blond-haired to be mine. Not enough brown blood—"

Pika feels it collapse—the dream upon reality—and reaches out for the source of the words—stops it. The air comes out the throat in the stop, the twacked-out Aztecan eyes get wider in the squeeze, Pika's own Polynesian-mad eyes maka sepa wider. Then the red screen in his head goes black and he blinks on a thought, thinking: I'm gonna ruin it all. Shit! Gotta breathe, man. Can feel it disappearing again, gonna get *made*, and he slaps Flaco across the face to finalize it and almost jumpstart his next move, an old one in two-month's time, taking to the farmroads again, the long winding anonymous search for Amity.

He deciphers the same claims and gangsta threats he's heard his whole life but it echoes up here, he thinks, inhaling the clean Oregon air because he can. That kinda nasty shit echoes any place where it's new. Or else where it don't belong. Bangin' off the old stuff like a pinball.

Benji

November 19, 2010

HE SPRINTS TO HIS ROOM AS TOLD BY HIS DAD and comes back to the kitchen table with the cards he'd snagged off his bed. His people are still in the same positions, sitting there like the zombies he's seen on the neighbor's TV and actually on three different neighbors' TVs and once he even heard an older boy on the playground say there's a video game where you shoot zombies. He's not a zombie. He's not scared of zombies, he just thinks they're dumb. They're always moaning and going, "Ahhhhhh." He jumps atop his Mama's lap, settles in, and shouts, "Okay, everybody! I'm ready! Wait! Wait!"

Now he sprints over to the living room and grabs the tin-framed pictures off the window sill, sets them up on the table's center like reminders to his people that they're his people, the only thing missing underneath the circle of family photos a lazy susan for constant showcasing.

He can feel her kiss his ear once from behind, and whisper, "Okay, hon. What do you want to play?"

"I only know one game, Mama. War. Don't you remember, Mama?"

"Yes. I do."

"You taught me that, Mama. Said it's the only game I can learn right now. Uncle Pika said he'll teach me Black Jack. You remember that, Uncle Pika?"

His uncle nods but nothing else and that's when his Mama looks up and around the table, and then she grabs the cards the way he once saw the bus driver grab a bus pass. He'd yelled, "Gimme that!" And also the boy who told him about the zombie video game was the boy who the bus driver took the pass from. He was waving the pass in the driver's face. He didn't like that, Benji thinks, even though a lot of kids were laughing. I don't think I liked it either. I'll never play that zombie video game with that boy.

"Okay," his Mama says. "Would you guys like to play? Can everyone play?"

"Yes!" the boy shouts. "They know how. Anyone can play War."

She deals now and it's not that the boy is not happy and excited to play War with his people, nor they with him, but he can see again that they are unhappy about each other. When you look someone in the eye, you are telling the truth. When you look down, you are lying.

Look up!

He gets his hand and pushes it toward the middle of the table.

"What's the matter, hon?"

"No."

"What do you mean?"

"I don't want to play, Mama."

"Come on. Why not? You forget?"

"No. I did *not* forget."

"What, what then?"

"No!"

"Benji, hon, please—"

"No! No! No! You play! No!"

"Top."

"No! No! No! No! No! No! No! No!"

He doesn't want to stay. He doesn't want to see their eyes. He runs off to his room again, but this time slams the door. Waits on his bed facing the wall for one of his people to come talk to him, but that doesn't happen. He tiptoes to the door, and puts his ear to the crack. No sounds from his people, not even of them walking or rolling off. He crawls into the closet because now he's worried they're dead or hurt real bad and so when he hears his mother's muffled voice he's happy and decides to squeeze through the hole and watch them because it's okay, Uncle Pika says, to change your mind now and then. Okay to see if you done something wrong and try to switch out on it. That's cool, Uncle Pika says. That's a cool cat who does that. So he wants to go back already, but he doesn't want to come in at the wrong time because they will send him off the same way he just left, and that will mean they won. That will mean their meanness won. What was in their eyes won.

"It's right there." His Mama. He can only see the back of her head but he knows she's crying. The way she's talking means she's crying. That's what it means. "Can't you feel it?—Don't you *see*?—Can be taken away so fast—Don't either of you *get* that?—By *now*?—Who else will help us but ourselves?—How many more reminders do we *need*?—Please—I can't—Please—Don't you see by now?—Don't you *see*?"

When the grown-ups look at the ground for a really long time, the boy thinks, they're thinking. When the grown-ups look at their laps for a really long time and not talking, that also means they're thinking.

Thinking is good, Mama. I think a lot about us.

Pika

Thanksgiving, 2010

IN THE CLEAN OREGON AIR HE'S BEEN UP ALL NIGHt and that's the way he likes it doing umu, twelve hours to get to this last phase. Gotta do it right. Buried Thanksgiving turkey and buried Thanksgiving whole chicken kicked down by the St. Vincent de Paul Food Bank and the goodly taxpayers of Ore-ee-gone. Mostly good people, mostly good cause, and that's good enough for Pika right about now.

You prepare for the worst, and hope for the best, he thinks. But the trick is not to shoot too high on that best thing. Fuck knows I've shot low enough with that worst thing.

The thin wisps of smoke are barely twirling out the mound of dirt like a volcano about to blow, and he knows it's time.

"Fa'afetai lava!" he shouts across the yard, digging into the raised avian grave with his shovel.

Feels all right, the no sleep thing nothing to be worried about—he's sharp, he's up, he's wide awake like a tweaker on a binge, although fuck tweakers: muscle-memory and cultural nostalgia and temporary victory over the rain in rain country is the brain's best caffeine. When he crashes later, when he sleeps later, he's gonna be out for days, Polynesian hibernation with meat in the belly, k.o.'d by the wild confluence of love and hatred in the Pac Northwest.

He scoops the dirt and tosses it behind him, stooped over but bent at the knees, powering it full speed to get to the dripping meat of these two birds. He didn't have lava rocks so he went to the South Yamhill with Malietoa as guide to snag a few river rocks yesterday morning. With a two-hundred-pound stripped pua'a you need two dozen rocks or more, plus ten to twelve hours in the ground, but with a bird, nah—you just stick one right in its cavity, wrap the banana leaf around the body, and bury it for six or seven hours.

He's getting there. They all are. Sissy suggested he run this whole Thanksgiving feast Samoan style, to make him feel at home, she'd said, and he appreciates it. Wants to do a hell of a job, even if they couldn't foot the bill to cook a pig the way he grew up doing. At work, he'd overheard one of the winery cats talking about feeding his yipster customers "roasted pork" to celebrate solstice, and the thought made him queasy. They all probably feel about me, he thought, the way I do about that.

Still, he's grateful. The kid, little Shotcaller: he's keeping us all in check, Pika thinks. Last night he'd begged Sissy to sleep out here near the umu, and Pika saw her look to that other guy for a nod, and he went and done it. Didn't roll off pouting in a hissy fit, didn't mention how he'd already lost the war long ago, letting his son visit the state prison, a boy not even out of diapers.

Cause no one knows where life is gonna go, Pika thinks now, the spade of his shovel scraping at the top of the tarp, where he sweeps the dirt into little mounds. Sissy was right the other day. Can't fuck with fate, man. Can't mess with time. Don't know what any day holds, as he hears the screen clap, the boy already screaming with excitement.

"Ohhhh yeeeeeaaaaaahhhhhh!"

Pika smiles. The kid barely slept. He kept jumping up out of his sleep and asking, "Is it ready yet, Uncle Pika? Should we dig now?"

"Wassup, Shotcaller."

He's got a baseball bat-sized purple and yellow plastic shovel, holy grail Christmas-gifted by the monks, he's been told by the kid half a dozen times.

"This is my shovel from the monks, Uncle Pika."

Half a dozen and one.

"Dig it." That's good shit: the gratitude and good kind of pride. "Now get digging."

The boy's scooping dirt so fast it reminds Pika of that line from *Cool Hand Luke*, an old school flic he'd watched locked up on Movie Night Tuesday, that dude Dragline telling his crew of Southern chain-gang homies, "Use that shovel like it was your spoon."

"Get the man, boys, get the man," was the line Luke kept throwing out.

He'll probably never see that film again, but he doesn't need to. This the deal right here. This the real thing. You cut me off from every other story for the rest of my life, he thinks, and I'm cool with it. Got this one right here to keep me kicking. Don't hover near it trespassing neither. Come in peace.

"Doing good, Uncle Pika?"

"Oh yeah, man. You digging like you hadn't eat in days."

"I'm a little bit tired right now, Uncle Pika—"

"Oh, are ya?"

"—but I'm gonna keep working, okay?"

"Okay, Shotcaller. Just stay there on the edge. Don't go to the middle of the pit."

"Yes, sir!"

He almost says, "Don't mix me up with your father, kid," but keeps quiet instead, just wedges his shovel between the tarp and the edge of the pit, thinking with the kind of gone-done-over with-uma-finality that if he lived with rapists and murderers and snitches in the pen—and he did, every day, just like every other mutherfucker in there—he can at least share a house in freedom with a rapist who this kid loves, and who the rapist loves back. That ain't a miracle, nah, but that ain't any harder than any other day of his life, not here in Amity, Oregon, or anywhere else he's ever been.

"Yep, yep. Okay, Malietoa. Here's what."

He nods for the boy to put his shovel down and the boy does, smart and earnest as he always is, little scholar of the non-verbal communication world of adults, who just basically failingly can't ever say what they want to say, what they ought to say, all plugged up with backstory.

"I'm gonna lift this tarp, flip it over to the other side, okay?"

"Okay, uncle."

"Now there's a fire in the ground still, and even though it doesn't look hot, it is. It'll burn you bad, you feel me?"

"Yes, sir!"

"Okay. Stand back then, pahtnah."

He flips the tarp one side over the other. The sacks of burlap atop the birds are dried and crisped of the water they'd once held to billow steam for the underground rottisary. He pulls them off, one by one, and tosses them like empty potato sacks into the yard, and hears, "You okay, Pika?"

"Oh, yeah, Sis!"

"Need anything?"

"Uh, yeah! I'm gonna send little sole—here he comes! Malietoa. Come here. Can you run inside and tell your mom to grab those tin pans she got at dollar store?"

The boy runs off before he can give any further instructions, but that's pretty much all he needs to say, anyway, and he's good with it. He reaches in and hooks into the chicken wire tied off on itself, and dead-lifts the light-as-hell-compared-to-a-pig-package of cooked birds, and starts toward the house his mother left him—and therefore her whole damned brood (without even knowing)—over five years ago. Little bit of a legacy, anyway, and he's cool with that. In less than a minute, it'll be his favorite part of the umu: unfolding the burnt-black, shriveled, curled-at-the-edges banana leaves like you do peeling barbecued corn, sticking your hands in the warm moist carcass, and pulling the bone off the meat like a seashell from wet sand.

"Coming through, yo, with a bird or two!"

The battered screen door slams battered yet again against the chipped wall of the front porch, and the boy comes sprinting out again—never tires, that boy: that's why he's Malietoa: kid's a Polynesian warrior from another life: got more life in him than a goddamned convict just set-free: he's better than me, this boy: I owe him my life, or at least the dripping meat of a dead bird: "Coming through, Malietoa!"—and runs along Pika's side like third-world kids tailing the first-world savior with food, and then he knows to sprint ahead yet again, run to the screen, shove it deeper into the chipped wall, and lean against it, shouting, "Here it comes, Mom! Here it is, Dad!"

What else a mutherfucker need up in this bitch than a champ-een bright-eyed boy full-speed on his high-octane hope?

Pika

Thanksgiving, 2010

AND HE'S ALWAYS KNOWN THE POWER OF FOOD. It ain't no joke. Wanna save the planet? Put a plate of umu'd bird in front of the President and his associates. Wanna visit the White House, you, from Russia? You, from China? Come on in then, gentlemen, gentleladies, but no words allowed, right? That's the rule. Just stuff your faces with umu'd bird, and then scoot. We'll talk all that nuclear shit later.

The hamos got that one right, he thinks, however much they get wrong in ahistorical America. But then, he thinks further, Samoans are Serbians are Cambodians. Same all the way around once you settle in these borders: plenty wrong, too much wrong, on-its-way-out-the-door-wrong. Tribal old world stuff gets washed out, eaten up. Story diluted by the crazy-ass mathematics of every other story on the globe competing for space in this place. Those stories are infinite, he thinks, but this country is finite. A late start. Everyone thinks that's great, enlightened and brilliant and shit, but maybe that's the problem.

By the end of the day, you can't get your head around all the possibilities of what we'll be on this playground, *who* we'll be, and are a little scared, really, at the null-set possibilities, too.

But so as not to get off too much in his head, he daydreams on the old theme: even in the joint, food ruled. At work, in the block, in the cell, all day hustling citrus for pruno in Hefty bags, bologna for mid-day spreads with the hamos, chicken to sell to any homie not working in the chicken farm. Fringe benefit of having Asians riding in your car, he'd learned and enjoyed learning, was how they'd come up with crazy-ass fish soups and rice balls out of nothing. Just like the paisas: something—a hell of a lot, actually—out of nothing. Lao and Vietnamese at absolute peace with one another until their bellies are full, and then it's back to the old school lines drawn over centuries.

Even vanilla-skinned, vanilla-cuisined palagis carry a flask of Sriracha to chow. Crazy, he thinks, the first time I saw that shit. '99. Turn of the century, ten years before the high-roller Cali transplant wine connoisseurs on Second Street even heard of it, and showcasing those chic yuppie shirts around. Nazi Low Riders drowning their stroganoff in blood-red.

Superimposed, Tut, he thinks. A good word for a bad image: swastikas on Mandarin.

"Let's eat, everyone!"

The boy knows wasssup. He's darting around the table the same as he does anywhere he's at with his folk.

Why else live up in this house (sinking in the mud of backstory, he thinks)? Why else keep the fire going (popping flames threatening to jump the mesh cage)? Why else sew the latest string to the family line (bastardized and warped and watered-down)? Why else say hope has any meaning? Whatever the truth of it is, he's gonna do his part, right?

Right?

She asks them on cue if it's okay then and they both nod without seeing the other nod in their respective breathing space and she says then to make a circle, and hold hands, to say the Lord's Prayer, the one in Latin that starts out Pater Noster and ends in Sed libera nos a malo.

She's the only one that knows this supposed language of God, she and the kid, and that's good enough for Pika. He ain't gonna switch it up, slide between his sister and the boy to keep it safe. Nope. Let home-boy-down-below make the move to abort this dream. So he waits like he always has and hears and feels no movement and then like a minor miracle (if he believed in em) says fuck it in his mind for the millionth time in his life and reaches out into what's probably nothing and then sure enough he's got homeboy-down-below's palm in his own. His in homeboy's. Hands like two flags hanging limp on a windless morn. And yet: cupped against one another. Skin on skin.

Goddamn it if he doesn't have to tug back on his own story. At least not yet.

More waiting to do?

Shit, he's trained to wait. Has proved that, anyway. Marrow in the bones sturdy as the pillars in the joint with waiting. Now Sissy and the boy are waiting, too, and it's all he can do to put his head down and nod again. Probably the same as homeboy-down-below is waiting: one little tug against me, dog, and then what? Is it *on*? Concede yet *again* to all the demons of yesteryear? Right here with the boy watching how the world will spoil on its own drippings in a second's time?

Neutral!

He's cool with that!

Goddamn it if he doesn't have to tug back on his own story this minor-miraculously sunny afternoon. What else to be thankful for his first Thanksgiving in freedom in half a decade, even if it is in this water-logged state?

Pika barely smiles. Doesn't look around, but doesn't care who's sharing it either. Loc'd up behind the boy is the way they play it, and gotta respect that. Everyone does. They're here. Being here's a non-negotiable wrap.

What'chy'all critics got to say then, huh?

To help the cause, he tunes into another station the way he used to secretly love the sound of the rain at OSP, listening to the lovely feminine humm of Sissy's voice in the Latin. He likes to zone out on the old world sounds, the beauty of what's basically medieval babble to him. He can say the prayer in Samoan. Stays quiet instead. He can hum along in a whole other tongue, but silence is where it's at this morning.

Amen, he thinks, and sits.

"Pika, it looks great."

"Right, right," he says, but nothing else, the cheek muscles of his tagged face unable to close down on the smile.

Michael

Thanksgiving, 2010

SHE'S ALWAYS SAID I CAN'T TALK, HE'D THOUGHT after their prayer and that true smile of her brother's despite the skin ink and also the best turkey he's ever tasted better even than Turkeyrama in Downtown Mac, and she's so damned right—isn't she?—I've got to work against the prophecy—don't I?—and so does. Has. Everyone, even him, listening to his stories about the valley. He can't believe he's doing this. He can't believe he's putting together the sentences in his head to be heard out loud and that the ground hasn't shaken and opened and swallowed him whole.

"And so my friend, Ryan—you remember him, Sis?"

"Yes," she says. "I always liked Ryan."

She hands Top a napkin. He's sucking on his fingers, and for good reason. "This is what I was waiting for!" the boy shouts.

They all laugh, nod.

"I can't believe how good this is, Pika," Sissy says, nodding. "So juicy. I've never had turkey like this."

"They're right," he says, forking a brown piece of wing, putting his story on hold.

"Is it some secret recipe from the South Pacific, Pika?"

"Nah nah."

"Well, what's the trick then?"

"Fat."

"Fat!" the boy yells, his jaws mashing the meat in his mouth.

"Again, big brother?" she asks, smiling. "More fat?"

"Yeah, you know. The old story from the south side of the neighbor-hood: greased both those birds. Stuffed em full with bacon and SPAM."

"So it liquefied, Pika?"

"Yep yep. Most of it. Ate the crisps outside, though. Sorry, y'all. Couldn't help myself."

"Chef's privilege," she says. "Truest benefit of being grill-side, Pika."

"Right right."

"Dad?"

"Yeah?"

"What's lick. Ee. Fied?"

"Melted."

"Sorta like turducken, Pika."

"There you go, Sis. A poor man's turducken. The Polynesian Man's Burden. A juiced up poor boy loosed on the intestines."

Sissy laughs at his latest litany of playful institutional nonsense, and then turns. "But what were you gonna say, hon," she asks, "about Ryan?"

He looks up from his plate, nods. "Well, you remember when he caught that fifty-three-pound salmon."

"Fifty-three!"

"Yep, Top."

"Dang, boy. That's what you call a fish right there."

She stands from the table, leaves it.

"How big is that, Dad!"

"Damned near big as you, Top. And he was carrying it around like a small child, too. That's exactly what he had in weight. What was more amazing, though, was that he did it fishing the shore. All those boats out there somehow missed that monster. Must've been at least a hundred boats. What fish could ziz-zag through that?"

"The South Yamhill, Dad?"

"No, no. Definitely not, Top. Salmon don't run it. Or haven't in a long time, anyway. We were fishing the Nestucca."

"Lures, Dad?"

He loves the kid for the question. "No, no. Salmon eggs."

"You use Borax on the pouch, Uncle Pika."

"Okay okay."

"That's how you make em hard, Uncle Pika. So they don't melt in the water like the pig bacon."

She's back from wherever she went, and hands a photo to Benji. "Here, hon."

"Wow!"

"Was I lying, Top?"

"Look at this, Uncle Pika! Look!"

Pika looks as asked, nodding, too, saying, "That's a lot of sashimi. A lot of fresh fish. We make lomi lomi salmon."

"Around here, the Indians smoke it," Sissy says, and Michael's happy for the save. He doesn't want to have to correct him already, contradict him two minutes into the story.

His eyes consider the edge of the table. "That's why I thought of it right now, Sis: last time I tasted something new like this was in Grand Ronde. Five Tribes. They do this ceremony at the season's first catch. Spring, I think. March. So, anyway, Ryan's dad was mad as all hell cause we took that fish out there. He wanted to stuff it. Ryan said, 'Hell with that,' and we went out, the both of us."

"That a reservation?"

"Yes, Pika."

"Back then, they didn't have the Center—you remember, Sis? The hospital, too, was just a field and a few shacks. Yeah, all that got built by the casino. Every citizen of Grand Ronde was poor until they brought in the white gamblers."

"Land and lives taken by greed," Pika says. "Land and lives given back by greed."

"Never thought of it like that, Pika. But that's exactly right."

"Even the mayor and the chief of police lived in shacks back then," he continues. "My mother warned me about going out there."

"That obviously didn't work, huh, hon?"

"Nope. Sure didn't. But a good thing to see. Was beautiful, actually. Sad."

"Dad?"

"Yep?"

"I love Michael Phelps, Dad."

They each one laugh without looking at the other, which means while looking directly at the kid, who somehow affords everyone equal eye contact, and holds it. More or less. But he's looking at me the most, though, Michael thinks. Hopes. I can't wait to see how he connects the tribes to Phelps: that's how his mind works: he's not afraid of connection. He's not like me. I love my son. "What made you think of him, Top?"

"He swims like a salmon fish."

"That's good, hon," Sissy says.

"I heard he never quits," Michael says.

"I love Michael Phelps, Mom, because once he swam a whole race blind."

"He's blind?"

"No, no, no, Sis," her brother says. "His goggles fell off when he dove in."

"Oh my God."

"But he kept going, Dad." Michael nods. It's true if the boy says so. He did. "He did, Dad."

"I know."

"He counted his strokes, that's all, Mom. Once down the pool and flipped right where he always flips, then back."

"That's amazing!"

"Because he's the best, Mom. That's why I love him. That's why I put him by my mirror. He's the fastest man alive, Dad. He's almost a dolphin. Have you ever seen him swim, Dad?"

"No. Never have."

"You should watch him."

He reaches out and rubs Benji's head. "Rather watch you swim, little man."

"Dad. He's the best. No one can beat him. His lungs are like balloons. That's what my swim coach says. We watched the video of the races. What's that mean, Uncle Pika?"

"What, sole?"

"That his lungs are like balloons?"

"Oh, just that he can almost breathe like a fish, you know what I'm saying? He holds his breath under water—that makes his lungs stronger than other people, feel me?"

"Like this?" Benji holds his breath, eyes bulging, and Sissy reaches out and pops his cheeks.

"Okay, baby. Work on your lungs later."

"Yeah. His lungs are the best in the world, Mom."

"Anyone want some apple pie?"

Someone's coming up their way now, so rare an occasion that they all turn to the window like birds on a wire.

"Sissy," he says. "Did you invite my mother?"

She looks down, nods. They can hear the deep engine of the car, as if it were growling through grit teeth, and then its idling grumble. Just as he gets out to his wife, "Damn it, Sissy, you had no right!" the tattooed lowlife he'd just given the benefit-of-the-doubt to is rushing directly murderously unstoppably at him for the second time in five years.

Pika

Thanksgiving, 2010

HE DOESN'T WASTE ANY TIME. Up on his feet at the grinding hood-bass of the six four Impala's muffler, as standard a sound in East San Jo as honking geese in this no-fly zone valley, he heads straight to the chair. Pushes and pins in one full-body thrust the half-body to the side and reaches for the gun at the belt line. Pulls it out without obstruction from the owner ("Heyyy!") and goes right to the door and out it.

"El Trece rider, punkass uso! El ese southsider Flaco!"

He hears the shot before he can really see the ese against the dark backdrop of his dark blue ride—*pop!... pop! pop!*—and so fires back low at the wheel—*toop! toop! toop! . . . toop!*—to keep him here, to kill him here, and whoever else drove his punkass here so no one here especially the boy gets fucked by a stray bullet—when he knows he's been hit. This makes his feet speed up not stop or slow but he can't see the ese on the road—fool's smart enough to turn his lights off. He knows the kitchen is framing his own body behind him—a mark, he thinks, and gets low to the ground. A target—and he wants to turn and shout, "Kill the lights!" but it's too late for that, even as it actually happens, even as he falls to a knee from a stabbing feeling near his heart—*pop!*—in pure darkness, no stars.

He rises but falls forward, takes a knee. Big uso on a knee in Amity, Oregon. Big oso on a knee—as the ese slams the door and floors the Impala, the lights not yet activated, blind through the neighborhood. Blind goes the ese like Phelps down the lane. A garbage can or something like it blows up, dragged down the road, and then at once the hardcore full-board suffocation of post-violence quiet. Silence he can't stand and so mutters, "Fuck," just to kill it, and then is saved by his ears. The trick-ling faucet of the creek and the chirping crickets along its banks and the piercing howling of his sister. Poor girl, he thinks, and then the scream-ing from the fale that he's always known.

Blind as homeboy rolling down the ramp right now, he thinks, in pure darkness, no stars.

Big bear. You successfully put a big bear on a knee, ese punkass, and then he sits Indian style to defy the thought, what his grandpa told him is actually called Samoan style in this fale because we do more of it than any Indian ever has, Pika Laikiki. We sit Indian-style all day long, uce! Tut used to claim from the ground on the yard, rolling dice for penny stamps after chow. Super-size yoga masters on a zen ride, cuz!

He smiles at the memory, he feels his eyes watering up at the memo-ry, or else also at the wincing biting boring pain near his chest, the one cutting off all his air.

"You get em, Sissy? You get em?"

"I got em, Michael!"

"Tell em send the EMT! 1352 Yamhill Street! Hurry up goddamnit! Man down! Man down!"

"Benji!" he hears.

"Keep him inside, Sis!"

"Uncle Pika! Uncle Pika!"

"Take him into the cellar and call 911! And stay down, Sis! Go on!"

"Uncle Pikaaaaa!"

"Leave the lights off! Get in there, Sissy!"

They're yelling for him even as they're retreating into the house and this is good, Pika thinks, because—

The chair with wheels is right here again—in his face, at his side—and homeboy maneuvers around in this chair like a rider on a live horse and kicks his dead legs out and swivels his lower body like a gymnast on a wooden horse—mutherfucking horses! Pika thinks. Homeboy can handle himself on horses!—and drops down in a hard grunting collision with the ground and: "You're all right. Where you hit? Where you hit?"

"Fucking chest, man." He can't say it now, can't say the whole thing now. "Can't breathe."

He lays down, and: "Don't do that!" but does it, anyway. He feels his heart sinking like a stone in water.

But he can see homeboy ripping his lumberjack flannel off and rolling it into a rope the way Pika makes donuts at the Red Fox Bakery and he can still hear them from the cellar.

Homeboy fastens the rolled shirt into his clenched teeth like a bit in a horse—Horses! Pika thinks. Love you crazy-ass northwestern horses!—and hops on two arms like a midget on crutches over to his side and rolls his upper torso alongside Pika, both breathless. Feels the snug rope tighten around the melting middle of his body, not held together anymore by muscle or bone but drowning in the melted muscle and bone and he can't talk now or ever again but: "Hang on there, buddy—hang on now—I'm with you—right here. There it is. There we go. Okay, you're good. Hang on now. Hang on. They're on the way, man. Oh, fuck. It's too much. Be here in no time, brother—no time. Shit: lost too much."

I'm not dead, he thinks, but the kindness softness of the tone seduces him into the realm of the possibility of anything even that and why speak now when homeboy lays down, too, face to the sky, and: "Ohhhhh, can hear em now, man. You hear em, bud? Like a fucking song of victory, man, I swear to God. What beauty, huh? What fucking beautiful sirens they are, huh? Hang on, buddy. Hang tight. I'm right here."

It's all good, Pika thinks. It's all good because—

"They will do right by you, I promise you that. I'm right here, man. Stay with you all the way out. We got it now, we got it."

He's flooded again by the old familiar sheen of his country's spinning red and blue lights and what he saw but can't say was the boy in safe tow into the underground cellar on his mom's arm or elbow or whatever, and that's what it's all about, ese punkass Flaco.

You feel me *now*, little boy?

You got what this uso's about, son?

Yeah.

Better.

Don't none of you misapprehending mutherfuckers ever forget it.

The Family

November 28, 2010

EXCEPT FOR THE PRIEST, THEY'RE THE ONLY ONES here at the newest grave in the Pioneer Cemetery. The day is Oregon gray, the kind of grayness warning of rain, like the turkey- and chicken-bones gone gray in their kitchen by now, three days after the shooting. The family table with the plastic-plane on plastic legs bought ages ago for three bucks at an Amity garage sale hasn't been touched: Dixie plates of fixings and stuffing and canned corn; half-full Dixie cups of Kool-Aid fruit punch; bird scraps.

"The monks," Father McFadden had said before the funeral mass, "send their condolences to the family. But they have their orders, too. They can't even leave the monastery if it floods." He'd shaken his head. "Well, not officially, anyway. Last seven monks of their order waiting out there to be drowned. Gotta love em and their devotion." He'd added, "Thought I'd share also that Brother John wept for him. And Brother Martin gave you this."

She'd taken the handmade Filipino rosary with its finite intricacies of the fourteen stations beveled like Morse code notches into the one-inch-by-one-inch squares of lacquered wood, and said, "Thank you, Father," and nothing else.

Now she tosses a modest grip of loose dirt on the box, the custom-made casket donated by these same monks bound to their monastery on the flood plain, and crosses herself. The boy won't go near the hole and so his father stays back with him, two tiny feet and two huge wheels heel-stuck on the packed dirt of the walk. The boy hasn't talked for three days and they're worried except for the fact that they haven't really talked that much either, not even about him not talking.

217

She thanks the priest, and her husband nods his acknowledgment of a kindness rendered, then spins on two wheels in his place, and pushes into the dirt.

"Come on, son."

The boy comes without any motion in his arms, and the boy's mother trails them. They're all three in the mourner's color, the one where every other color gets mixed in like a soup, the nothingness that no morning light can penetrate. She looks back and stops, says, "Wait here, okay?"

They watch her walk over to the gravesite. Three paisa men are already shoveling giant scoops of earth onto the box, sealing the bullet-riddled body and its folded arms unto itself, the cement stone soon to be lifted and fitted in, like a plug in the drain of the bathroom tub.

She gives one of the men the rosary just given her, and the paisa is nodding nodding nodding so truly that his shoulders are bobbing up and down in unison, and the other men have stopped their work to respect not just the gesture but her presence, though by the time she turns to catch up with her husband and son, they're hunched over and digging again.

They walk now, the three of them, the boy and his people minus one. His arms still don't move. His arms follow him along in the same way his feet are following along his father. He's looking down, guided by the sound of his father's rubber wheels on pavement, constant depression of the half-body's weight against the ground. He can hear his mother behind him, and then he can feel her, an arm pulling him in so that he walks with a slant from the waist up, the arms still motionless.

The air is caveat chill, the bursting rolling nebulae in constant closer threat. No one's at the makeshift skate park, which is nothing more than the foundations of a Lewis statue on one side, Clark on the other, and the plywood slats of a puzzle-pieced ramp in between. The city council didn't pay for it, but they didn't condemn it either. The evergreens surround the family but that's the same as any other day. The trees that have already outlived them times seven or eight, the ones that give them oxygen to breathe and wood to burn and a small-town Oregon logging history to talk about when there's nothing else to say. Which has always been often. The ones that fall down now and then, and as strong and steady as they are, give no real protection from the stronger and steadier rain.

She kisses the top of her son's head. He's upright again from the waist up and separates to breathe as deep as he can, his arms alive with movement and utility for these few steps of transition, but that's it. At the tracks, she catches her husband up and leans his chair back so that he doesn't fall forward, pushes hard across the divots. A rusted train loaded with industrial garbage from Portland sits unmanned at the crossing, like it did yesterday and the day before that, as if the difference between a day and a hundred fifty years were nominal. They walk on, unnoticed. They make it across without an incident, like the spill that happened four years ago, how she'd stood paranoid in the middle of the deserted road and flagged a car down for help after at least a quarter hour had passed. Four deep bumps in all—Badoomp, badoomp. Badoomp, badoomp—two rails, successfully overcome.

Coelho's is open but empty, and they know this from the time of the day and because the parking lot itself is empty. They don't look into the windows, having never been inside the tasting room, anyway, and turn right on Main Street where everything's empty and closed, too, even the market. The abandoned squad car still warning drivers to slow is rusting now, the weeds and grass knee-high around the sagging tires.

They take the trail along the lightly graffitied stairs leading to the creek below, her whole body and the boy's whole body leveraged against the chair. They're both in their mud boots for exactly this exercise of fighting the forces at work trying to pull the wheels down, where the pools of rainwater are drowning the unkillable tangle of catch-me vines. He's gripping the rubber harder than anything he's ever gripped before, aiding the process as much as he can, his neck muscles straining against the black collar of his jacket.

They reach the bottom and don't rest at all, just switch positions with a kind of automation rivaling their Sundays at mass. The boy is enveloped by his mother's arms, pushing from the center-middle, she from the outer-higher. He pushes, too, his neck still straining, and up they go, inch by inch.

Five minutes pass like this and they make it to the flat-land yard before their house and, again, don't stop to rest. They reach the base of the ramp and he pushes ahead to indicate that he doesn't need their help, which is different, he'd once said to his son, than not appreciating their help. You can appreciate, he'd added, the boy still standing there worried about his father's permanent condition of need, and not need to focus on the appreciation. You can go on, he'd concluded, without feeling guilty about helping me, Benji, or doing what you've just done. You don't have a damned thing to feel guilty about, son, remember that.

He keys the lock to the door and they enter the house like strangers. Not to each other, but to the house itself. Slowly, each of them go in—slowly—in their own way. The boy walks off to his room, closes the door without a sound until the click, and they stay in the kitchen.

"I should clean up," she says.

"I'll help."

"Okay."

He wheels her the dishes to wash, forks and knives and spoons, the Dixie plates and cups stacked on his lap to be dumped outside, and by the time he's returned, she's soaking everything in water so hot her hands are curled like the disfigured claws of the creatures she believes hell to be infested with. She can't think on the demon-man that killed her brother right now because her knees would give out in despair and anger and her mind would ponder the pointlessness of having brought him back to the house in the first place (Tried to reverse course on personal history, she thinks. What mortal can do that?), but she knows this is wrong, that he paid greater than she for their desperate unification behind the boy, and that she should merely clean this spoon, lay it on the rag to dry, and then that is it. The season's first real rain starts, pelting the rooftop in the first burst, ten a hundred a thousand fingernails tapping on the coffee cup.

I'd called for him, she thinks, and he came.

"Are you hungry?"

"I can eat a little," he says, his slacks unspilled on, yet ringed black around the groin with sweat.

"I'm just gonna watch."

"Mmm-huh."

"I'll getchu some spaghetti."

"Okay."

"Want me to fry SPAM?"

"That's all right."

She puts the aluminum can under the automatic opener and lets the machine take over, changing her mind about eating before it's done. She gets two Dixie plates and gives him two-thirds to her own third, and then sits across from him exactly the way he likes so he can see her without twisting down and around on his own shoulder, the Joe Cocker pose, he calls it, when mocking himself.

"Will he be okay?" she whispers.

He says yes with a prolonged blink and barely traceable nod and she feels no relief whatsoever. She can't eat, and so slides her cold Chef Boyardee spaghetti across the table. He can't eat either, but the rain is hitting the rooftop so hard now that he may eat soon, she thinks, just to take his mind off the sound, which is no longer of fingernails on porcelain, but of knuckles on the door, on the wall, on the tabletop. So loud and heavy you think that the roof must be sagging somewhere. That the world's been turned upside down. Surrounded, in the end, by water.

Just then she hears the click of the bedroom door behind her, and before she can really register the answer to the question, he rushes past them both slumped over their untouched plates, and goes straight out the front door naked to the waist, barefoot. Down the steps, across the muddy yard and up the battered field already flooding like a small creek—when he suddenly stops, damned near soaked to the bone in two-minute's time from the same old skytears of western Oregon.

She stands and he grips the wheels. They come out to the porch. Watch him, wait. As still as this son of Amity, stiller.

He's right there in his uncle's drenched loincloth, face up to the rain, stout in the heart of the storm.

A Tip

I'd like to "tip" this book to the awkwardly silent Lebanese guy who'd made me coconut-infused white teas in his pristine underground store downtown, where I wrote about 82 percent of this book beneath the painting of a bespectacled crow, two local artists on anonymous display. I don't know how long your culturally authentic indie tea shop with homemade baklawa on Chinese platters will make it in this remote Pacific Northwestern valley, but I hope you'll stay open as long as you can, if only for me and my next book! By the way, I saw you reading novels between customers at least a hundred times, and I'd wanted to talk shop like they did in the olden days, introduce myself, say, "You know, Faulkner there was despised in his native Mississippi, just like Steinbeck in Salinas," but for some reason didn't; and then I won't forget when you once refused a tip because you'd said Americans don't appreciate the gesture, how the money is always expected here, which makes it lose its meaning, and I'd just nodded since you were right from a certain sandstorm, bartering, '60's French-existential vantage of the village first, and who am I to enforce the minimum-wage chaos of our picketed American streets on you and your charming store? I pocketed my three-buck tip for a hardcore Tapatio-drenched chorizo burrito at the taco truck later. Anyway, don't want to shoot too low in my own acknowledgment in my own book, but I'm cool with this tip being at the end of the line of your reading list. To me, it's always been about the long slow haul to a pair of patient, world-weary eyes at tight little spots no one but a few curiosities had enough curiosity to find.